From Beyond the Crooked Spire

Marjorie P. Dunn

Other Books by Marjorie Dunn

For the Love of Children

Children's Books

Flambo the Dragon
The Wild Rocking Horses of Ringinglow
Mr Fisher's Ducks
Horace Returns to Dore
Lancelot Rides Again

Historical Novels

The T'alli Stone
The Reluctant Traveller
Abe's Legacy
The Maggie Kelly
Call of the Lapwing

Cover picture: Chesterfield Market Square c.1805
Courtesy of Derbyshire County Council and www.picturethepast.org.uk

From Beyond the Crooked Spire

Marjorie Dunn

© 2011 Marjorie P. Dunn

Published by **The Hallamshire Press**
for and on behalf of **Marjorie Dunn**

Typesetting and design
Pauline Climpson

Printed in Great Britain by
Berforts Group Limited, Stevenage

British Library Cataloguing in Publication Data:
    A catalogue record for this book is available from the British Library

ISBN 978-1-874718-72-7

To my Grandchildren
Vikki, Alex, Cai and Marc

Acknowledgements

My thanks to Lesley Phillips and members of staff of Chesterfield Local Studies Library for their help and interest in this project.

I am especially grateful to my editor Pat Whitehead for her skill and guidance, and to Pauline Climpson who had the faith to publish my books for so many years.

Thanks to my husband Bob for his help and patience, and to my daughter Heather Dawson, whose computer skills far exceed those of mine on a typewriter.

An example of a model ship made by French prisoners during the
Napoleonic wars, 1793–1815.
It is constructed of mutton bone, metal, wood and thread.

Reproduced by kind permission of the Burton Art Gallery and Museum

In the year of our Lord 1802 the quiet backwater that was Chesterfield heard with great relief that England's war with France was over. Although this news brought great rejoicing, the majority of her inhabitants continued as before in a spirit of determined self-preservation, knowing quite well that it might be an uneasy peace which wouldn't last.

The small town, hazy with smoke, cluttered with lowly cramped dwellings, shops and factories was beginning to spread over the surrounding meadows and valleys. Only cloth manufacturers, munitions factories and producers of other necessities of war had prospered in the ten years since hostilities had broken out with France. Now the town's tanners, potters and craftsmen looked forward to the prosperity that peace should bring. Where taxes had risen to pay for the war and grain prices increased through shortages, the poor had become impoverished. Now, with luck, these same shortages and prices should level out easing the burdens placed on the ordinary man and woman on the streets, and men would return home from fighting to the comforts of family life. There was an air of optimism spreading within the town!

On a small farm at Brampton Moor on the outskirts of town, George Silcock and his wife Elizabeth had more reason than many to be cheered by the news, for now their son William could return home having been spared the ravages of battle. George himself was getting old and the farm was in need of the strength and enthusiasm of a younger man in order to overcome the neglect that had slowly crept up on it. Over the past four years, particularly since William's departure, there had been harsh winters followed by unproductive summers and these had taken things beyond George's capabilities and his health had suffered badly.

George looked towards the town. There the familiar outline of the old church's crooked spire stood proudly against the evening sky as if surveying the smoke-covered buildings on the lower contours of the town with disdain. He drew heavily on his well-sucked pipe. Oh how he hated the French for the shortages they'd caused and the human misery which had been the result. More than that he hated them for taking his son away, but it was over now and William would soon be home and all would be well again.

This was not to be however as, barely a few weeks after peace had been declared, came the shattering news that William had been injured in the last skirmish before the cessation, injuries from which he never recovered.

George had naturally taken the news of William's death badly, and the farm was now struggling to survive without him.

It therefore came as a further shock and blow when, less than fourteen months later, England declared war on the French due to their constant violation of the Treaty of Amiens, and hostilities resumed once more.

Chesterfield, tucked away in the hills of North Derbyshire as it was, saw no immediate threat to its inhabitants by the resumption of war, and yet it wasn't long before a remarkable and unusual turn of events occurred within her boundaries. A French invasion of a kind did take place!

Over two hundred French Army and Navy officers, their staff, together with other captured prisoners were sent 'On Parole' to Chesterfield, to be billeted there until the war ended. A few of these men were exchanged for English prisoners in France and sent home, a few died, one or two married whilst others absconded, the remainder lived as best they could until the war ended in 1814. One of many towns chosen to hold these prisoners, Chesterfield led a strange existence with an unusual peace taking place between the inhabitants and the French prisoners.

The following story is drawn from actual accounts taken from newspaper reports and records of the period 1802 to 1815 referring to this 'French Invasion'. The characters of Henri Pichon and the Silcock family are fictitious, and, by expanding on what is known of

John Bower, several times Mayor of Chesterfield, and his family, the author endeavours to portray an accurate insight into this extraordinary part of the town's history.

The circumstances behind the capture of many of these prisoners are both tragic and revealing. There are always two sides to any conflict but 'a man is a man' no matter on which side he fights, and how he behaves often depends on the pressures placed upon him.

The cessation of the war between England and France was tragically short-lived, although neither side had actually expected peace to last. The English Parliament had no liking for the Treaty of Amiens which had brought peace about, and Napoleon was merely seeking time to re-organise his forces before he could declare war again. However, England's unexpected decision to resume hostilities took Napoleon by surprise. For, whereas he had made good progress with his plans towards an invasion of England, in doing so he had neglected his Navy and even despatched a large contingency of ships to the West Indies in order to ensure that the rich French investments there were safe. England on the other hand had taken the opportunity of the break to re-stock and repair her Navy, thus giving her the advantage when war resumed on May 16th, 1803.

The British Navy therefore lost no time in apprehending any French vessel at sea, one of the first being the frigate *Franchise* which was taken off Brest as it made its way back to France from San Domingo at the end of May. As it happened, on board were several high-ranking Army officers, their staff and other ranks, some of whom were destined to be parolees sent to Chesterfield, General Boyer and his servant Philip Jager being the first to arrive.

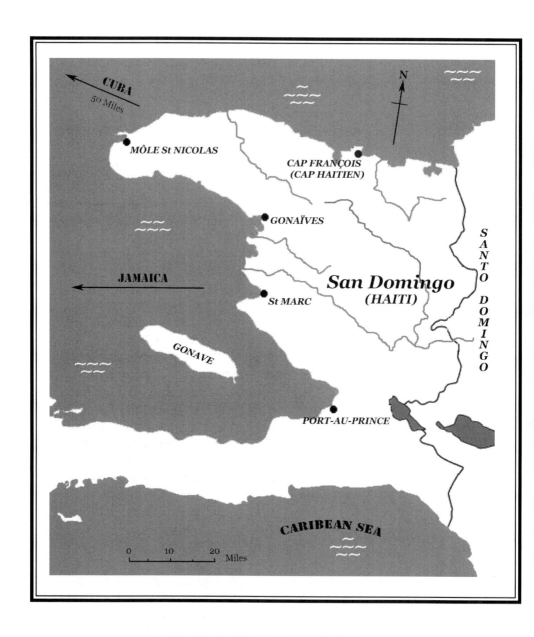

The Island of Hispaniola was divided into
Santo Domingo (Spanish) and San Domingo (French) in 1697.
After the rebellion of 1804 San Domingo became Haiti.

Chapter 1   1803
West Indies — July

Captain James Walker of His Majesty's Ship *Vanguard* received the news of renewed hostilities with delight, as he could once more patrol the seas in earnest, seeking his old enemy, the French.

He watched from his usual station on deck as Port Royal on the island of Jamaica disappeared slowly from view, whilst his ship headed towards San Domingo through the Windward Passage. 'There's bound to be several of Bonie's ships anchored in Cap François,' he remarked, rubbing his hands together in anticipation as he turned to the Lieutenant of the Watch by his side. He was glad to be at sea again with a firm purpose in mind and a fresh breeze playing on his weathered face. 'The heat on San Domingo and the mosquitoes will be taking a toll of the Frenchies by now,' he went on. 'If they've any sense they'll not want to be blockaded in the harbour by us for long.'

Surveying his ship with pride, James Walker noted the set of the sails and the good order of all on the deck just below him. She had once been Nelson's flag ship until being demasted in a violent gale, then, as she drifted helplessly towards the rocks off Sardinia she'd been saved only by the crew of the *Alexander* who had somehow got a towing-hawser on board the crippled *Vanguard* and taken her in tow. They could so easily have let her go and left her to her fate but with great determination she was saved and then refitted. Now she was his responsibility, and he relished every moment of it.

The *Vanguard* sailed on for several days in the Caribbean in company with HM Ships *Bellerophon*, *Elephant* and *Theseus* presenting a splendid and inspiring sight as they sought any vessel flying the French flag. All were well stocked and ready for action, the crews working optimistically, and looking forward to sharing any prizes resulting from the capture of enemy ships.

On reaching the vicinity of Port Picolet the Squadron replenished provisions; *Vanguard* transferred to *Bellerophon* and *Theseus* thirty tons of water, twenty bags of bread and over forty bushels of peas, receiving in exchange several casks of rum along with prisoners captured from several schooners encountered and taken during the present sortie from Port Royal.

Towards five in the afternoon the following day the fine moderate weather changed suddenly, becoming squally with very strong winds. The Squadron now took station off the Bay of Cap François intending to blockade any vessel sheltering there. Two enemy ships and a frigate of the line could be seen standing in the harbour, together with other smaller vessels.

The sudden blockading of the harbour by the British Squadron thwarted the plans of the French captains including Commodore Julien Querangal of the 74-gun troop ship *Duquesne*, who had been ready to leave for France.

On board the *Duquesne*, Brigadier General Charles D'Henin with his staff would dearly have liked to go back to Europe now that war had broken out on the Continent again. He was exasperated by the loss of good men to the ravages of sickness, this being compounded by severe shortages of supplies. He had also witnessed heinous crimes on San Domingo, committed by the native insurgents and the French occupying Army, which he knew would result in even worse reprisals against whoever lost. Charles was a compassionate and fair-minded man who was popular with his men, all of whom were by this time, in poor health and disillusioned by the overwhelming futility of trying to maintain the colony for Napoleon.

The revolution in Paris had liberated the downtrodden peasants of France and these same people now saw the encaptured black slaves as fellow sufferers. As a result, most would prefer to fight for the freedom of the slaves of San Domingo than against them. Many a soldier therefore arrived on the island with high ideals, only to find that the double-crossing and constant mischief-making by Napoleon, the cunning of the British and infighting amongst the islands own black generals, destroyed his faith in the ideals of the Revolution.

The burning sun and humid atmosphere of July was no respecter of rank and fever had cut through General D'Henin's men like a farmer's scythe. Apart from his aides, none of the troops on board were his own men; he was Commander of St Marc, a fort in the Southern Bay of Gonaïves, the men there were ill-fed and sick and in need of supplies. He had made the journey north to Cap François by sea to confer with Rochambeau rather than cross the mountains and risk the dangers therein. Now the journey back would perhaps be just as hazardous and he was worried about the state of the men still trapped at Fort St Marc. Here on the *Duquesne*, the troops were sitting like ducks on a pond in the stifling heat, trapped by the British blockade through which no supplies could pass.

'If our three vessels make a break for it together,' General D'Henin suggested respectfully to Commodore Querangal, standing beside him on deck, 'there is every chance that we might make it through the blockade, rather than sit here and rot. There's trouble behind us, you're needed in Europe and we are nearly out of supplies. I fear replenishments will not get through even if they are sent!'

'I agree,' the Commodore replied. 'Better to risk capture than perish one at a time in this hell-hole.' He turned away from D'Henin and instructed the Watch Lieutenant to gather his officers into his cabin immediately.

Meanwhile General D'Henin looked ashore, his eyes following the road that ran along the shoreline until it rose to the heights of the town. It was a place of much misery and greed. He had much admired the efforts of the previous black leader General François Toussaint Louverture, who had sought to erect fine buildings and to educate and civilise the black labourers; this same man who had been so cruelly deceived by Napoleon and his cohorts. Toussaint had been tricked into going to France away from his people where he had died through deliberate neglect, in prison. This act had broken the bond between San Domingo and France, and Jean-Jacques Dessalines, the new black leader, sought to despatch all whites from the island. France had responded by sending the sadistic Generals Rochambeau and Boyer to deal with the insurgents, and to re-introduce slavery.

Apparently the dead Toussaint had written numerous letters to Napoleon before his forced departure, begging him to send experienced officers, administrators, good machinists and workmen in order to build and strengthen the French Colony through good government. However, Bonaparte always had at the back of his mind the re-introduction of slavery but it was too late, slavery would not be tolerated anymore and the insurgents had risen again. Charles D'Henin had respected the surprisingly ugly-featured Toussaint, seeing him as a remarkable man, always courteous and charming in his manner. Bonaparte would have done better to have taken this man on his side and worked with him. Instead, thousands of good Frenchmen had lost their lives as a result of his intransigence, and for what—sugar! The French were now finished on San Domingo, if only they were wise enough to see it. General D'Henin knew he had to get his men away.

Turning, Charles D'Henin saw a longboat wending its way between the flotilla of ships, the frigate *Guerriere*, the *Duquay Trouin* and the *Duquesne*, and suspected that action would soon follow. He felt his spirits lifting.

Word was finally passed round that the crews should prepare themselves quietly for the breakthrough and to stand by, ready to slip anchor on demand. As luck would have it a squall arose, and soon a choppy sea and blustering wind helped to conceal their intention to escape from the harbour and elude the British ships blockading outside the bay.

The storm worsened, generally reducing visibility and the British Squadron off shore took the full force of the storm. They were therefore taken by surprise and insufficiently prepared when the three French ships made their sudden dash for freedom.

The captains of the British Squadron hastily made sail to chase the fleeing enemy but the storm caused the ships to pitch terribly in the contrary winds and off-shore currents, with the result that the enemy were lost for the time being.

However, in the turmoil of the storm the three French ships gradually separated and the *Duquesne* thus lost contact with her companions in the fading light, her Captain realising that he would, in all probability, have to make his way home to France unescorted rather than return D'Henin to St Marc.

At the first glimmer of dawn, Captain James Walker quickly joined his fellow officers on watch as they searched the horizon for any sign of the rest of the Squadron, and in particular the fleeing French vessels. He was a little disappointed in himself for he should have anticipated the desperate need anyone trapped on the island would have to escape. At this time of year yellow fever would be rampaging through the white population, whilst the black insurgents were gathering their forces and in no mood to tolerate or respect any European after the intense cruelty meted out to them by the new French Governor, General Rochambeau, and his cohorts. News had reached Jamaica of the murder and mayhem that had taken place and that Napoleon intended Rochambeau to re-instate slavery on San Domingo, then to exterminate the Mulattoes, half-white half-black, who out-numbered the whites on the island. Such was Rochambeau's hatred of the Mulattoes that he allowed his troops to use abominable cruelty without restriction.

With the weather now improving, *Vanguard* raised more sail and set out to locate and capture the escapees, James Walker and lookouts scanning the horizon intently for sight of any ship's topsails.

'Blockading the island and depriving it of supplies, will make Napoleon wish he'd never heard of San Domingo,' he remarked to the Lieutenant of the watch. 'Supplies there must have dwindled severely and if General Rochambeau had any thought for his men he would withdraw.'

In quick succession came cries from aloft announcing that the remainder of the Squadron was now in view. All were now sailing along the shore off Môle St Nicolas and by twelve o'clock the weather had become clear and breezy, enabling them to witness and hear *Tarter* exchanging shots with an enemy ship. It wasn't long before the schooner hoisted her colours and surrendered. James also saw two more enemy vessels engaging *Theseus* in an affray which before long was also brought to a quick and satisfactory conclusion.

'Sails, twenty miles distant fine on port bow, Sir,' Midshipman Jones reported. It was shortly after noon. 'She's running East-North-East, Sir. Are we to make chase?'

James, who had finished his lunch only moments before, responded immediately, 'My compliments to Lieutenant Valentine please to signal the Commodore that we're making chase, and tell the Master to set all sails. We're not going to let them get away if they're French'.

On the French ship *Duquesne*, Charles D'Henin spent most of the morning looking aft over the shimmering waters of the Caribbean in case the ship was being followed. Occasionally he cast an eye on the soldiers who were sprawling lethargically on deck in large numbers, perhaps praying for death as a way of escaping the misery of seasickness.

'At least the British won't find it easy to catch all three vessels, divided as the flotilla now is', D'Henin said with some satisfaction to Commodore Querangal, who had joined him on deck.

'We need to make good time whilst the wind is in our favour', Pierre Querangal replied as the steady breeze filled the billowing sails. 'But we're over-laden with troops which will hold us back in a skirmish. Every strike from the enemy is bound to kill or maim some of them!'

'I'm afraid the pitching of the ship is making many of them sick,' D'Henin replied thoughtfully. 'They're undernourished as it is, and some are ill. Seasickness is only adding to their misery. I'm not a good sailor myself so I can sympathise with them. At least I'm feeling more optimistic now that we've successfully broken out of the blockade. I wonder how *Duquay* and *Guerriere* have fared, we've had no sight of them since last night?'

'I'll probably not know that until I reach Toulon, but without a good wind none of us will make France without incident.' Julien Querangal watched the lively rise and fall of the bow, it was an action that had never upset his stomach and he found it hard to understand the other man's discomfort. He suddenly felt the need to partake of something nourishing. 'As the watch is changing, shall we go below and indulge in a bite to eat?' he suggested in case the General was of a similar mind.

'I think not,' Charles D'Henin answered wryly, 'but I thank you! It would possibly be asking too much of my already churning stomach.'

'You'll excuse me then,' Querangal said, 'if I go to my cabin?'

'Certainly, the mere thought of food disturbs me at this moment.'

The increasing heat of the afternoon sun beat down on the haggard-faced troops propped against any fixture that kept them out of the way of the ship's crew as they hurried about their tasks. Charles D'Henin was joined on deck by his Lieutenant Colonel Pierre Legay, whose face was as grey as the sails above him. 'I don't know which is worse,' he said, 'this, or dying of disease, or even worse, on land!'

'I think you know the answer to that,' Charles D'Henin said ruefully. 'Didn't we all think that equally on the voyage out from France?'

'So much has happened since we arrived on the island, Sir, that I began to wonder if we would all go mad even if we did survive being murdered by the blacks.'

'I fear for those left behind,' D'Henin rejoined. 'What a terrible waste of good men, and now I believe we might not be able to return to them at Fort St Marc, we may have to go back to France on this ship!'

A shrill voice and whistle was heard suddenly from the look out on *Duquesne's* mizzen topsail yard, drawing the attention of the Watch below.

'Sail on the horizon to starboard aft,' the piercing, agitated voice called. A heavy silence settled over the ship; all who heard the cry paused tensely, wondering if it would be the *Duquay-Trouin*, the *Guerriere* or the enemy.

A midshipman ran to inform Commodore Querangal who was already coming in response to the call. 'A ship spotted, Sir!'

'She's coming up fast, Sir!' an excited voice called down. 'And making good speed!'

'Identify man, identify,' shouted the first mate.

'She's not alone either!' The same voice called down. 'A larger vessel about a mile to her port side.'

'Right! Make haste with more sail, we need any advantage! If they're together then they're searching for us!' Julien Querangal could now see their topsails himself, and watched intently until it became evident that the distant ships were not the *Duquay* and *Guerriere*, besides which a third set of sails was now in evidence.

'They're heading towards us Sir, and are definitely British,' reported the mate.

'We're going as fast as we can but I suspect it is only a matter of time before they get within range, Sir!'

'Prepare for action then, run out all guns and hoist the Tricolore,' Commodore Querangal ordered. 'We'll not be taken without a fight.' He knew that in battle a single ship stood little or no chance against an enemy Squadron but he'd be damned if he'd give in without putting up resistance.

On board *Vanguard*, Captain Walker smiled confidently. 'The Squadron should take her,' he remarked to Lieutenant Valentine, whilst watching the vessel ahead. 'We're gaining on her—it has to be the seventy-four gun ship of the line out of Le Cap* harbour or she would be heading in the other direction.' The latter he muttered almost to himself.

'She's making more sail, Sir,' responded the Lieutenant. 'Do you think she'll surrender without a fight?'

'Not if she's fully armed—but we don't know what supplies she had on board before she fled. I suspect most of her seventy-four guns will be at the ready, though when we get closer I will signal offering

* *Cap François*

to accept her surrender. The problem with the French Navy is they spend so much time in Port that through lack of practice they can't manoeuvre their ships quickly. Nevertheless their strikes could do a lot of harm. I'd like to take her without too much damage, if we can, as she'll be a valuable prize.'

'She's aiming to outrun us, Sir. She looks heavily laden, although by their hasty departure in the squall she may not be fully provisioned for a long sea-journey, or a fight!'

'That is mere conjecture, but if so she might even be relieved at being taken. However, these Frenchies are proud and won't give in without a fight. Who can blame them, I'd do the same myself. Beat to Quarters and clear for action Mr Valentine!'

Later, shortly before three in the afternoon *Vanguard* came up fast behind *Duquesne* who, in answer to a warning shot, replied by firing her stern guns in an attempt to deter further action. In quick response *Vanguard* attacked with fire from her bow guns. As the exchange of gunfire intensified the French man-of-war shot away *Vanguard's* fore topgallant yard.

'The damned French do tend to fire high!' James Walker complained, as debris was being cleared from the foredeck. 'Have we lost any men?'

'One man killed and another wounded, Sir,' Lieutenant Valentine reported as a further shot tore away the top-mast studdingsail yard and damaged the fore and main topsail yards. The mizzen topsail yard was also damaged.

'Damn!' James Walker cursed again. The enemy ship wasn't going to be overwhelmed as easily as he'd hoped. 'She intends to do as much damage as she can before being taken.' It was only a matter of time, of course, before *Bellerophon*, *Cumberland* and *Tarter* would close in but he was disappointed by the damage done to *Vanguard*.

'*Bellerophon* approaching fast Sir, two miles distant!'

In desperation *Duquesne* used her stern guns again to which *Vanguard* briskly returned fire and, as the two vessels drew nearer, the French ship turned slightly so as to be able to fire a broadside at *Vanguard* which again was quickly returned. It was a brave, defiant action by Julien Querangal but with insufficient supplies with which to reach France and so many men to care for, the sight of other ships of the British Squadron rapidly approaching convinced him to reluctantly strike his colours. The *Duquesne* then shortened sail and hove to.

The skirmish had taken an hour and a quarter from start to finish and tragically cost the life of Joseph Lovelock and wounded Thomas Wood on the British ship. The sortie had ended successfully but Captain Walker was more annoyed than dismayed on surveying the damage done. 'Tell the Master to see to the damage, Lieutenant. We're not likely to meet any opposition here now, Bonie's got enough to do defending Brest and Toulon, and he'll be lucky to get his ships out of the other blockaded ports of France. He'll not be wasting any more of his energies on San Domingo I think, and those Frenchmen still there will be lucky to see their homes again.' To some degree he was pleased by the day's efforts. 'A seventy-four gun man o'war is an excellent prize to take, and by removing her from French hands this operation lessens their fleet and increases ours,' he added, smiling broadly. 'T'was well done, Lieutenant.'

'She's certainly the vessel out of Le Cap,' Lieutenant Valentine responded with a satisfied nod.

'Right then! Get a party of men together to board and take possession of her, Lieutenant, and arrange to transfer the prisoners. Let's just hope they don't bring the fever on board with them. There's always that risk.'

While *Vanguard's* crew valiantly made a great effort to clear away the tangled ropes and broken timbers resulting from the short battle, and attempted to repair what they could of the rigging, a boat was lowered taking Lieutenant Valentine and several men to take possession of the prize.

The reason for the Frenchman's unexpectedly quick surrender was soon apparent to the boarding party as they climbed aboard. The decks were crammed with men who were predominately of the military and in poor condition, some now wounded from the battle with *Vanguard*.

By early evening 823 prisoners had been safely transferred from the *Duquesne* to HMS *Tarter* and *Vanguard*, but unfortunately in doing so a seaman off *Vanguard* fell overboard. In consequence the *Duquesne* then lowered a boat which was accidentally swamped and Lieutenant Terry also drowned. It was a dark day for mishaps casting a shadow over the triumph of the afternoon.

It always saddened Captain Walker to lose a man, especially an officer of close acquaintance, but life at sea was one of chance and the loss of life whilst performing one's duty was not unexpected.

Hoisting up the last of the boats used to transfer the prisoners amongst the ships returning to Port Royal, *Bellerophon* and *Cumberland* parted company and went on their way. *Vanguard, Tarter*, the captured schooner, *Duquesne*, and other captured 'prizes' then made sail for Jamaica in convoy.

As James Walker looked out over the choppy grey sea, his thoughts weighing heavily on his mind, he was informed that a schooner was coming before the wind and showing a flag of truce. Yet another prize! One more to add to those the Squadron had taken on this expedition, he was gratified by this. However, worsening weather and a spell of thunder and lightning quickly brought him from his darker thoughts—there was work to do!

The squadron and their prizes passed Donna Maria Point on San Domingo before heading across the open sea towards Jamaica and when at last Morant Point was rounded, the harbour of Port Royal eventually welcomed them home.

Once the French prisoners had been inspected for fever and taken to their respective places of confinement on land, the crew of the *Vanguard* repaired damage and replenished her stores in the calm waters of the Port.

Charles D'Henin and all the other French officers had been disembarked immediately, and after interrogation were permitted a controlled freedom as befitted their station. However, Charles still fretted about the fate of the men left behind on San Domingo.

'This should be your Fort, Charles,' Julien Querangal remarked one day as the pair studied the strong, buttressed red brick and stone fortification of Fort Charles, 'she's named after you!'

Nodding, Charles D'Henin smiled wistfully. 'That France should have such good fortifications and relations with the island's inhabitants is to be envied!' he said thoughtfully. Three weeks had passed since their capture during which time a strange mixture of emotions had crept over Charles D'Henin, as he pondered on the purpose of France's involvement in so many countries, and grieved over the terrible waste of human life. These thoughts were taking a toll on him; he loved France and all things French yet he wondered if she wasn't in danger of losing her real identity. He was a man of honour, a loyal officer who knew his duty but he was also a thinking man, and a tired one. He'd fought a good campaign in Egypt but the waste on San Domingo was causing serious disquiet in his mind. 'Thank God the men are treated fairly well here,' he said to his companion, 'the sick are hospitalised, and all are being fed'.

Julien agreed. 'We would appear to be lucky, but I'm afraid we shall soon be shipped to England and incarceration there. I judge this will be another long war!'

'I was told this morning that a vessel docking from the Bay of Gonaïves carried reports that the blacks are massing behind General Dessalines and that our General, Rochambeau, is perpetrating unimaginable cruelties on them. An English officer told me quite openly that Dessalines has the fort of St Marc surrounded on three sides and intends to annihilate our troops there, up to 900 in number!' The gravity of this news had depressed Charles all morning. 'There must be something we can do, by negotiation. I am most concerned for the safety and conditions of my men there!'

'But what can we do without ships? We're prisoners and have no influence whatsoever!' Both officers discussed the problem for some time until Charles came to a decision.

'What I have experienced here so far gives me the impression that there is a humanity in the British officers equal to our best. Perhaps it wouldn't hurt to discuss the possibility of rescuing our men in Fort Marc?'

'You can try,' Juilen replied, 'there will certainly be no help coming from France. We have been abandoned to the furtherance of the war elsewhere, I'm afraid! Do what you will!'

Charles bit his lip, considering carefully what to do next. To negotiate with the enemy for the lives of 900 men, even if it meant their eventual captivity was surely a better thing to do than to let them die a horrible death. What kind of man would he be if he sat back and did nothing?

Chapter 2   1803
Fort St Marc

Within the confines of Fort St Marc on San Domingo the French soldiers despaired of their future, knowing that they all might be killed or left to die of disease or starvation, for no ship would be allowed to rescue them. Life seemed hopeless.

For some time now, Lieutenant Henri Pichon, erstwhile Aide-de-Camp to General Boudet, also had questioned his patriotism to the new Republic of France, having witnessed at first hand the betrayal of what the revolution had been all about. What the ordinary men and women had wanted for all citizens, everywhere. Freedom!

After his arrival on the island it very quickly became obvious to him that Napoleon Bonaparte had no idea of the conditions and pressures his troops were under. Neither could he have any concept of the strength of feeling, or an understanding of the fierce determination of the black population on the island, even when informed of it by his Chief of Staff there. That, or he simply refused to listen when told the truth, as power and commerce were all the First Consul was concerned with. He just could not see or would not accept that the ultimate aim of the black ex-slaves was freedom, and that they were prepared to die to achieve it.

The black revolutionary armies which had earlier been trained by the French were now led by their own Generals and becoming extremely clever, cunning and desperately brave. Towards the end their ingenuity had won Henri's respect but it also left him in fear of his life!

Although the walls of the fort offered Henri some protection from the blazing sun, the humid atmosphere laid him low. He was comparatively lucky, yellow fever had claimed the lives of many of his comrades and the worst of the season was not yet over. It had taken many men only two or three days to die from the fever but he had survived, although the pains in his bowels and the persistent shivering had left him weak. Henri sometimes thought it might have been better to have succumbed to the fever rather than be incarcerated in the fort with no hope of salvation. They were surrounded on all sides by revolutionary black armies who were baying for their blood, while behind them lay the sea by which there was no apparent means of escape. With the British Navy constantly prowling the seas ready to pounce, no French ship would be allowed to approach them and it could only be a matter of time before the hordes of enraged black ex-slave insurgents would move into action. He shuddered!

His head was still fuzzy, and his limbs were hardly able to take the full weight of his body, so Henri lay back on the cot and rested a moment before trying again to rise. Who could blame the blacks of San Domingo for hating them all, the French, the English, all the whites, even the Mullatoes—all of whom had at various times betrayed them. No matter how many thousands of men Napoleon sent to quell the insurrections that constantly arose through lack of understanding and mistrust, France would never again win the islanders' loyalty. Any man of sound mind could see that slavery and cruelty would achieve nothing at this late stage. The plantation owners and the white overlords had in fact bred cruelty into the labourers, and the prospect and taste for freedom and independence was too sweet in the mouths of a people hungry to rid themselves of their greedy oppressors.

'This cursed war,' Henri muttered to himself. First it had been gold, then sugar which had brought the Europeans to the West Indies, wiping out the indigenous population only to replace them with unfortunate black slaves—hundreds of thousands of African men, women and children, torn from everything they knew and understood, to live in inhuman conditions, conditions which Henri knew few white men could ever have withstood or survived.

For all he feared the revenge of the blacks, Henri felt a compassion for them after witnessing first hand the cruelties em-ployed by Rochambeau and General Boyer on hundreds of thousands of them.

Madness now pervaded the Island amongst both blacks and whites, and distrust ruled out all pity. A feverish hatred and fervour for revenge permeated the countryside. In the two years Henri had been on the island he'd seen the black leader Toussaint lead General Rochambeau and his troops on many a wild goose chase in the

Grand Canos mountains before completely disappearing, after employing guerrilla tactics which confounded and depleted Rochambeau's forces. He had seen Toussaint betrayed and replaced while Frenchmen in their tens of thousands had perished from disease and battle on the island.

Rochambeau, however, was now getting his comeuppance, as, during his attempt to capture the fortress of Crête-à-Pierrot from their new General, Jean Jacques Dessalines, the natives had shown extraordinary cunning. Leaving his fort apparently unmanned, Dessalines and his men advanced to meet the French yet refused to give battle. Instead he teased the French forwards as he himself retreated towards the fort: the men with him then reached a ditch surrounding the fortress and to a man jumped in and hid. A terrifying volley of cannon and musket fire from the fort then decimated the French, leaving hundreds dead or dying.

When General Boudet brought up reinforcements, which included Henri, the same trick was employed and even repeated when further reinforcements arrived. Three days of bombardment ensued before the fort was eventually taken at a cost of 2,000 French lives. General Boudet was wounded at this time, as was Henri along with hundreds of others.

Despite the care of the doctors in the hospital, Henri's wound had at first refused to heal, but his commander, General Boudet, soon recovered and was despatched back to France without him in order to explain the hopeless situation the army was in on San Domingo. Henri remained in the hospital until he was fit to fight again and so missed the opportunity to return to France with the General. Unfortunately, Henri then caught yellow fever and was trapped in the Fort of St Marc. Rochambeau was now exterminating the blacks with unremitting vengeance whilst General Boyer, who was almost as bad, had been captured off Brest by the British Navy on board the *Franchise* on his way back to France.

Henri was just one of 850 French soldiers under siege in St Marc; all were emaciated, weak and barely able to defend themselves. The new black leader Dessalines was determined to put the garrison to death, and fear was undermining the men's morale. Never before had Henri felt so physically and mentally afraid; he'd been a true and loyal servant of France but this catastrophe, born of the horrors and tortures he'd witnessed wormed its way into his gut and soul. What made matters worse was knowing that not a man trapped in the fort could do anything but simply wait for death.

While *Vanguard* was being repaired and provisioned at Port Royal, Captain James Walker was at liberty to go ashore and enjoy a temporary break from routine; not that he enjoyed being on land for too long, for he soon yearned to be out at sea again. There were plenty of foreign vessels out in the Caribbean Sea, all waiting investigation and possible capture by the Squadron, prizes for himself and his crew. He hated idleness in the hot, unhealthy towns of Port Royal and Kingston when he could be out where the air was fresh and fever beyond reach of himself and his men.

After two restless weeks on land he was suddenly summoned to attend a meeting with Sir John Duckworth, Commander-in-Chief of his Majesty's Fleet in Jamaica. This 'request' came quite out of the blue as *Vanguard* was almost ready to sail and he had already received orders as to his actions on leaving Port Royal. He was therefore not surprised to be ushered immediately into the presence of the Admiral.

'Come in, come in, Captain,' Sir John said, rising from his desk as James entered his office. 'I'm afraid we'll have to change your orders, something important has cropped up.'

Although James knew Sir John quite well from times when he submitted reports to him, and also on the several occasions they had both been to social functions on the island, he realised that this meeting must be over a very urgent matter to warrant such personal attention. '*Vanguard* is practically ready to sail, Sir,' he informed the Admiral.

'Yes, and I'm pleased to have her back in commission, James, as you no doubt are too. Now then, I have a special and important mission for you. Apparently the Black General, Dessalines, on San Domingo has been sending out messages under flags of truce to ships cruising off the island with the specific aim of despatching letters here to General Nugent and myself, asking for sufficient arms and ammunition to enable him to rid the island of the French. He also wants free commerce for San Domingo and British troops to be garrisoned at St Marc to stop the French returning.' He saw James raise his eyebrows, half in disbelief. 'I know, I know, if we hadn't been forced to evacuate St Marc ourselves in the last war he wouldn't have been stuck with the French there now. Notwithstanding all that, I don't think it worth the risk to agree to garrisoning our men there. However, he knows the French intend to re-establish slavery and wants to rid himself completely of them. It seems too, that the French General Rochambeau is spreading lies about the British aims in the area, so I want you to go to Gonaïves with the express purpose of learning more of Dessalines' views and get him to explain more fully what he requires.'

'Do you want me to go onto San Domingo under a flag of truce, Sir? Or for him to come out to *Vanguard*?'

'I am authorising you to do whatever is necessary Captain, to take despatches from General Nugent and myself to Dessalines, and to negotiate a satisfactory agreement with the man. We have constantly asked for protection of the whites on the island, and for them to be re-instated on their estates, which he refuses, saying they have been influenced by the French and that they and their negroes would stir things up against his Government of the island. Foremost he wants to be rid of the French and claim independence for San Domingo!'

'Sir, I understand from the captured French General D'Henin, late commander of St Marc, that he is himself extremely worried about the conditions and safety of his men there. As you know, news filters through, and it appears no supplies have been getting to the place for some time due to the success of our blockades.'

'Yes, we are well aware of the situation and I authorise you to come to an agreement between both Dessalines and D'Henin whilst protecting our interests in the matter and, if possible, evacuate the French prisoners trapped there. Take General D'Henin and his aides with you—the man seems to be an honourable and caring man. In addition, take Dessalines the arms and ammunition he wants, it will save us the trouble of getting rid of the remaining French ourselves. Their presence in the area takes up too much of our valuable time and resources.' Sir John lifted several despatches from his desk and handed them over to James. 'These are from General Nugent and myself to Dessalines, together with an outline for yourself as to the limits of your authority. Remember, Captain, it is Dessalines who has written to us asking for supplies and help—not the other way round. He knows that if we were to continue harassing shipping to prevent supplies from reaching the island he will never succeed in his ambitions—we hold the upper hand.'

James took the despatches and after a few moments of polite conversation left the Admiral's office and hastily returned to his ship, deep in thought over the task ahead.

With *Vanguard* once more heading towards the open sea, James Walker was happy to discharge the pilot who had taken them out of the Naval base of Port Royal and led them safely through the dangerous coral reefs known as the 'Cays' of Jamaica.

This time he was sailing directly for Gonaïves Bay on San Domingo with ten barrels of powder and forty-eight stands of arms for the rebel General Jean Jacques Dessalines. The present British relationship with the island's leaders, who had little time for the British, was tenuous. In order to maintain commercial negotiations and their supplies, and because the British Navy threatened to blockade the Ports of San Domingo if not allowed to trade, agreements had previously been made, agreements which Dessalines appeared to want to extend.

There was, however, more at stake on this passage, for on board was General Charles D'Henin and two other French officers who hoped to negotiate for the lives of the troops trapped in the Fort of St Marc. James Walker was to assist by mediating on their behalf. James trusted Dessalines no more and no less than anyone else on the island, as each side played false when it suited, and providing his ship came to no harm he was authorised to help relieve Dessalines of his French oppressors. He actually felt some sympathy for the plight of the ordinary French soldiers who were at the mercy of the insurgents and merely pawns in the hands of the power-mad Napoleon Bonaparte.

The weather on their journey to Gonaïves varied from periods of gusty breezes to raging tropical storms, with lightning and torrential showers of rain, but no time was lost in their efforts to achieve a rescue before a massacre took place at St Marc.

Fortunately the British Navy enjoyed domination over the Windward Passage, that vital stretch of water separating Cuba and San Domingo, thus allowing a successful blockade of the island and a furtherance of British influence in the area.

On arrival in the Bay of Gonaïves on the evening of August 27th, *Vanguard* dropped anchor to await developments and was immediately visited by a messenger bearing a letter in French from General Dessalines, informing James that he proposed to besiege the Fort. Despite the many pressures of the long day and the lateness of the hour, James replied immediately in order to calm the situation down. He informed the General that he carried despatches from the Admiral in Port Royal and had the power to negotiate on his behalf. He also indicated that he had the arms requested should Dessalines still need them.

Whilst *Vanguard* lay at anchor in the Bay for a further day awaiting a reply, General Dessalines himself arrived in the town of Gonaïves and eventually indicated that he was willing to meet with the Admiral's representative.

'Send for Mr Cathcart,' James ordered, having read the note and knowing that Cathcart was standing by ready to leave when requested. 'Tell him I'm ready to go ashore!' He then took the despatches, which he'd taken the precaution of wrapping in water-proof cloth, and waited impatiently for Cathcart to arrive. 'Are the guns and powder shipped safely?' he asked, more of a way of calming his anxiousness than anything else.

'The longboats are loaded as you ordered, Sir!'

When Captain Walker and Mr Cathcart stepped down into one of the waiting boats to be rowed across the harbour to the town, James wondered just what obstacles Dessalines would place in their way and just how flexible he would be to Sir John's proposals.

It was a smooth and quiet journey as the oarsmen rhythmically dipped and pulled their oars with their usual efficiency and, for once, James was not inclined to small talk, such was the responsibility he felt laying upon his shoulders. He trusted, however, that Mr Cathcart understood this well enough. James was not himself cognisant with the contents of the despatches, only with the instructions on the separate papers given to him. This much he knew, that Dessalines' requests had been countered by British demands, and that his suggestion that British troops should occupy the vacated fort of St Marc required far more concessions than those he would be willing to accept.

James was even less talkative later in the day when returning to his ship after a meeting with the General which had confirmed many of his doubts. Dessalines was unwilling to allow the British to occupy land around the fort, in complete safety, for the growing of vegetables and other crops needed for survival, nor would he return the estates to the whites. He was also quite prepared to put the French troops in the fort to the sword. Having urged Dessalines not to proceed with that, pending further negotiations, James delivered the ten barrels of powder and 48 muskets in good faith, agreeing to return the following day to recommence the talks.

As these negotiations were somewhat controversial and difficult, James Walker and Mr Cathcart were forced to return to Gonaïves yet again on the third day when Dessalines finally consented not to put the fort's garrison to death. In addition it was particularly stipulated that if they surrendered, he should march the men under guard in safety round to Môle St Nicolas where *Vanguard* would take possession of the shipping there and distribute the prisoners amongst them.

This was therefore much to Charles D'Henin's relief and he was taken ashore protected by a flag of truce to negotiate the rescue and arrange the evacuation.

Captain Walker watched anxiously as the boat carried the party on its mission of mercy. Would Dessalines keep his word or would he simply arrest the French officers? What were the black General's real intentions? He was a magnificent soldier, crude and coarse perhaps, and stained with crimes, but dedicated to the freedom of the black population of the island. His hatred of those who deserved to be hated and destroyed, sharpened his wits and made him a man of intense determination. Would he actually allow the men in the Fort to leave in peace?

'Let us hope that Dessalines means precisely what he says,' James muttered as he watched the boat disappear amongst the other vessels in the port. 'It depends how much he needs our help!'

'A prayer would be in keeping, don't you think?' Mr Cathcart replied soberly. 'Dessalines may not be able to control all the insurgents even if he wants to. The men will be prey to the weather and renegade islanders.'

For James' part, *Vanguard* was got underway with the express purpose of heading to Môle St Nicholas to await the arrival of the prisoners.

On her eventual arrival, a strong squall of wind and rain delayed communications between Captain Walker on board his ship and General D'Henin on land, but finally on September 2nd both agreed to and signed a Document of Trust allowing the commencement of the evacuation to start the following day.

Fort St Marc—San Domingo

A sudden gust of wind woke Henri with a start. He could hear things, untethered things, rattling around in the yard outside. The wind dropped as quickly as it had arisen, only to blow again seconds later rapidly gathering strength. Then the rain started, driving rain lashing against the barrack walls, but now at least the air was cooler and he could breathe more easily.

This was the hurricane season during which violent storms could go on for days at a time getting stronger and wilder, flattening trees and bringing rain that soaked everything in an instant. However, it broke the monotony and would hold the insurgents at bay, for a while at least. But it would not last indefinitely, and once the storm ceased the urgency of the Fort's situation would become more acute.

Henri's strength was returning but his progress was slow, mainly due to the lack of food. Every day brought fresh rumours regarding the possible arrival of relief troops from France, but no one believed this would happen any more. Morale was at its lowest ebb and fear was beginning to overtake reason.

Now that Henri was able to walk about again he'd begun to mix with his fellow officers in the mess-room within the fort where the subject of their plight was constantly the subject of conversation. Today however, the tone was more subdued than normal and the mood was one of resignation.

The silence was suddenly broken by a weary voice. 'Where are we going to find sufficient food to feed the men?' one officer asked despairingly. 'Without having eaten the flesh of horses we would already be dead! We cannot go on! We really have no choice but to surrender to Dessalines in the hope that he will show us mercy. Otherwise we will die a slow death.'

'Under the circumstances I can see no reason why he should show us any pity after what Rochambeau has done to his people', someone muttered bitterly.

'Then we have a choice, to surrender or starve, or die of sickness. I'm sorry, but I think we have to surrender with honour', another officer replied.

A gloomy stillness descended on the men until this was broken by a deep sigh from one man who could not bring himself to imagine what might then befall them all.

Once again the sound of driving rain penetrated the silence. 'It's a blessing, at least, to be out of the heat for a while', Henri ventured, in an attempt to raise spirits, before slowly walking away to seek the privacy of a small office where he sat, his head placed in his shaking hands, pondering just what to do next. There was no possibility of help arriving from any of the other besieged forts or towns, it was every garrison for itself.

Eventually, he left the room simply to breathe the cooler, damper air outside, knowing it wouldn't be long before the heat returned and with it the flies and dust. Repeating nothing of what he'd heard in the mess to the men sprawled on their iron beds endeavouring to pass away the time, Henri eventually returned to his quarters, his strength exhausted. Still weak he took to his bed, not intending to sleep for if he did there was the danger he would stay awake throughout the tedious and long drawn-out night. He wasn't mentally tired but before long he succumbed, lapsing into a deep slumber.

Some time later Henri awoke disorientated and thirsty, and realised that the Muster Call had sounded. This is it, he thought, God help us if we are to surrender!

Together with those who were still able to, Henri stood in silence in the central yard of the garrison, hoping to hear that the fort was to be relieved.

'Men', the officer temporarily in charge of the Fort shouted. 'I know we hate the English but I have to tell you that God has seen fit to give us hope through them! We have received a messenger under a flag of truce to tell us that General Dessalines at Gonaïves has agreed with our General D'Henin to allow the blockading English ships to take us on board.' He paused, allowing the men a moment or two to digest this momentous news, and when the buzz of conversation died down he continued. 'However, we have to march to Môle St Nicolas where the ships are anchored, and from there they will evacuate us. In our physical condition it will be a long, arduous walk and some of us may be too weak to make it—but it is our only chance. The choice is to become prisoners of the English, or die. Be ready to march as soon as the heat of the day has subsided. Take only necessities, we'll eat what there is before we leave and use any hand carts or wagons light enough to pull for the sick who cannot walk. We are also to travel unarmed but will be escorted by Dessalines' men, we have no choice other than to trust them. Prepare as best you can!' Dismissing the ordinary ranks he ordered the officers to gather in the mess-room where orders were given for the surrender of the fort.

To the ordinary soldier there was a sense of relief leading to bewilderment at the news, but little feeling of joy. Most were subdued, all of them were unkempt with long straggly hair and wearing stained, worn-out uniforms, their pride too seemed to vanish as each man came to terms with the news. Was it a trick to get them out of the fort, out into the open where they would be vulnerable to attack? Why would the British even care what happened anyway?

To Henri and the other officers, however, the fact that the order had been signed by General D'Henin was a reassurance that all may indeed not be lost.

Carrying only essentials or personal effects which wouldn't hamper their journey, the occupants of Fort St Marc soon set out on their long trek to freedom. The road was rugged and muddy from the recent rains and at any moment they could be ambushed, if this were to happen there was nowhere to run even if they were capable of doing so. The blacks knew the mountains intimately and a white face could not hide for long; it would be better to die on the road than face their anger.

As the long crocodile of weary men plodded on, some falling on the uneven surface of the road, the sick carried on carts pulled by the stronger, Henri shivered at the thought of what might lay in the trees beyond the track. Taunting calls and wild cries made deliberately to frighten and terrify came out of the dusk, and his whole frame shuddered with each new sound. As the long, gruelling journey drew to a close the men grew wearier and weaker, only the sight of the English ships, now visible in the distant bay, gave them the strength to keep going.

When James Walker saw the long, straggling line of refugees finally reach the small town of Môle St Nicolas he felt only pity. Later, as they came aboard he knew from their emaciated, gaunt appearance that they would have been incapable of existing or even defending themselves for much longer in the Fort. Nor would they have survived an ambush during the march. This gave him the satisfaction of believing that in showing humanity here, England had rid herself of some of the shame that war brings to any nation. That which man was compelled to do in wartime out of duty, out of necessity, was often not a matter of choice. Nevertheless these deeds had to be done or campaigns would be lost to the enemy.

By the time the entire contingent of Frenchmen had embarked, distributed between *Vanguard*, the seized corvette *Papillon* and the transport ship *Trois Amis*, James Walker was more than ready to leave the Môle for Jamaica.

With a relieved and grateful smile, General D'Henin finally boarded *Vanguard* at three o'clock in the morning on the 4th of September and handed James a receipt for the 850 men now in the charge of the British Navy. 'It is done, Monsieur Capitaine, we have done it!' There was a catch in his tired voice and his eyes misted over. 'Now we are all your prisoners—but I am not afraid. On behalf of my men, and France, I thank you!'

Replying in French, James replied. 'A satisfactory conclusion, General, although prison in England may not be quite as comfortable as you would hope for.' James thought of the prisoners who, apart from the officers were battened below deck, most of whom would eventually be incarcerated within the prisons and hulks of a colder and wetter island, England.

He turned to Lieutenant Valentine. 'Well done', he said simply.

Together with several other vessels including the captured *Papillon* and contraband carrying schooner *Mary Sally*, the latter caught attempting to break the blockade by landing forty or fifty barrels of powder on the island, they sailed out of the Bay into the clear aquamarine waters of the Caribbean.

Whilst the majority of the prisoners sank listlessly and despondently on the cluttered lower decks where they'd been sent, Henri as an officer was able to sit, exhausted, in the fresh air above. For a time he watched the northwest headland of Cap du Môle slowly disappear from view, until gradually the feelings of peace and relief brought about by the rescue took over and his eyelids, heavy with lack of sleep, slowly closed.

He was woken sometime later as fresh drinking water was handed to him. When eventually he stood up and looked astern, San Domingo had almost disappeared from view. Only a thin dark outline of the island's mountains remained visible on the far horizon, and Henri on board *Papillon* was relieved to have left her shores for good. His experiences there though, would never leave him! Gone were the once luxurious valleys full of sugar plantations worked by imported black people who had never wanted to leave their own native soils. These same plantations and valleys were now ruined, deliberately scorched and destroyed. The slaves had been cruelly mistreated and betrayed, but at last had found their feet and were determined to throw out the white French oppressors. San Domingo, a land of so much sorrow, hatred and fear, was no longer one of the richest countries of the world and was headed towards an uncertain future. Henri wished her people luck.

En route to Jamaica it soon became common knowledge amongst the prisoners that the Captain of the escorting vessel, *Vanguard*, was responsible for the negotiations that took place between General D'Henin and General Dessalines in order to secure their release from the Fort. To Henri these two men were now worthy of his admiration and respect, and he was more than willing to comply with orders given by his English rescuers.

Although not a good sailor, this voyage did not disturb Henri as much as it did many of his fellow prisoners. Nevertheless he was more than a little relieved to see the British Standard fluttering a welcome as Fort Charles came into view. After anchoring in Port Royal harbour amidst the great variety of vessels already there, Captain James Walker was keen to discharge all the prisoners into the hands of the Port Authority as soon as possible. With the sick taken into quarantine as a matter of urgency and the ship fumigated and scrubbed clean, he could be well satisfied.

As the bedraggled remnants of Napoleon's San Domingo forces eventually left the ships, James eyed them with detachment. He had no love of the French nor the sound of their native tongue but he saw the men as a shepherd sees his flock safely penned, and wondered how many would ever see their homeland again. The barrels of powder from the captured *Mary Sally* had been transferred into the safety of the powder magazine in Fort Charles, where their contents could not now wreak havoc against English shipping in the area, and James looked forward to returning to his normal duties.

Having given his report to the Port Admiral, Sir John Duckworth, immediately on arrival, he now set about writing a similar dispatch for the Admiralty in England. As he did so, he felt sure that the volume of ships captured or destroyed by the British Squadrons must be having a detrimental effect on Napoleon's Navy and his deployment of troops, thus helping the success of war to Britain's benefit.

To Henri the red-bricked bastions of Fort Charles were an imposing sight as he marched with the others along the main road from the harbour, through the nearby fishing village and on to the extensive parade ground and barracks, where they were to be held until transported to England. During the march it was noticeable that the behaviour of some of their accompanying guards was more hostile towards them than had been the case on the *Papillon* but he was in no position to complain, being still weak, and he just did as he was told. He must have shown signs of being unwell for he found himself being taken to the Naval Hospital instead of the barracks where he was examined.

'All the men are extremely emaciated Sir,' a young assistant quietly observed to the Medical Officer who was examining a prisoner. 'Many are sick and wounded, and all are in a bad way.'

'They're lucky to be alive, by all accounts,' the officer replied without looking up from the open wound he was examining. 'Food and peace will gradually cure many, but as for the really sick only time will tell.'

The wound he was treating was already beginning to ulcerate. 'If such wounds as this aren't dealt with before he is shipped, he'll not survive,' he declared in a low voice. There were so many in need of treatment that the doctor had no choice but to work quickly and impersonally, and the minute he'd finished he waved a hand indicating to the prisoner to move on. 'I'm informed that what some of these men have experienced will affect them for the rest of their lives. Some wounds I can heal, minds I cannot!' He sighed.

Henri had been watching the officer as he worked on the man before him, and saw the muscles of his face working as he concentrated on the task, showing little emotion as he used his skills. He wondered at the man's thoughts as he treated the enemies of his country, men who may have killed one of his own kind. Sitting in a chair in an English Naval Hospital miles from home, Henri stared subconsciously at the officer's face and was shaken when he suddenly looked up and their eyes met unexpectedly. The man's face was strained, however his eyes were friendly enough and in that brief exchange Henri saw compassion and resignation, and realised that there really was little difference between one man and another, excepting in language. In that moment Henri decided that if he was going to be a prisoner in England then he would make an attempt to communicate with all those he met and to use and expand what little English he already had.

From then on Henri sought every opportunity to engage the attention of medical and other staff so as to pick up any words that would be useful in the future. On hearing him do so a fellow prisoner sneered, 'Sucking up to the English then?'

Henri shook his head in denial. 'If we're sent to England it might prove useful to understand what is being said,' he replied, 'and who knows, it could even be of service to France!' He spoke to the man as if sharing a confidence. 'Besides it will occupy my mind.' No more was said and Henri began to be convinced that by learning the language of his captors he might just be able to achieve something worthwhile.

With better food, good medical supplies and being a young man, Henri recovered well. He was still painfully thin, but as the Naval establishment on the island of Jamaica had more prisoners than it cared to hold, those fit to endure the rigours of the Atlantic were despatched to England as soon as possible, Henri amongst them.

Throughout the long voyage to England, whether battened down below deck or exercising above it when allowed, Henri kept himself to himself whenever possible. As he was of a higher rank than the majority of the prisoners, this was quite easy to do as, since General Boudet and his retinue had returned to France without him, it meant that he was the only member of his own Brigade on board.

At every opportunity possible he listened and learned what he could of the English language, but time hung heavily on his hands, and as their journey progressed from the warmth of the Caribbean Sea into the cooler waters of the Atlantic he often felt depressed. Seeking shelter below deck from the wind and waves above, he frequently found himself thinking of his parents who could have no idea whether he was alive or dead, or what had befallen him. Even so they would probably hear rumours and reports of San Domingo that would distress them. He wondered how his mother in particular, in her delicate state of mind, would receive the news of his capture, perhaps simply with relief that he was at least alive. His last letter home had been written when the first signs of yellow fever in him became evident so, duty bound, he'd written a short apologetic note assuring them of his devotion. Since then, when St Marc became cut off by the insurgents, there had been no way in which further communication could be made. His parents might now be fearing the worst.

At the age of twenty-eight he should be in the prime of life, well established with a wife and family in some provincial town in France. Instead, all his expectations for the future had evaporated completely, and he was to be imprisoned in England, for God knows how long.

His parents, Joseph and Marie Pichon, were simple but honest people who worked on land belonging to the owner of a Chateau near Saumur in the Loire Valley. They were poorly paid and Henri had been sent to work at the oldest of Saumur's churches as a very young boy, where he'd found favour with one of the Abbés who took him under his wing. This led to Henri's eventual ability to read and write well, for the Abbé soon recognised that his young assistant had an able mind and so took the trouble to instruct him in his spare time.

From being a small boy Henri had always admired the horses at the École de Cavalerie stables of the Military Riding School and spent many an hour imagining himself riding one of them, perhaps in some battle charge or other. This simple dream had become in part a reality, in spite of his lowliness of birth and his parents' impoverished circumstances which would not normally have allowed him such an achievement. The Abbé, however, had seen to it that he was able to use his education, such as it was, to his betterment.

When Napoleon began conscripting young men for his Grand Plan for Europe, Henri was thus at an advantage, and this, together with his ready acceptance of hard work allowed him to rise eventually to the rank of Lieutenant. Finally he was promoted to be an Aide-de-camp to General Boudet, Chief of Staff to the hated General Rochambeau on San Domingo. Henri obeyed orders and got on with his duties but, as time went by, he began to dislike and distrust Rochambeau who he felt betrayed the true spirit of the revolution. This officer, together with another, one General Boyer, had an evil side to their personalities which Henri despised and he had no desire to renew acquaintance with the sadistic pair ever again. As to the present whereabouts of his own General, Boudet, he had only surmise and rumour to go by, and hoped that he'd evaded capture and reached France.

Thinking again of his parents he wondered if they had given up hope and now wept over his demise; and what of Hortense,in the the girl who had promised to await his return?

Finally the shores of England came into view and Henri, with only his thin, tattered uniform to shield him from the cold winds, watched with mounting apprehension and gloom rather than relief as his long journey across the Atlantic neared its end.

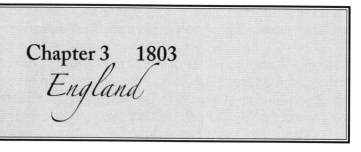

Chapter 3   1803
England

By the time the ship upon which Henri sailed reached England, on a cold, damp November day, some of his strength and resilience had returned although he was still very thin.

There were so many prisoners disembarking at the same time that he found himself being herded along with men he scarcely knew. All too soon they were rowed out to the creaking, rotting prison hulks that lay in the lee of the Isle of Sheppey on the River Medway, between Chatham dockyard and Sheerness. After weeks at sea in the clear fresh air of the ocean he was dismayed at the dismal sight before him.

Five, once fine, vessels were now moored securely, slowly rotting, shabby and without masts, totally unseaworthy but making convenient places to house both criminals and enemy captives alike—as Henri was about to find out.

He could smell the foulness of the marshes beyond the hulks and realised escape would be almost impossible. So, this was to be his home for the duration of hostilities! He was depressed even more by the knowledge that, because Napoleon was such a determined and ruthless man, this war could go on for years.

All the new prisoners were sent immediately below decks and the hatches battened down. Henri wasn't a tall man yet even he found it impossible to stand upright on the lower deck on which he was to live and literally sleep as all the hammocks appeared to be occupied and the deck around them was crammed with palliasses for the many new arrivals. He sat down and looked around this stinking, rat-infested place, his mind becoming numb with despair and hopelessness.

Men returning to France from English prisons in the earlier war had told of inhuman treatment, lack of good food, shortage of clothing, foul air and boredom. All these were conditions he knew would be his to endure if the present war went on for any length of time.

The men already there, coughing and wheezing as a result of their incarceration in the fetid and damp atmosphere, had been little helped by the poor diet and lack of exercise. They were being turned into broken old men. Would he become like one of them? Even now he could feel a familiar tightening of his chest, which sometimes caused prolonged coughing.

Lethargy and boredom became Henri's worst enemy and within a week he had given up trying to converse with the other prisoners who lounged about him, shoeless and unkempt, their grey faces hidden beneath straggling beards. He was always cold and the air he breathed was foul with bodily odours. The constantly coarse and filthy language of those near him he found unpleasant and he began to feel isolated. He didn't fit in with these men; he didn't gamble, seeing only the futility and misery of it. Men gambled not only the clothes they had on but the very rations meant to keep them alive, and what he hated most of all was his inability to curb their foolishness. He sympathised with their plight, they had wounds which refused to heal, and coughs which contributed to the general malaise. He needed stimulation but was determined not to resort to gambling as a way of distraction. He could not understand why, as an officer and aide-de-camp he was not entitled to better treatment, yet to complain might further alienate him from the other prisoners.

Occasionally a name would be called out, summoning a man to go up on deck and from there be taken ashore, never to return, his fate unknown.

Further time passed, then the hatch was again suddenly drawn back and a harsh penetrating voice called, 'Henri Pichon!' Henri was immersed in musing on his misfortunes and didn't immediately register the name, until, for a second time, a louder, harsher cry repeated the name. 'HENRI PICHON!'

Startled, Henri jumped up. 'Oui,' he shouted, grabbing his coat and hurrying to the foot of the ladder beneath the hatch. 'Oui, Henri Pichon!' he shouted fearing the man would go away, and hastily began climbing the ladder. The brightness of the light outside blinded him. 'Henri Pichon!' he gasped, quickly donning his coat against the keen fresh air. Even so he could still feel the fierce

December wind against his body. 'I am Henri Pichon,' he repeated.

'Fetch your belongings,' the guard ordered. 'Immediately!'

'Oui, Monsieur!' Henri replied respectfully and hurried back down to the lower deck to retrieve the remaining few possessions he had. The appalling smell of the lower deck struck him even more after the outside air and he instinctively clamped his lips together. His dirty but serviceable clothing had not left his body since he arrived, nor had anything of value, these were in the sabretache across his chest even when he slept, in case of theft. He had only removed his coat earlier in order to try to wash and was glad he had seized it before going on deck or that would have been the last he would have seen of it. The small book he had managed to carry on the march to the Môle he kept under his straw palliasse, knowing it was of little value to men who could neither read or write. At the last moment he remembered the tricorne hat which he was unable to wear due to the low beams, this had been secreted under his pillow. He seized it and hastened again to the foot of the ladder.

'Never trust the English,' a voice called out from behind him in the shadows of the hold. The sound of rattling bowls and pannikins grew louder but Henri understood that the prisoners were merely relieving their boredom by acting this way.

Emerging a second time, Henri swallowed hard, a feeling of optimism returning with each new intake of breath. He didn't fear what lay ahead, nothing could be worse than the incarceration he had endured, and he did not believe he would be killed.

'I am ready,' Henri said politely in hesitant English, much to the surprise of the guard.

'Follow me!' the man ordered, leading him to where several other prisoners stood by the top of the gangway ladder waiting to be taken down into a longboat. He recognised one man he'd seen during the sea voyage from Jamaica. He nodded to him but had no time to speak before being ordered to climb down the ladder.

Seated at last in the boat the two men found themselves alongside each other. 'We go to our deaths, maybe?'

'I don't believe that will happen.' Henri replied with a glimmer of a smile. 'Why us when we've done no harm, and why bring us so far?'

'Perhaps you are right,' the man agreed thoughtfully. 'I am Louis Brecon, I saw you on the voyage. You speak a little English I know, what do they want with us?'

Henri shook his head, 'I really don't know, I am simply happy to be out of that lousy, stinking hulk. Let us hope that we don't get sent back there—or anywhere worse.' He folded his arms, wrapping them round his body to fend off the biting wind as the boat rocked in the rough water. Eventually they reached a jetty and once on land were marched to a large building where they were made to wait.

No explanation was given as to what was required of them and Louis whispered, 'What was it like on the Island of San Domingo, was it as bad as they say?'

'Worse than bad! Death surrounded us, starvation was almost upon us and without the English who rescued us we stood no chance.' Henri paused then asked, 'And you? How did you come to be on board?'

'I am a midshipman. My ship was seized off Cap Français, we tried to break through the blockade but stood no chance.'

'Ah,' Henri said, 'that's why the movement of the boat affected you very little. I'm not a sailor.... ' A sharp voice interrupted.

'Quiet! No talking!'

With the order to be silent, Henri waited patiently until his name was called.

'Henri Pichon!'

At the command, Henri rose and followed the guard to the door of a small office where he was asked his name. 'Lieutenant Henri Pichon!' he replied, 'Aide-de-Camp to General Boudet!' His assessment on arrival had been cursory and it was probable that it had taken some time to finally arrange his immediate future. He produced several papers of identification from his sabretache, these were examined closely and, after answering various questions which apparently satisfied the officer in charge, Henri began to relax.

A second officer who spoke fluent French then entered the room and addressed him. 'As one of General Boudet's retinue, you are entitled to be put on parole. If you agree to the conditions that I will read to you, you will be sent to a small town where you will live within that community. This will be a position of trust which if broken will result in your detention in a prison.'

The officer allowed Henri several seconds to reflect on the idea before explaining the terms. 'You will have the liberty to walk on the Great Turnpike road within a distance of one mile from the extremities of the town, but not to go into the fields or cross roads, nor be absent from your lodgings after 5 o'clock in the afternoon during the winter months, that is Oct 1st to March 31st, nor from 8 o'clock in the evenings during the summer months. Once the form has been signed everyone is obliged and required to suffer you to pass and re-pass without hindrance or molestation providing you keep within the limits and behave according to the law.' He paused for a moment before continuing, 'Any attempt to break Parole would immediately occasion your arrest and imprisonment. You will receive a weekly allowance of eight shillings and nine pence per week to pay for lodging and will have certain privileges. Also, repatriation will sometimes be arranged depending on circumstances as time passes.' He paused again, looking at Henri, 'Breaking Parole is a serious breach of trust. Punishment will mean incarceration at Norman Cross, or a return to the hulks. However, considering that our two countries are at war this is a very fair offer.' He waited while Henri read the full French version of the declaration himself. 'Escape from England is almost impossible, being on an island, and great vigilance is taken at all ports to prevent escape. It is not worth attempting. If you agree to the terms then sign the form and we can proceed with preparation for Parole.'

Hardly daring to believe what he'd heard, Henri was willing to agree to anything rather than return to the hulk where he would probably die. He wasn't a man to give a promise lightly however, believing that half the world's troubles sprang from mistrust and the broken word. He also had elderly parents to whom it was his duty to provide care in the future. He could hardly do this if he were to die.

Finally he nodded, 'I give my word not to break Parole,' he declared, and taking the pen he signed the document, albeit with some trepidation.

'Will it be possible for me to notify my parents in France that I am alive and well?' he asked hopefully.

'You will be able to write to your family from your destination. However, all correspondence must be sent through and inspected by your Agent. You must also pay the costs yourself.'

Having signed the Parole Form and received sufficient cash for his journey, Henri was taken to the barracks where he remained until issued with a ticket to travel. He was also provided with sufficient clothing to replace such of his own that was no longer usable and his boots, which had rotted and barely hung together were also exchanged together with a pair of socks. His uniform, although worn and soiled did not, however, warrant replacement. He now eagerly awaited instruction as to where and when he was to go.

On the same day on which Henri was being offered parole in England, across the ocean in San Domingo, France's domination of the Island came to an infamous end. General Rochambeau had angered the black Generals and insurgents with his threats and cruelty to such a degree that a full-scale revolt was taking place.

After several bloody military defeats Rochambeau and the French troops had been forced to retreat into the forts around Cap François and were under siege from mobs of crazed, ragged and mentally inflamed blacks; people desperately trying to rid themselves of their oppressors. By this time both black and white populations were almost out of their minds. The blacks, recklessly and courageously advancing on the besieged French were being torn apart by muskets and grapeshot, but nevertheless they repeatedly advanced in the brilliant sunshine towards the Forts. Even the observing Rochambeau was stirred by the sight of their courage. Only a sudden outburst of torrential rain brought the fighting to an end.

That night Rochambeau held a Council of War and decided to negotiate with the black leader General Dessalines in order to evacuate his troops from the island.

Dessalines, dissatisfied with Rochambeau's demands ordered him to leave the Island immediately or his ships would be bombarded with red-hot shot and burned. However, he did agree to allow Rochambeau to surrender to the British Fleet and said that he would take care of the wounded French soldiers who had to be left behind. Once Rochambeau had gone he massacred them all.

Rochambeau was shipped to Jamaica, as had been Henri, and then finally on to England and prison.

When the French fled San Domingo, once one of the richest countries in the world, they left it ravaged beyond recognition, the plantations destroyed, her ports and towns devastated, and a population seething with a hatred of anything white, a hatred that would linger for 200 years.

The result of the surrender was a national humiliation for Napoleon who had lost nearly 60,000 men on the island. Immediately, General Jean-Jacques Dessalines declared the colony independent and subsequently the old name Haiti, her original name, was re-instated.

Eventually, clad in his new boots, enjoying the feel of wearing a clean shirt but still wearing his faded uniform and tricorne hat and carrying his meagre belongings, Henri was marched for several days with a group of other prisoners until they reached London. Here he was put on a Mail Coach under the supervision of the driver, shortly to leave on the northern highway for the town of Chesterfield.

The coach left the yard of the Bull & Mouth promptly at one in the afternoon on a journey that would take almost twenty-two hours.

Hour upon hour he endured the jolting and swaying of the coach as it rumbled along the deeply rutted roads. He was not dismayed, for an army traverses all kinds of terrain in order to reach its destination, hardship was a soldier's lot. However, Henri would have preferred to have been on horseback rather than inside a coach.

As they travelled through the rolling countryside he tried to sleep to avoid the curiosity of his fellow passengers who obviously knew what he was. His own inquisitiveness however, prevailed, and he looked frequently through the side windows of the coach; the trees were bare of leaves and the hedgerows decorated with frost, in stark contrast to the humid heat and burning sun that he had experienced in San Domingo. He marvelled at the comparative freedom that was now his lot, but whenever the coach halted to change horses the newly boarding passengers would at first stare at him, then furtively glance in his direction when they thought he wasn't aware of it.

There appeared to be little of the resentment or hatred he had anticipated, although occasionally he would sense coolness in their attitude, but he was never quite sure whether or not it was all in his imagination. It was impossible to hide the fact that he was an enemy soldier, perhaps his shabby appearance aroused their pity.

Having no desire to offend anyone he refrained from attempting to speak English but instead contented himself to listen and in this way, learn. Henri left the coach when told to do so by the coachman and endeavoured to behave in a manner which would not draw more attention to himself than necessary. Nevertheless he desperately wanted to know more about his surroundings and his final destination, Chesterfield. Was it a small or large place, important or sleepy, and how would the people of the town feel on seeing him walk amongst them? Surely they must resent having the enemy in their midst whilst their fellow citizens were being killed!

As the day wore on it became too gloomy to see out and, notwithstanding the increasing chill in the coach as night dragged on, he was able to sleep fitfully. Suddenly the sound of the coach horn woke him with a start!

He thought himself back in Fort St Marc and the fears of that time came flooding back. Trying to suppress this and to control his shaking hands he lifted his head and peered out into the darkness. He could just make out the silhouettes of the many buildings lining the road; houses, factories and mills, shadows against the pale winter moonlight. Then as the coach penetrated deeper into the town the skyline gradually became hidden by fog.

'Birmingham!' The coachman shouted as the horses snorted and finally clattered to a halt before the *Albion*. 'Birmingham!' the man called out once more before climbing down and handing the reins of the horses to a yardman.

Henri sat for a few moments after the other passengers had alighted; was he to follow or sit awaiting instructions? He knew he should change coaches at Birmingham but that was all.

'You too!' The coachman called through the open coach door, and saw the rather puzzled look on Henri's face. 'You want the 5.45 to Chesterfield via Lichfield and Derby. The Innkeeper will let you know when it arrives.'

With aching back and stiff joints Henri climbed down and looked about him. He had been given sufficient money to buy refreshments but was unsure what kind of reception he would receive once inside the Inn.

'You don't leave the *Albion* until the branch coach arrives!' the coachman said, not unkindly. 'You stay in there,' he repeated, pointing to the doorway, unsure if the Frenchman fully understood him. 'No running away now!'

Although Henri wasn't totally sure if he knew what the man meant, it was obvious that he was not going to get the chance to take a walk in order to stretch his legs. Instead he simply followed the other passengers into the warmth of the Inn where he was able to purchase a drink before standing gratefully by the fire to await the arrival of the branch coach. He longed for some exercise but as it wasn't possible to take a stroll he eventually moved to where he could doze quietly in the corner of the room. Unfortunately the laughter created by the two women travellers who had journeyed with him in the coach from London, disturbed him. The pair had earlier chatted incessantly throughout the night causing another occupant, a gentleman and obviously a man of the cloth, to sigh with distain and eventually lean back into the shadow, becoming almost invisible in the dark. It was impossible for Henri to follow the prattle between the women and having now thawed out somewhat he felt his eyelids closing.

He was awoken suddenly when someone tugged his sleeve. 'Frenchman, your coach has arrived, and the horses are being changed. Up you get!' Henri strived to orientate himself as he rose and reluctantly left the warm room for the chill outside. This brought on a bout of coughing as the biting cold night air came as a shock to his system. He climbed aboard and found to his relief that the two women were not to accompany them.

The coach rumbled out of the town and with the eventual arrival of daybreak he became interested again in the passing terrain which changed slowly from softly undulating fields and low hills to more defining higher ridges.

When the branch Mail Coach in which Henri was travelling finally reached the small market town of Chesterfield it was in the late afternoon. He could see the clustered houses of the township on a low hill dominated by the strangely twisted spire of a church, the sight of which took him by surprise. It was not its unusual shape which struck him but the familiarity of it, for within the Loire Valley where he'd been born there were several such spires, one also distorted like the one before him. He pondered, had it been struck by lightening or fire? Nevertheless it was a poignant reminder of his homeland.

The coach finally drew up before *The Angel Inn* in the Market Square. 'Chesterfield!' The driver repeated loudly before climbing down and handing the reins to the ostler who led the horses through an archway into the yard behind.

It was a drab, damp afternoon and Henri's limbs were almost numb as he climbed tiredly down. He flexed his legs and feet in an effort to revive his circulation before taking stock of his surroundings. The buildings around the large Town Square were of a better style than those on its approaches and it was a strange, uncomfortable feeling to be standing there alone, dressed in the uniform of a French officer, in a place belonging to the enemy of his own country.

As there was no luggage to collect from the roof or box of the coach, the driver sensing Henri's bewilderment, said, 'Come with me. Have you got your papers with you?' He hoisted the mailbag over his shoulder and indicated that Henri should follow him.

'Ah, Oui! Thank you!' Henri replied hesitantly, and sought the folded papers in the sabretache across his chest as he went.

'Come inside Lad! Mr Lovett will tell you where to go,' the driver explained, leading Henri towards the heavy oak door which had been left open by a previous customer.

Pausing for a moment to let his eyes adjust to the change in light, Henri saw several men sitting in the parlour, close to a log fire. All raised their eyes in curiosity at his appearance but soon resumed their conversations. Henri, however, in spite of his limited understanding of the language realised that he was of course the subject of their thoughts. Ignoring them he stood quietly by as the driver exchanged words with the Innkeeper, William Lovett, who listened and nodded in understanding before turning to look enquiringly at Henri. The driver then withdrew and made ready to leave.

'Thank you, Monsieur,' Henri called after him, then turned to face Mr Lovett. 'Please, this man?' he asked, offering his papers and pointing to the information which had been included with his travel details.

'A Frenchman?' Lovett asked, although it was obvious from Henri's blue uniform and tricorne hat that indeed he was.

'Oui!' Henri nodded. 'Please to buy a drink and use a latrine?'

The man smiled agreeably. 'Come with me!' he replied, thinking that here was another potential customer, albeit a prisoner, who would need to buy food and drink once he had established himself. Henri followed gratefully and, on his return to the parlour accepted the ale which the man offered, refusing to accept payment; a gesture of goodwill which immediately struck Henri as a decent thing to do, an act which he would not easily forget.

'Merci, I thank you!' Henri raised his tankard in a toast and then drank deeply, realising how dry he was. He would have preferred a glass of sparkling cool wine from the Loire Valley, but he was cheered by the offering.

As Henri relaxed, the Innkeeper called out to a youth in a backroom, with whom he had a brief conversation during which the name Bower cropped up. The boy then left, only to return several minutes later shaking his head. 'I knocked on his door in Church Lane but there's nobody there—the man next door says he's gone home!'

'Take him to Mr Bower's at Spital Lodge then,' Lovett ordered, adding with a knowing look, 'and don't linger on the way back!' Turning to Henri he said, 'Follow the lad, he'll take you!'

'Merci!' Henri responded, 'Thank you!'

'Call again, your fellow countrymen are welcome here!' Lovell responded heartily.

Although not fully understanding all that was said, Henri gathered from the openness of the man's face that there was no animosity there. He then proceeded to follow the boy who seemed reluctant about being seen in public with a French soldier and instead trotted ahead, hesitating every so often to make sure Henri was still with him. He was quite unable to disguise his natural curiosity which was evident in the boy's eyes.

When the first French prisoners had appeared in Chesterfield two months previously, there had been a feeling of indignation and some fear in the town. But slowly, like everything in a country area, life had gradually resumed with a quiet acceptance. In fact a mutual respect was growing between some of the landladies and their lodgers. There were some prisoners whose haughty manners caused resentment and dislike, but others behaved like gentlemen.

Jeering youths, however, still received considerable satisfaction from taunting the Frenchmen who, generally, ignored them. The lifting of tricorne hats, the kissing and embracing which went on when the prisoners met still amused the locals, who thought the foreigners a little soft or feminine.

Crossing the Square the pair then wended their way through several narrow alleys and streets, all the time descending to the valley bottom where the noise of factories could be heard. As they crossed over a bridge spanning a small river the unmistakeable smell of leather tanning and glue emanated from one of the properties. Looking down into the River Hipper, which flowed peacefully from the surrounding hills at a leisurely pace, Henri thought how different it was to the strong Loire river which passed by his home town and often flooded large areas where he lived in France.

If he had needed a good walk Henri was certainly getting one now, and at times he wondered just how far the boy was taking him. He was led him over several watery meadows to where the land began to rise again until eventually they reached the gateway of a drive at the head of which stood a pleasantly modest house, standing back in the trees. Taking Henri up to the doorway of Spital Lodge, the lad used the knocker to announce their arrival. Several seconds passed without response, causing him to knock again.

'Alright, alright! I'm coming!' a voice called from within. The door opened to reveal a middle-aged gentleman who looked enquiringly at the youth and his companion.

'Mr Bower, I've brought thi a Frenchie,' the lad replied, pointing to Henri as if he were invisible. 'Mr Lovett sent 'im from *t'Angel*. You weren't at t'office when a went. Can a go now? Only 'e said be quick about it!'

John Bower chuckled to himself. 'Right, you can leave him with me lad, off you go, and thank you.' he said, handing the boy a coin from his pocket.

The boy took it and grinned. 'Thanks Mister!' He gave Henri a glance and scampered off.

'Come in, come in, I'm John Bower,' the man informed Henri in French as he held out his hand. 'Welcome to Chesterfield. I am the agent for French prisoners on parole here.'

'Henri Pichon, Lieutenant, Sir,' Henri said as he shook the outstretched hand before scraping the mud from his boots on the iron scraper by the door. He then handed over his Parole papers before entering the house. He was encouraged by the friendly reception and pleased to hear his native tongue spoken so well. He was also cold and hungry. 'Where do I go?' he asked in hesitant English.

'Ah! Good! A Frenchman willing to speak our language,' John Bower exclaimed. 'You could be useful here as a go-between for me and your countrymen,' he said, reverting to French in order to save time. 'You look weary, man,' he remarked as he led Henri into a dimly lit room and invited him to sit down.

'Merci, Monsieur, I have travelled for twenty-two hours without proper rest. Please, where do I go to sleep?' Just then the church bell rang out across the valley. It was 5 o'clock in the afternoon, and was known as the 'Frenchman's Bell' heralding the start of the daily curfew.

It was getting dark outside now. John Bower shook his head and looked towards the window. He thought for a moment and began lighting several lamps within the room, the light from the fire becoming insufficient for their needs. It was certainly too late now to wander out with the curfew already upon the prisoners. 'You'd better stay here until morning!' he said. 'I'll find you lodgings in the town then. I think Mrs Bower can be counted upon to provide you with a meal, and you can have a wash first to take the dust of your journey away.' He was used, as an attorney, to quickly summing people up and his impressions of Henri were favourable. As a result he was willing to give him the benefit of his intuition and find him a bed. 'I'll not be a moment,' he informed Henri, 'I must arrange things with my wife. Meanwhile, warm yourself by the fire.'

When Mr Bower left the room, Henri glanced round and judged the agent to be reasonably well provided for, nor was he without education judging by the number of books lining a case on the nearby wall. It was a pleasant room in which Henri felt comfortable for the first time in many months.

Several minutes later Mr Bower returned from another part of the house. 'All is arranged,' he said, smiling as he entered and seated himself in a comfortable chair beside the fire. 'As a man representing the Law and as agent for any prisoners sent here,' he explained, 'I am responsible for their welfare and behaviour. I find them lodgings, pay their allowances and see to it that they obey the rules of their parole. Prisoners have been arriving in large numbers this week and finding accommodation for them has been difficult.' He could tell that Henri was tired but felt obliged to put the man at his ease. 'I don't know how long this cursed war will last. If you don't mind me asking, how did you fall into English hands?'

'I was taken off the Island of San Domingo with over eight hundred of my countrymen.' These painful memories caused Henri to grimace and frown for a moment.

With an understanding nod, John Bower continued. 'Many of the men here, about eighty so far, were taken at sea as they left San Domingo. You may know some?'

'They were amongst the lucky ones,' Henri responded, 'to get away before the worst part began.'

'Not so,' the Agent replied, 'many were in a bad way as a result of fever or wounds which have left them with infirmities. They also have inner scars which will be a long time in healing.'

This was no surprise to Henri who was well aware of the mental horrors from which he himself suffered occasionally. 'I can understand only too well. I owe my life to an honourable English Navy Captain. Our entire garrison would have been slaughtered if he had not negotiated to take us off that island. We were all sick and emaciated from lack of rations and despairing for our lives.' He paused for a moment and John Bower waited patiently, realising that Henri was finding some relief in talking of his experiences. 'We struggled,' Henri began again, 'to walk from the Fortress of St Marc to the peninsula at Môle St Nicolas where his ships awaited us. For that I honour the man.'

This outburst of emotion had taken John Bower by surprise, and he replied, 'I can understand why the prisoners resent having been captured, even their dislike of us, their enemy, but if someone like you who speaks our language can foster a little better understanding between them and the whole community, it would make things easier for all concerned.'

Henri agreed, then fell silent. He was exhausted, and the conversation at times had been difficult to follow but he now felt relaxed in the company of the man in whose house he sat. The gentle firelight gave the room a cosy effect, and the warmth from the fire grate had eased his stiffened muscles. Before long he unintentionally dozed off, making a forlorn figure.

John Bower quietly left the room and the sleeping Frenchman. He realised the risk he was taking in keeping the stranger in his home, however, in the man's condition, without money, in enemy uniform and with a strong foreign accent he felt Henri must realise that he was better off in the house than attempting to flee in the dark. John simply went to his study to sort out some of the paperwork he'd brought from his office that afternoon, leaving Henri to sleep.

Hunger must eventually have woken Henri, that or the smell of food cooking from another part of the house. He was momentarily disorientated and unsure what to do next, such comforts after the months of deprivation made him want to stay exactly as he was. Instead, he sat up straight and coughed out loud, hoping to attract attention, which it did.

'I think your Frenchman is awake,' Isabella Bower said, popping her head round the door of her husband's study. 'Will you show him where he is to sleep so that he can wash first. Or shall I feed him?'

'Perhaps the latter, dear,' he replied, 'a little dust and dirt won't hurt for a short while longer.' He rose from behind the desk at which he'd been sitting for almost two hours and followed his wife from the room. There was not a lot of money to be made from being the local agent for the prisoners, but there were a few perks included and, as he was about to regain his position as Mayor in the town, it gave him a little more prestige in the eyes of the Town Council.

There were plenty of women in the town willing to take in lodgers, all were in need of the extra money it brought. Some ladies simply wanted to enhance their children's education by having a foreigner in their midst to teach painting, music and language skills, and the presence of an educated French officer in a household was also a symbol of social status. These prisoners were always easier to house than seamen or servants who had to be placed in hostelries or poorer homes.

So far John's wife, Isabella, had resisted any suggestion that they offer accommodation to the higher-ranking officers. This no doubt was because she thought that with three daughters living in the house this might cause problems. John himself would have liked the company of an educated Frenchman, although Lieutenant Henri Pichon was not quite of high enough rank to suit his coming position as Mayor. Nevertheless, until accommodation could be found in the morning they had a guest for the night.

As he entered the room assigned to him by Mrs Bower, Henri looked longingly at the bed, being the first proper one he'd used since leaving France. After lumpy camp beds, ship's hammocks and the straw palliasse provided in the hulk, this was luxury indeed. He removed his stained and travel-worn clothes and washed carefully so as not to soil the clean linen placed on the bed by his hostess.

Earlier he had eaten carefully of the meal kindly placed before him, in case his stomach reacted to the unaccustomed goodness, and now replete he stretched out feeling almost human again. His dark brown hair contrasted with the white of the linen as his head sank into the pillow and he promptly fell asleep.

'He's very polite,' Isabella said to her husband later in the evening after Henri had gone upstairs. 'I feel quite sorry for him. He does at least speak some English which makes it easier to communicate. How old do you think he is?'

After a moment's consideration, John Bower shook his head. 'I've not yet checked his papers and it's difficult to tell when a man has been through such a lot, it ages one so! I'd say about thirty. He's lucky to be alive having survived yellow fever and near starvation whilst they waited, expecting to be massacred. Apparently our Navy rescued his party just in time off that island.'

'No wonder half of the recent arrivals look drawn and have an air of shock about them. I hadn't appreciated that things had been so bad. I wonder how many more we'll have to house in this small town?' Isabella asked as she prepared to retire to bed, 'Who are you thinking of placing him with?'

John began extinguishing the oil lamps. 'I've been through the list of people willing to accept a lodger, but at the moment it's a short one.' He paused, 'Perhaps he could stay here?'

'Not likely, John!' she retorted. 'What do we want with a French prisoner here? And you about to be Mayor again. People will say your sympathies are misplaced. Besides we have the girls to think of, it would be most inappropriate!'

'Mmm,' he muttered, unconvinced. 'I just thought a little extra income would come in handy.'

'What's more to the point, in eleven days time, as Mayor, you'll have enough to think about without a stranger in tow! In any case, he's a complete stranger, how do you know that you can trust him?'

'I'm a pretty good judge of character in my job, but if that's how you feel, Isabella, then so be it.' He extinguished the last lamp while his wife led the way upstairs by the light of a candle.

Once in bed, John Bower lay in the flickering light from the bedroom fire contemplating his fourth term of office as Mayor for the Borough of Chesterfield, a role he immensely enjoyed, then slipped easily into sleep.

In contrast, Henri woke several times during the night, each time with the familiar nightmares that often troubled him. Towards dawn he stirred finally and the comfort of his present situation brought him almost to a point of contentment. He was not a particularly religious man, and his experiences of the past year or so had greatly disillusioned him. This morning, however, he acknowledged the bounty that was his compared with what might have been and prayed silently in thanks for his good fortune. In this state he must have dozed off again.

He woke later to the sound of knocking. It was still dark in the room due to the heavy damask drapes at the window, and when John Bower knocked again then called advising Henri to rise, he did so hurriedly.

Henri acknowledged his host and then drew the curtains to one side in order to see where he had placed his clothes, pulling them on quickly as the room was icy cold. That done, he returned to the window and saw that the sun had fully risen but the ground was still hard with frost.

The house appeared to be in a rural backwater surrounded by fields and broken woodland beyond the driveway. The small town to which he'd been brought the previous day was scattered on the opposite hill and covered by a haze of smoke, above which the clear bright sky seemed out of place.

Glancing back at the comfortable bed which had given him such well needed rest, he was alarmed to see that his unwashed hair had left a grubby mark on the pillow. He was a proud man and ashamed to think that he'd repaid Madame Bower's kindness by soiling her linen so badly. Just as an army marches on its stomach, so they say, a soldier also puts his head down anywhere without much thought at the end of a wearisome march. He must apologise and wash his hair at the first opportunity. After tidying the room, Henri opened the door and went downstairs coughing so as to warn those below that he was on his way.

John Bower came to greet him. 'Did you sleep well?' he asked, looking at his guest's grave face.

'Oui, Monsieur,' Henri replied, nodding. 'But I have to apologise to Madame for soiling the pillow with this hair of mine!'

Seeing the genuine look of concern on his guest's face, John waved the matter to one side. 'I will explain to her, I'm sure she will be grateful for your concern.' Then as a gesture of appreciation asked, 'Perhaps you would like a bath before I take you into town to look for prospective lodgings?'

Henri smiled. 'That is kind of you—I will of course your kindness pay for, I have a little money.'

By now the pair had entered the kitchen where Isabella, having despatched her daughters from the house on an errand, was preparing his breakfast. Henri bowed courteously, while her husband explained about the pillow.

'Tell the good man,' she replied, 'that it will wash out but that I appreciate his concern. Now, would he like to eat before he leaves? Did he sleep well?'

'Oui, Madame! Thank you!' Henri replied directly. 'I do sleep well and am hungry!'

Throughout the meal his confidence in his ability to converse with his hosts increased so that between them a tolerable conversation took place. Mrs Bower, plump as a partridge with greying hair and a pleasantly rounded face, reminded Henri of his own mother. 'Please do you have paper on which I can write?' he asked. 'Perhaps my mother thinks I am dead!'

Seeing that Henri had finished his breakfast, John got up. 'Bathe first, then we must go to my office where I can register your arrival. I've plenty of paper there for your letter and we can despatch it to the Transport Office once I have ensured that what you have written complies with the rules.'

The luxury and near-forgotten enjoyment of sitting in a hip-bath of hot water made Henri feel almost human again and once bathed, with his long hair now sleek and tidy he re-entered the kitchen, his appearance much to the approval of Isabella Bower. He bowed and kissed her hand, thanking her. The colour rose in her cheeks and she quickly left the kitchen with a smile on her lips, relieved that she had sent her daughters from the house to visit their sick aunt in the town.

Together Henri and John Bower set out for his office in Church Lane—this time along the roads. The surface was in fact crisp from the frost and crunched sharply as they walked. It was a far less muddy route than that which the boy had taken him across the fields the previous afternoon, perhaps against Parole Rules.

Alternating between French and English, John Bower, who was a good conversationalist, fell easily into explaining something of the locality as they went. 'Don't forget you are only allowed to go a mile beyond the town's boundaries,' he said, 'you'd best be mindful of this because to go beyond it would break Parole with the result that you could be taken to Norman Cross, a hell-hole of a prison which you would not like to enter.'

'I have no intention of breaking Parole,' Henri commented reassuringly. 'But I am a son of France first and was a revolutionist seeking freedom for all men. Sadly, I fear what was planned and fought for has been betrayed by Bonaparte, but neither do I think that the English really want to end slavery?' These thoughts spoken out loud were sincerely meant and by no means a challenge.

However, John Bower quickly responded, 'Just a word of caution! There is a strong movement and a great strength of feeling here towards abolishing the slave trade altogether but there are some who do not agree, so, I wouldn't express your opinions too openly if I were you, it may make your countrymen restless and alienate the citizens of this town against you!' Then in a more conciliatory tone, 'Your biggest problem is going to be boredom. You need to find something to occupy you, perhaps by making things to sell to augment your allowance. Many are already turning to gambling to while away the time.'

'I'm certainly not a gambler!' Henri assured him.

By this time they had re-crossed the river and almost reached the brow of the hill. A few eyebrows were raised en route but it was possibly simply due to him being in Mr Bower's company as there appeared to be no abuse or animosity directed at him.

'Not far now,' John Bower informed him. 'You will never guess what a strange resident we've acquired since your countrymen arrived. A monkey, of all things! One of the prisoners brought it all the way from San Domingo! Naturally the children are fascinated so it is breaking down a few barriers.'

Henri was horrified. 'Poor thing, it won't enjoy the frost!' His sensitive view on captivity made him speak a little sharply.

'Someone made it a jacket so I wouldn't worry,' John Bower replied with a laugh. 'Here we are, Church Lane and my office. In we go.'

The sleep, the food and the walk had done much to restore Henri's spirits and lift his expectations. So far he'd met only kindness since his arrival but soon he would have to go out alone in the town. It would certainly be a strange new experience.

'Sit down,' John Bower ordered in a businesslike fashion once they had entered the building, and he shuffled through papers on his desk. 'I need your details for the records and to exchange your travel papers for a permit to reside here at liberty,' he said. Once Henri had handed over his papers he was given the necessary permit along with his first week's allowance as a Lieutenant, from which Mr Bower would deduct the cost of despatching his letter to France. The Agent took a clean sheet of paper from a drawer and offered Henri a space at his desk at which to write. At this point he left Henri to his thoughts and worked at some other business needing his attention.

Henri's letter was short yet not without sentiment, and conveyed all that was necessary to allay his parent's fears about his welfare. He would write again, at length, when he was in more conducive surroundings. He finally handed the sheet to Mr Bower to check before it could be addressed and posted to the Transport Board from where, along with many others, it would be despatched to the continent.

'If I can't find you private accommodation, I'm afraid you will have to lodge at an Inn with others of your countrymen.' (He hated using the word prisoner directly to a man's face.) 'There have been many more arriving recently and you will appreciate that accommodation is becoming scarce.'

Henri considered this. 'If possible, I would prefer not to lodge at an Inn,' he commented, 'unless I know the men concerned. You see I would like to improve my knowledge of your language. I have quiet habits and read a lot.'

'Well,' said John, rubbing his chin and eyeing him thoughtfully. 'There is one billet which might suit you. As I feel I know a little about you from your behaviour in our acquaintance so far, I think you would fit in there quite well, whereas others might not. The place is just within the mile limit at a small farm where an old couple are having trouble making ends meet. The money you pay for your lodging would help them.'

'This farm, it sounds interesting. My parents worked the land and I helped them as I grew up. Perhaps I could help them in other ways too and stave off my boredom.'

'They couldn't pay you I'm afraid, but you'd probably eat better there than in town.' Then John hesitated. 'There is just one problem though. Their son was wounded in Egypt, but sadly he died on his way home and was buried at sea. On reflection, I think it is more an ordinary English lodger they want!'

At this Henri raised his eyebrows in surprise. 'I really don't think they would tolerate a French soldier in the house! I might be made to feel guilty for the death of their son,' he said quite reasonably. 'In war things are done of which one is often ashamed.'

'I understand you perfectly. There is one other place, nearby, but with a crotchety old widow who also needs the money.'

'You have been most kind to me,' Henri replied, 'but I think perhaps I will take the latter if the lady is willing.'

'Then we'll go there immediately. Remember you must always use this office for all your correspondence otherwise it will not be sent.'

Together the two men went directly to Glumangate where a Mrs Parsons had a small but clean and orderly house.

'Come in,' she said on seeing the solicitor and the Frenchman. 'You've come about the lodgings?'

'Oui, Madame,' Henri bowed respectfully.

'Good morning, Mrs Parsons,' John Bowers said, lifting his hat, 'Lieutenant Pichon has just arrived. He stayed at Spital Lodge with me last night but he has no luggage and has a limited knowledge of our language.'

'Well then he can teach me French!' Mrs Parsons responded a little bossily. She let them into a small front room with a window that gave a view directly onto the street.

Mr Bower ignored her remark and got down to business. 'Three shillings is the most he can pay per week, with breakfast included.' He waited while she thought about it, then added, 'But not a penny more.' He could see she had been about to argue. 'Not a penny more mind you, if you want to come to some agreement about other meals, then that is up to you, but he doesn't have much money to exist on.'

'That will have to do then,' said the lady with some spirit.

'If you need me to translate at any time or answer any questions, Mrs Parsons, you know where to find me. Now, I must go, this fellow has taken up a good deal of my time already.' He lifted his hat, bade them both farewell and opened the door to leave.

Mrs Parsons called out to him. 'I certainly will call if I need you!' she said pointedly.

This caused a slight feeling of apprehension in John Bower as he walked away from the house, but he had other pressing problems to concentrate on and deal with, so he continued on his way back to the office.

Mrs Parsons was a tiny woman with a thin, pinched face topped by thinning grey hair. 'Come with me,' she said to Henri and pointed to the stairs. The room she showed him was quite small but adequate for his needs, particularly as he had no luggage or possessions to spread about. 'Dinners are more money!' she said, as he held out the unfamiliar English money for her to take the three shillings agreed to. When they'd done negotiating he looked at the few remaining coins in his hand, hoping that what was left would be sufficient for his needs. It seemed a paltry amount for a man to manage on.

Seemingly satisfied now, Mrs Parsons smiled thinly and left the room, closing the door behind her.

There seemed little enough for him to do in such a small and tidy room, so Henri decided to take a walk in the hope that he might meet a fellow countryman in the town to exchange information with.

'Don't miss the Frenchman's Bell at five o'clock,' Mrs Parsons called out as he prepared to leave the house. 'And remember, supper is at six o'clock!'

The words bell and supper were new to him, and seeing the bewilderment on his face she pointed to five on the old grand-daughter clock standing in the corner, and gestured as if ringing a bell.

'Ah, oui! Thank you!' he replied, wondering if he would be allowed to return before that, or if he might have to wander the streets until then. He closed the door behind him and walked down the street, pausing every so often to peer into the windows of several shops on either side. He again considered the small amount of money he had left and concluded that his worst enemy would now be poverty and hunger.

Fortunately, in common with many of his fellow officers he still had in his possession half a dozen gold pieces hidden within the buttons of his uniform, and a watch of which he was particularly proud. This was still stitched into the lining of his coat for fear of theft. Other than his sabretache, everything else he owned had been lost or abandoned one way or another, during sickness or confusion or was found to be too cumbersome to carry.

The air was cold and frosty and he wore his tricorne hat in order to keep warm. Although of medium height, his upright posture gave him an air of military distinction which could not be disguised.

At the bottom of Glumangate he entered the Market Square and looked about. To his astonishment he saw several French soldiers gathered before the door of *The Angel Inn* where he'd arrived the day before. He approached them slowly, hungry for contact with men of his own world but experience had taught him that men brought down by misfortune and degradation, as in the hulks, should be treated with caution.

Turning, one man recognised the uniform of a Lieutenant and exchanged a courteous salute with Henri, whilst several others proceeded to embrace him, drawing stares from passers-by who, attracted by their noisy chatter, watched with embarrassment at this open show of affection. Questions were asked of him. When had he arrived and where from? How had he been captured? Each man had his own tale to tell, and all had different backgrounds but were bound together on enemy soil.

Henri decided from the outset to keep his own council; to watch, listen, observe and learn. He needed their knowledge of life in the town and did not object to drinking with them, however it soon became apparent that unoccupied hands and minds, together with a lack of funds was leading to a disintegration of their faculties. He excused himself and declined to gamble, explaining that he had nothing to gamble with and that he had urgent business to attend to with the Agent. His rank gave him an added protection with the military men, and their respect gave him privacy.

Thus, after a short while he left his new companions and explored the alleys and narrow streets off the Market Place, noting where things could be obtained when he had the money to buy them. Eventually he found a jeweller and watchmaker's shop and, after making sure he was not observed by any of his countrymen, he went in. He produced a small piece of gold which he'd removed from one of the buttons earlier, and offered this to the man behind the counter.

'English money, please?' he asked politely. After examining the piece and weighing it on his small scales the shopkeeper held out several coins, the value of which Henri could only hope was fair. 'More?' he suggested hopefully. The man shook his head. Reluctantly and with a sigh, Henri took what was offered and left the shop to go in search of items he desperately needed.

Taking care not to give the impression that he was in possession of wealth he bought a pen, ink and paper in one shop before purchasing more personal items elsewhere. He knew that what pieces of gold he still had about his person would need to be used sparingly. However, he finally gave in to his hunger and bought a pocket-knife, some bread, a piece of cheese and a small bottle of wine.

One thing he did learn from talking to other prisoners was that he needn't wait until curfew before returning to his lodgings, so, as he was now thoroughly chilled by the raw December air he decided to take his purchases home. Mrs Parsons let him in and he went straight up to his room. It was clean and tidy but sparsely furnished, with a comfortable-looking bed, a straight-backed chair, a small table, one armchair, a chest of drawers, a commode and a mirror, and that was it. Compared with the prison hulks, this was luxury indeed, but what was he to do with himself on a regular basis for the duration of his stay? Inactivity did not suit him, it would drive him mad! Over the previous months he'd been too ill to care or else intent on surviving. Release from the prison hulk had been so sudden and unexpected that when offered parole he'd accepted it in an instant, but now that he had gained a form of liberty he felt guilty. Should he not think of escaping? He was after all a Frenchman, a soldier and a child of the Revolution. How could he rest easy like this when France needed him; when there were so many others of his countrymen imprisoned in hideous conditions not that many miles away. These thoughts depressed him. Would he not indeed be better off in a shared house instead of total isolation after the curfew bell had gone?

There was a fire-grate in the room but no wood with which to make a fire and he was cold. He ate his frugal lunch of bread and cheese, washed this down with some of the wine and reluctantly went to bed in order to warm himself. He woke three hours later in time to wash before going down for his evening meal.

'Bonsoir, Madame!' Henri greeted Mrs Parsons with a cautious nod.

Mrs Parsons looked up and eyed him, her face flushed from the heat of the kitchen, a couple of strands of grey hair hanging down over her forehead.

'I help?' he asked instinctively without really thinking.

'No, thank you kindly,' she replied, a nervous smile hovering on her lips and he realised that she was actually slightly unnerved by his presence. Was it because he was foreigner or was she simply unused to the company of a younger man? At her behest he seated himself at the table, noting at the same time the sparseness of the wood on the fire. The food placed before him was meagre too, although when he tasted the piece of meat pie he found it was quite well cooked, as were the potatoes. At least Mrs Parsons produced a hunk of bread and a piece of cheese to finish with, but Henri could have eaten more.

Communication between them was difficult and made harder by his lack of experience with old ladies who nibbled quietly as if obsessed with the food before them. Under what circumstances would his own mother have taken a stranger into her home? Poverty of course! This poor woman was reduced to sharing her home with a foreigner, and he resolved to gather any fallen wood he could find whilst out and bring it back to make fires, plus anything else that would make life easier for the pair of them.

He coughed, drawing her attention from the plate in front of her. 'Thank you, Madame!' He rose. 'I wash the clothes?' he asked as he stood pointing to his breeches and anticipating an outright refusal.

Eyeing his garments somewhat critically, she surprised him. 'Yes, they need it,' she nodded, 'you give them to me tonight!' She then left the room abruptly after indicating that he should wait her return. Before long she did so with a pair of old trousers. 'My husband's, he doesn't need them anymore—here, take them!' Henri took the offering which smelled heavily of camphor. 'They will fit, he was a big man!' she insisted almost bossily, and observed him with wry amusement while he hesitated. 'Go on—take them!'

Doing as he was told he took the breeches to his room and changed into them. Mrs Parsons was right, they fitted him and would have probably taken in another man as well. Nevertheless, they were clean and would suffice until his own were washed and dried. He also took his shirt downstairs in anticipation, keeping his coat on for modesty. He held it out apologetically and when she took it, he said, placing a hand over his heart, 'Madame, from here I thank you!' To which he received a defiant sniff.

He returned to his room knowing that he looked slightly ridiculous in the over-large breeches and needing to clutch at his faded jacket, but was relieved that no one would come calling and see him thus attired. When he went downstairs the next morning both shirt and breeches were drying round a small fire, and from their appearance Mrs Parsons had spent a considerable amount of time and effort endeavouring to clean and repair the stained, well-worn clothes, an almost impossible task.

'They are nearly dry,' she informed him, mumbling, 'but I can't do miracles, at least they are clean.' It was becoming apparent that between them they were developing the art of speaking out loud, both suspecting they were probably not understood by the other but it was better than nothing. Mrs Parsons lent him a brush with which to tidy his coat and a cloth to sponge it with. He felt rather like a young boy being bossed about by this tiny determined woman and found himself quietly obeying her, as he no doubt would have done in the presence of his own mother.

Finally, attired in clean and tidy garments for the first time in many months he felt better equipped for the weekly muster of the prisoners that took place in the Market Square. There they responded one by one to the roll-call made by the Agent John Bower, who had stressed to Henri the importance of attending. To fail to do so without good reason was counted as absconding. In fact when Henri arrived at the appointed time he was quite surprised to see how many were already gathered there, looking odd and out of place, part of the remains of Napoleon's San Domingo Army. He was embarrassed by their situation, arrayed as they were like a motley crowd of ruffians in full view of a gathering crowd. In addition there were amongst them, Officers, aides, ship's Captains and seamen whose misfortune it had been to be in the wrong place at the wrong time, not losers of some glorious battle. Maintaining dignity was vitally important if they were to survive, even in the Market Square, and all ranks exchanged salutes respectfully.

Mingling freely with those near him, Henri's attention was suddenly drawn to the familiar figure of one man in particular. This sight made him catch his breath, and he strove not to stare but his brief glimpse confirmed his worst fears. It was the one man, other than General Rochambeau, he had hoped never to see again! A shudder of revulsion swept over him and his face blanched white at the sight of General Boyer.

All sorts of memories and emotions swamped Henri—why of all men should Boyer have ended up here in Chesterfield? It was the cruellest of ironies, and any peace Henri had been feeling was gone in that one moment. All his nightmares flooded back. He moved carefully into another group of men as far away from the General as he could and immediately the count had taken place, slipped from the Square and strode briskly back up Glumangate, back to the safety of the house.

The moment he entered, Mrs Parsons knew something was wrong. Henri's face was ashen, his eyes almost wild. She was greatly disturbed but strangely not afraid.

'You poor man,' she said, 'I hope you're not going to be ill on me?' She had almost said 'die on me' but held back just in time. Henri waved his hand in denial to allay her fears. 'You go up and lie down and try to sleep,' she suggested. 'Would you like a cup of tea?'

He shook his head and mumbled his thanks. Once within the bedroom he quickly finished off the wine which remained from the previous evening. His hands were shaking and the strength of his emotions made breathing difficult. He rose from the chair, the room was cold and the wine was making him melancholy; he needed to sleep and to try to escape from his past memories. He closed his eyes time and time again unable to blank out certain thoughts which persisted in tormenting him. San Domingo! That accursed place— the cause of his illness, his disillusion and his present predicament.

Every time he dozed off Henri saw both blacks and whites murdering each other in the most brutal fashion possible, and could see Boyer and Rochambeau with his trained dogs hunting for victims. These ferocious animals tore at flesh wounds caused when Boyer deliberately slashed open a black man's stomach to entice the dogs into attacking. He saw men dying of disease, and remembered the disgraceful state of the hulks in England and the pitiful state of men held therein. He could not hold back his tears as the fiendish memories flooded back again and again, until finally, exhausted, he fell into a fitful slumber.

Downstairs Mrs Parsons fretted, wondering whether to disturb Henri, almost afraid that she might find him dead in his bed. She'd heard the bed creak at first as he tossed and turned, then finally nothing. The silence stretched into several hours. Should she go up or fetch help? She decided that if she hadn't heard anything more from him by tea-time she would send for John Bower. By then, however, Mr Bower would probably have returned to Spital Lodge and it would be dark. This was a quandary!

All afternoon she listened keenly for the slightest sound, all the while thinking the worst until, around 4 o'clock, she heard a welcome creak emanating from the room above. She sighed with relief, and was even more satisfied when, soon after five she actually heard him moving about, and this prompted her to prepare their evening meal.

When Henri had finally woken up he looked at his pocket watch and realised that it was too late to go outside again. He was depressed, his head ached, and his stomach yearned for sustenance, so he washed his face and tidied himself before venturing below where his landlady eyed him keenly. His face was pale and he still seemed distracted.

Quietly acknowledging his presence, Mrs Parsons did not pry. She'd learned from years of experience that a man would tell you when and what he wanted you to know and no more. However, as he sat picking at the food before him, she could contain herself no longer. 'Is there something wrong with the meal?' she asked.

Although needing to eat, Henri found himself balking at each mouthful. At first he didn't hear her, such was his disturbed state of mind.

'Is the food not to your liking?'

Realising with a start that Mrs Parsons was questioning him, he quickly reassured her. 'Please excuse, Madame. I am not well!' He continued to peck at the plate like a bird, when normally he had a good appetite. He finally rested his fork on the plate before him. 'Today I see a bad man. A very bad man. I am unhappy and very worried.'

Mrs Parsons drew back, more than a little disturbed herself. 'Will he kill you?'

'Non,' Henri shook his head, 'not me Madame, but he killed many men in San Domingo, yes!'

'Ah, you knew him there? But there is no war here—you are safe! Now eat, my dear, I have taken care in preparing this dinner for you.'

The calming influence of Mrs Parsons' tone helped Henri who could ill afford to miss the meal before him. It was the same next morning at breakfast; he ate all he was given but had little interest in it.

He was reluctant to leave the calming influence of the house in Glumangate, not out of fear of General Boyer himself but from the dread of those memories his presence brought about. Having overcome the first shock of seeing him, anger now took over, yet there was little he could do to relieve the burden. His task would be to try and avoid contact with Boyer. After hearing Mrs Parsons leave the house he thought no more about her departure, and was more intent on fathoming a way of keeping clear of the General without being thought disrespectful of his rank.

The Agent's office in Church Lane was only a short walk for Mrs Parsons, however she met so many people en-route with whom she passed the time of day that it was almost half an hour before she was eventually able to speak to John Bower.

'Good morning, Mrs Parsons,' he said brightly, 'what can I do for you? There's no trouble with your lodger, I hope?'

'No, no! But I am very worried, Mr Bower.' Her small grey eyes were troubled.

'Oh, why is that?'

'The man is very quiet, he's a well-mannered gentleman and I don't see him causing me much trouble. Only I'm concerned that he might be ill. When he came in yesterday, his face was white as a sheet and he was shaking.'

Her concern worried him, for she was noted more for her strong opinions than her compassion. 'Perhaps it is the result of the fever?' John well knew how long-lasting the effects of yellow fever could be.

'No. This morning he seemed disturbed in his mind. I felt quite sorry for him.'

'Do you want me to ask a Doctor to see him?'

Mrs Parsons hesitated, 'Hmm, he doesn't know I've come. He seems physically strong, although very thin. I thought yesterday that he seems to be suffering mentally. Do you think he might harm himself? He ate everything I gave him but he picked at it as though he'd lost interest!'

John Bower was puzzled. 'He seemed to be a level-headed fellow, that's the reason I sent him to you, instead of to someone I knew nothing about. He stayed at Spital Lodge for a night and even Mrs Bower took to him.'

'I thought he was going to die on me he was so ill when he came in yesterday. Really bad he looked,' she paused for breath. 'I didn't pry, but this morning he said that he'd seen a wicked man in the Square. A very evil man. Sometimes it's hard to follow his English, so I thought I'd better come and see you.'

'You did right, Mrs Parsons. Did he say who this bad man was?'

'He said something about a General and things that happened in San Domingo!'

John Bower knew the problem immediately but decided the least said in front of Mrs Parsons the better as he didn't want all of Chesterfield to know of it. 'Mrs Parsons, you have to understand that many of these men have been through much suffering as well as the distress of being captured. They have witnessed things which we cannot even imagine the barbarity of. They suffer nightmares and sometimes have difficulty in distinguishing fact from fiction. Let's hope time will prove a healer. A lot of patience may be needed, but I do appreciate your concern. Give him time!' Hoping that this might satisfy her, he went on. 'Thank you for coming, I shall of course investigate things further.'

'I do hope so, I can't be doing with one of them dying on me!' Mrs Parson's was now more relaxed after his comments.

John Bower chuckled. 'I don't think there is any fear of that!'

He saw her to the door and returned to his desk. This was one of several complaints he'd had about General Boyer in the short time that the man had been in Chesterfield. He was a nuisance, behaving badly and attempting, quite deliberately, to harass his enemy, and John could understand that. However, Boyer cursed in English everywhere, even in the presence of ladies, and several of the prisoners were refusing to have anything to do with him because of what they'd witnessed in San Domingo. Sighing and making a decision, John put pen to paper and wrote to the Transport Board explaining his reasons for requesting General Boyer be removed to any place away from Chesterfield. 'I must go and have a word with Pichon myself,' he muttered, 'and see if I can set his mind at rest.' He took his letter with several others to the Post Office in the High Street, and made a point of calling at Mrs Parsons' home on the way back.

The weather being wet and windy there was nothing for Henri to leave the house for. Suspecting that his landlady would be out for some time he was quietly reading his book yet again when John Bower called.

'Entrez, Monsieur!' Henri said as the two men shook hands. 'This is a pleasure!'

'I was passing and thought to make sure you had settled in.' John Bower replied. 'I didn't get a chance to speak to you in the Square yesterday, the Muster roll gets longer every day.' He refrained from mentioning Boyer in the hope that Henri would raise the matter first, which he did, much to John's relief.

'I was preoccupied yesterday in the Square. Very disturbed in fact! I left as soon as I was dismissed.' Henri's voice rose as his inner tension increased.

'You were disturbed? Nothing serious I hope—is there anything I can do to help?'

Henri hesitated. 'Perhaps I have no right to complain, but I find the presence of General Boyer most distasteful. He is a man of evil disposition and I have seen him do things to human beings that make me ashamed to be French.' The tremor in his voice betrayed the depths of his feelings. 'I will not associate with him so I am avoiding his company.'

'Ah, yes. General Boyer!' John Bower nodded in understanding. 'I have had similar complaints from several people who feel as you do, but his behaviour here is also disruptive and unpleasant. I have taken steps to see if anything can be done. It may, however, take time.' He refrained from mentioning Mrs Parsons' visit earlier in the day and decided to change the subject. 'How are you settling in here?'

'I consider myself fortunate, however the money will be insufficient for all my needs. You were right, boredom will be my cross to bear.'

'Perhaps you would like to borrow a book or two? Tell me your tastes and I will see what can be done.'

'You are most kind sir, and as the weather is so bad I would be happy to read anything you have to offer.'

'Well, I have a lot to do and must be off,' John said, feeling a little sorry for the young man, and resolving to examine his bookshelf for something suitable.

'Please understand,' Henri said as he took the Agent's hand, 'I am not ungrateful to be here under the circumstances, perhaps when the sun shines and the wind drops things will be better.'

For several days after John Bower's visit, Henri avoided the Square whenever possible in case he met Boyer and took to walking in various directions on the roads out of town. Whenever he found small broken branches of wood lying by the side of the road he picked them up and took them back to the house to dry out for firewood.

Once beyond the immediate vicinity of the town he enjoyed himself and, providing he kept walking, he felt warm. However, for a man used to marching his walks were short and limiting and it wasn't long before he'd covered most of the area within the bounds of his parole. The longer he stayed with the widowed Mrs Parsons the more he began to understand why she was so frugal with the food and wood. Life for a single woman in wartime was not easy with all the shortages, and his being with her was, he knew, of benefit to them both.

Very early one morning, seeking to augment his meagre rations, Henri decided to gather up as many snails as he could find. Lifting stones and following slime trails he hunted them down and placed them in a cracked and broken brown stone jar left near a pottery factory on the outskirts of the town. He was quite looking forward to having them as a tasty addition to his dinner and proudly showed them to Mrs Parsons.

Looking into the jar which he held towards her on returning to the house, Mrs Parsons let out a horrible cry. 'Agh...Agh! Take those disgusting things out of my house immediately—Out! Out!' She waved her hands frantically at the door, indicating what he should do with them.

Henri, not amused at her reaction, hung on to the chance of an addition to his meal, and protested. 'You can eat!' he tried to explain. 'Good food!'

'Out!' She persisted firmly, 'and don't bring any more! And no frogs either!'

He shook his head in disbelief. After all the searching he'd done on the cold ground in order to collect them! His fingers had almost frozen in the act. However, having no choice now but to get rid of them Henri decided they should not be wasted. He went down to the Square and sought out the first Frenchman he could find. After explaining what had happened he parted with the snails.

'These English don't appreciate good food,' the man said, seizing the offerings with gratitude. He said he would take them back to the communal house where he and some other prisoners cooked for themselves.

'I could have done with them,' Henri mourned, his mouth watering at the prospect. 'The short rations I get wouldn't feed a cat.'

The man grinned. 'Little does anyone know, but we were so hungry last week that we caught a cat and skinned it. It didn't go far between eight of us, but it was better than nothing. Tasted like rabbit, it did. Anyway, thanks for these!' The man departed happy enough, leaving Henri to return empty handed to Mrs Parsons.

Henri wasn't very pleased with Mrs Parsons and ignored her continuing remonstrations by going directly to his room, half expecting her to follow. Much to his relief she did not and he settled in his chair, trying to read. Whilst he would never be rude or short tempered with the lady, Mrs Parsons' reactions to his efforts to supplement his diet with free food bewildered him as much as anything else. And she had treated him like a child. At his age he wasn't used to being ordered about by any female, young or old!

Slowly mellowing, remorse set in. He actually felt ashamed of his behaviour. Damn the woman! Damn the war, and more than a curse on Bonaparte and his grandiose ideas. What on earth was he himself doing in the middle of a war, living freely as if the enemy were friends? He was angry, frustrated and ill at ease. In prison one was allowed to hate the gaoler, to protest and revolt. This Parole undermined his reasoning and his self-respect, yet he had chosen this course of action. Now he had lowered himself to speak abruptly to an old woman and was thoroughly displeased with himself as a result.

The pangs of hunger were always there. Admittedly he still had the gold pieces secreted in his buttons, but how long these would have to last was impossible to estimate, once they had gone there would be no more. Anyone else would already have sacrificed these but he had always been prudent and cautious, even now when his weekly allowance was barely enough to cover the cost of his lodging and victuals he kept to his habit. After taking all his essentials into account there was nothing left to spare for occasional refreshments or replacement of his clothing, and certainly none for entertainment. Nor was it easy to find the wood that he tried to bring back to the house, it would seem that everyone had the same idea. If only he was allowed into the fields and woods he could have done better but the parole forbade it. The large number of prisoners arriving during December had virtually swamped the town with impoverished Frenchmen all on the look out for anything they could find to make ends meet.

Once winter was over Henri would be able to manage on less food and without a fire. However, that was three months away so until then he must be prepared to sacrifice another piece of his precious hoard.

Having passed many of the lodgings and communal houses where other prisoners lived he also realised that he would be no better off with them even if it cost him less money. Most of these dwellings were shabby run-down buildings with deplorable and insanitary yards and the men were even more hard up than he was.

He waited expectantly for a reply from his parents in France, although he knew there could be no help from that quarter as he had always subsidised their income from his army pay. Had they even received the letter? Were they still alive? Every so often these melancholic thoughts were driven away by a feeling of guilt. He was at least alive, his health was slowly recovering although his chest still troubled him, and it was his duty to survive for his parents' sake.

Taking off one of his coat buttons he forced it apart and removed the gold hidden within. He left the house and returned to the jeweller who had purchased the previous gold from him. Apparently, according to the date on the board outside, the jeweller had been there for years and Henri had no reason to suspect duplicity. He made sure he wasn't seen so that no one would know that he had anything of value, or else he would quickly be waylaid and robbed—if nothing worse. So far this had not happened and it was far better to trade at apparently reputable premises than bargain for more money elsewhere and be at risk.

With the precious money in his pocket Henri left the shop and decided to obtain one item of luxury with part of it. He passed several poultry dealers, making note of the prices and conditions of the stock hung up. Finally he selected a rabbit, sniffed it and took it home as a peace offering to Mrs Parsons.

Taking the animal from him, Mrs Parsons bent her head as if examining the thing closely. 'Thank you, Mr Pichon,' she mumbled with a catch in her voice, 'I'll cook it tomorrow!'

There was a noticeable improvement in the size of his supper that night, and just before he retired to his room, she handed him a cloth in which she'd wrapped a hot brick she'd warmed in the oven-range. 'Put it in the bed,' she said softly, slightly embarrassed by her feelings of compassion towards her lonely lodger. Their private war was over—no more was ever said about his snails.

The January weather became extreme to say the least, with biting cold winds and heavy falls of snow that failed to melt even in the winter sun, making outdoor gatherings impossible.

Heeding John Bower's earlier warning that by isolating himself from his comrades Henri might feel lonely, he decided to seek out meeting places not likely to be frequented by Boyer. He knew from several men with whom he was on speaking terms in the Market Square that Boyer and his cronies frequented *The Falcon Inn*. Henri therefore tended to join a smaller group in a place in Bedlam Yard, off Saltergate, two minute's walk from home. These occasional meetings boosted Henri's morale. He soon found that he was only one of many wishing to avoid the General after doing no more than salute him, as was proper to his rank.

In all respects Henri was very circumspect regarding the General, giving no-one cause to pass his thoughts on. He also wondered, had John Bower kept his word regarding looking into reports about Boyer's behaviour, which by all accounts was becoming more resented and noted. The man strutted pompously about the town and spoke loudly in a vulgar manner, bringing the name of France into disrepute. Perhaps now that John Bower was Mayor of Chesterfield he had better things to concern himself with than the behaviour of one man.

Returning one morning from one of these gatherings, Henri found a letter from France that John Bower had left with Mrs Parsons for his attention. As neither of his parents could write, Henri had no idea who the letter would actually be from; Hortense to whom he was promised, was not able to write either.

Tentatively he broke open the seal, but the well-formed handwriting within the letter indicated nothing as to the writer's identity. He read on. It was in fact written by a local priest at the request of Henri's father who had probably paid good money for the cleric's work. Joseph Pichon was pleased to hear from him, to know that at least he was safe: there was no mention of his mother Marie at this point, but things had not gone well for the family and times were hard. Then the blow! The shock of not knowing whether he was alive or dead had been too much for his mother—she had died of a broken heart.

Henri put the letter down, the rest could not be of such importance and he would come back to it later. He might have known, his mother had always been fragile of mind and had worried over him ever since he had been conscripted into the Army. The constant thought of having a soldier son in battle had slowly worn her down and she lived always with the fear of losing him. The news of him having Yellow Fever quickly brought her down to her final conclusion.

It was as if part of him had died too. The sight of comrades mown down in battle, wounded men suffering untold agonies, deaths from disease; he had seen it all and, having witnessed so much by the age of twenty-eight, considered himself almost immune to emotional pain. This, however, was very different; it touched a part deep within; the link between all that was tender and lovingly supportive was gone! Emotionally he was now alone as never before. His poor father must also be having similar thoughts but there was nothing Henri could do to help in any way. He held his head in his hands at the table and closed his eyes, trying to shut out the memories which swamped him. He just wished he hadn't been the instrument to have in all probability brought about his mother's demise. Like so many mothers she'd always cared for him, but he was a man now and death could have come to him from many sides. He blinked back the tears that welled up in his eyes and sat for some long time thinking of her, then took up the letter and continued to read. It wasn't a long letter. His mother had been dead three months already, and his father, stoic as ever, was looking no further than beyond the winter. A winter without the joy and comfort of his wife.

After a while he went downstairs to inform Mrs Parsons of his loss. In a forlorn voice, he said, 'Madame, today a letter comes from France. It is bad. My mother is dead!' His face was etched with sadness, his eyes mirrored his inner loss, but no tears fell.

'You poor man,' Mrs Parsons replied softly as if afraid of hurting him more. 'Come and sit by the fire, and I'll go and make us a drink.' She left him alone, unable to say anything for fear he would misunderstand her words in the state he was in. He sat by the fire, mournfully staring into its glowing embers, awaiting her return as he had no desire to be alone at this time.

She found him deep in thought when she returned. 'Here my dear, take this!' Mrs Parsons handed him a beaker of tea into which she'd put a tot of Brandy from the sacred bottle, normally used only for 'medical purposes', or for occasions such as this. He sipped gratefully at the drink and thanked her.

Its contents took him by surprise and, as the liquid went down, its warmth began to slowly dissipate his chilled spirits. The old lady drew another chair towards the fire and sat beside him. She didn't speak then, instead she simply drank from the cup in her hand and quietly observed the same flickering flames of the fire.

After several minutes Henri sighed with resignation and leaned forward to ease the itching soreness of his feet.

Seeing his discomfort, Mrs Parsons looked questioningly at him. 'Are you in pain?'

'It is the legs, the feet—the cold!' he said lifting one leg of his trousers as if trying to explain.

'Chilblains! That's what that is,' she exclaimed, recognising the swollen red patches on his lower calf and she rose immediately. During the past few weeks instead of trying to explain her intentions to him, she had started simply to get on with things in the hope he would understand better that way. She returned once more from the kitchen, but this time with a small bottle in her hand. 'Essence of mustard,' she said. 'Rub it on!'

Placing a few drops on his hand and recognising the fluid from its colour, he nodded. 'I had two good mothers. Now I have only one, thank you.'

Quite unused to such demonstrative words, Mrs Parsons kept quiet, almost as if she hadn't heard, whilst within she felt deeply moved. Eventually she broke the silence. 'I have to go out for a time.

Sit here by the fire and see to your legs. Don't go up to your cold room.'

Henri had forgotten to light his own fire on returning, being distracted by the letter and its contents, and he hadn't even noticed the chill of the room upstairs. He resolved to go and light the fire and then return to attend to his swollen feet while the room warmed up. His appreciation of Mrs Parsons' hospitality was a growing source of comfort. Things could have been so different, and he owed much to James Walker of the *Vanguard*, John Bower and now Mrs Parsons.

Chapter 4   1804
New Arrivals

Several days later, near the end of January, Henri went to John
Bower's office with the reply he'd written to be posted to his
father in France. It had been a difficult letter to write simply because
his parent had never been an emotional man, and Henri had felt
inadequate in offering the comfort needed.

Entering the Church Lane office intent on handing over the
letter as required, he found that John Bower was pleased to see him.

'Just the man!' the Agent exclaimed. 'I have some good news for
you!'

Henri was bewildered by this exuberance as he had no idea how
any news would affect him for the good, if at all. 'Is it another letter?'
he asked.

'No, no! Not a letter for you, but for me from the Transport
Board! General Boyer has been given a pass to travel to Bath for the
benefit of his health. He leaves on Friday.' His relief and delight were
evident. Then, as if remembering his position as Agent, he added a
cautionary note, 'I trust you won't inform your comrades of my
delight, I'm supposed to be unbiased in my dealings with you all.'

This was just the news Henri needed to spur him on through
the rest of the winter. January had been a long and bitter month, with
snow and dull dreary days. The information was indeed a boost,
especially after his recent bad news from Saumur. 'I too am very
relieved at his going, it will make my own stay here more bearable.'

'I am greatly pleased to be rid of the troublesome fellow, no-one
other than his servant Jager will be sorry to see the back of him.
However, what brings you here? Did you get the letter I left with
Mrs Parsons?'

'I did, thank you,' Henri replied, 'although I would have wished the contents other than they were.' John Bower looked at him expectantly as if awaiting an explanation, even though Mrs Parsons had already informed him of Henri's loss and he considered discretion now to be the best option, for her sake. Henri went on, 'Sadly, the letter brought me the terrible news of my mother's death.'

'Oh my dear fellow, I am sorry!'

'She died about the time I was being shipped from Jamaica. All that time ago and I had no idea.' There was a catch in his voice, the loss was so fresh in his mind. He sighed. 'I want to send this letter to my father, please.' He passed the letter across the desk. 'Thank you, how much am I to pay?' He reached into his pocket and handed over what was asked.

Having taken the money, John Bower said, 'Please accept my condolences over your loss, it must be very difficult for you being so far from home. I will check your reply and take it to the Post Office today.'

Henri left the office with a stronger, more purposeful step than when he'd arrived. He walked down Lordsmill Street towards the river and finally along the canal, to where long narrow barges were being filled with crates, the contents of which were a mystery to him. Each crate seemed very heavy and the barges settled very quickly in the water.

Where, he wondered, did the narrow canal and its equally narrow craft go, and how far? Canals and small rivers usually flowed into bigger ones, and these eventually led to the sea and ships, ships which sailed far away. This trend of thought was becoming dangerous. That he should even consider breaking his promise to the Parole Board was an abomination to his code of honour, yet he couldn't stop himself from questioning and dreaming.

A scurrying rat in a nearby bush broke his trend of thought, bringing him back to the harsh reality of his position.

Confirming with others that the transfer of General Boyer to Bath had indeed taken place the day before, Henri felt more inclined to mix with his fellow prisoners. He drew the military cloak closer round his body, thankful that he'd earlier sacrificed some of his remaining funds to buy it from a prisoner who was in desperate need of money to pay his gambling debts. His own cloak had been abandoned somewhere on San Domingo where it hadn't been needed in the heat and humidity.

This time he went direct to *The Falcon*, where several Frenchmen were huddled before the log fire and, after purchasing a jar of ale, Henri joined them. They acknowledged him casually before continuing their conversation which, he gathered, had been about the widely welcomed departure of General Boyer. However, there appeared to be other news of which he was unaware. He listened quietly as had become his habit, until curiosity overcame him. 'Why the excitement?' he asked the man sitting near him.

'There's a new batch of men just arrived from Portsmouth. Another General and his retinue, including a black man,' the man said, turning towards him, 'they looked frozen stiff in this cold.'

'Any idea who they are?' Henri hastened to ask. As long as it wasn't Rochambeau, Henri didn't mind. The man shook his head.

'I heard the name D'Henin mentioned,' another voice interjected.

If this were true it was extremely good news. Here was a man Henri could respect, the man who had helped save his life along with the rest of the men trapped at Fort St Marc. He listened carefully now, hoping to catch other names with which he might be familiar but the conversation drifted away to talk of cold accommodation, bad English weather, lack of food and inevitably to gambling. After a while he made an excuse to leave and went home in an even happier frame of mind, with Boyer gone and the news of General D'Henin's arrival.

Each new day brought more French prisoners to the town; they came in batches after being marched from Portsmouth or Tiverton, suffering the verbal abuse of townsfolk en-route. This was an indignity Henri had been spared due to his good fortune in being selected to travel by coach from London.

The news of the arrival of other high-ranking officers and their staff offered him the potential of associating with men of his own calibre. Things were looking up! Although he didn't know General D'Henin personally and could hardly force himself upon a senior officer, Henri was eager to meet him. He awaited the next weekly muster in the Market Square with great anticipation.

When that time came he found the place awash with blue uniforms, tricorne hats and a mixture of other dress, the crowd so numerous that there appeared more prisoners than citizens in the town.

Henri scanned the scene before him until finally he saw General D'Henin amongst a group of officers. The General's appearance was certainly less dishevelled than many around him, for which Henri was grateful. The man deserved no less in his eyes for negotiating so successfully on behalf of the Fort of St Marc.

Moving across the gap which separated them, Henri waited patiently until an opportunity arose to salute the General. He had seen him only fleetingly when the surrender at the Môle had taken place and had been so exhausted by the march that he was simply relieved at being rescued. He was, therefore, surprised when the General returned his salute and spoke to him. 'Have you been here long?' he asked, seemingly interested and awaiting Henri's reply.

'Seven weeks, Sir! I was one of the 850 men you rescued off Môle St Nicolas.'

Charles D'Henin smiled, his interest awoken. 'You look far better now than some of those who came aboard from the island. Every man I saw was a worrying sight!'

'Yes, Sir, and may I thank you, Sir, for your efforts to save us!' Henri pressed on, 'But I wonder, can you tell me—have you heard anything about my own Chief, General Boudet? Did he reach France safely, do you know?'

'I think so. Unfortunately I have no idea where he is now— perhaps he had better luck than we did. All we hear are rumours! Even the news reports are full of mis-information, so that I am unable to tell you what befell him.'

'Thank you, Sir! I am Lieutenant Pichon, one of the General's aides. The General and I were amongst those injured and taken to Le Cap hospital, but I later developed Yellow Fever and could not leave with him. The rest you know.'

With the large numbers mustered in the Square it took far longer than usual for the men to collect their allowances, but General D'Henin didn't appear anxious to part company with Henri. 'You must meet up with my officers when you can,' he said, 'I would like to find a place for us all to meet as soon as possible.'

'That would be much appreciated, Sir. I believe that we all would benefit from some organization. I see some of the lower ranks frittering away their time, unable to help themselves.'

'Well, we'll see what we can do then!' The General moved towards the muster clerk and turned to another officer by his side.

'Thank you, Sir!' Henri replied as he saluted, then drew back to allow the General to proceed. His impressions of Charles D'Henin were favourable. With Boyer gone, perhaps there might now be a possibility of bringing the men together constructively. He accepted that there were some wasters and unscrupulous characters amongst the lower ranks for whom nothing, save gambling, would please. That would be up to them. With these thoughts in mind he began to feel that his existence now had purpose.

Even Mrs Parsons noticed a lightening of Henri's demeanour as they sat together later at the table. 'You look happier now that horrible General has left,' she said, trying to converse as simply as she could.

'Oui, Madame, and today I meet a man, a very good man. It will be better now!' Henri's English was becoming less stilted, his confidence growing. 'My legs are better also!' A relaxed grin spread across his face, taking years off his once haunted features.

He's a handsome fellow, Mrs Parsons thought as she watched. Slowly over the weeks she'd seen the change in him, yet she worried that he spent too many hours alone in his room. The tiny five-roomed house was too small to have him under her feet all the time, so what, she wondered did he do when alone up there for so long?

Self-discipline had always been Henri's main forte, this he considered was the reason he had succeeded where a mere peasant's son normally would not. It was an attribute that had disadvantages too, and although it kept him away from gambling it often kept him in isolation. To offset this he had recently determined to keep a daily journal, and also to record as much as he could remember of the earlier parts of his life, his achievements and anything interesting that had happened up to the present day. This preoccupation was becoming increasingly pleasurable even if it took a toll on his money, for paper and ink were not cheap and could not take priority over his need for food.

The time had come to organise his life. If he was exchanged for an English prisoner and returned to France, then of course he would be prepared to fight once more. If not, he did not intend to live like a pauper and to this end he was willing to work. The sight of pigs, sheep, horses and cattle, along with cheeses and other produce displayed in the various markets held in the town had already lost their fascination to him. So far he'd been a silent observer, watching and listening in the background, thereby increasing his English vocabulary—in spite of the strangest of accents. He frequented the local bookshops in order to study the written word and occasionally to buy a newspaper to gain an idea of things happening in the wider world. He now had an eye to buy what he saw, rather than simply to admire things which were beyond his purse. Perhaps John Bower knew of someone whose children were in need of tuition in French?

Although extremely busy when Henri called, the new Mayor of the town was not displeased to see him. Not all the new arrivals were as peaceable or as easily satisfied as Henri had been. Some were making John Bower's life difficult with their complaints and constant demands. Henri was of a different category; he was an officer as capable of showing respect as earning it. His installation in Mrs Parsons' lodgings was one of John's more successful achievements with the prisoners, the other was in persuading Mrs Bower to take in General D'Henin as a lodger on a permanent basis.

'Good Morning,' Henri said, in English, 'I am come to ask for help.'

'Oh, dear, is there something bothering you?' John Bower looked crestfallen, expecting bad news.

'No, but I am wanting to earn money. To teach French to children, no?'

This news brought relief to the Mayor. He could see the determination on Henri's face and heard the dramatic improvement in his spoken English. 'I'll ask around and let you know,' he replied.

'Thank you, Sir!' Not wanting to hinder the Agent, who he could see was busy, Henri turned, intending to leave.

'Are things better now that General Boyer has left?' John asked, detaining Henri a moment. 'Have you met General D'Henin yet? Or Commodore Querangal?' he asked, reverting to French, 'He was Captain of the *Duquesne* on which General D'Henin was captured.'

'My mind is at peace now, and I spoke to the General at muster only yesterday. He is the officer who negotiated with the British Captain to rescue us from San Domingo.'

John nodded. 'The General and I have talked at length on the subject of San Domingo, and I know he was very relieved to have the men off that place.' He paused, 'Did you know he is staying at Spital Lodge with us? You must come and visit sometime.'

'I am obliged to you, Sir. It is no more than the General deserves to be so billeted. I believe he would like to find somewhere for the officers and men to meet, a clubroom or the like. Has he mentioned this to you?'

'It's a sound idea! I'm sure it will prove beneficial all round and be very good for morale.' There appeared then to be nothing more of interest to discuss and John Bower decided to send Henri on his way. 'I'll see what I can do about your desire to teach French,' he said, holding out his hand in farewell. 'Give my regards to Mrs Parsons, will you? She's a good woman at heart.'

Leaving the office, Henri saw that the sky had darkened considerably and a flurry of snow was beginning to leave a layer on the cobbles at his feet. As the flakes swirled about him he experienced a feeling of exhilaration. This was a childlike sensation, as though the pure white flakes were gradually obliterating the tired old world and cleverly hinting at a new beginning. He hurried along the street, not just to escape the snow but because no one could stand still in such conditions. The thought of Mrs Parsons' small terraced property, hemmed in as it was on either side by people he hardly knew and all huddled by their fires, strangely comforted him. He felt elated by the changing events.

Later, as he sat at the small table by the window of his room, with his pen poised ready to write, he watched as passers-by struggled along the main thoroughfare that led down to the Market Square. There was a fire in the grate, not a large one, but one sufficient to warm the room. He thought to write to Hortense, but knowing that she would have to get someone to read the letter out to her made it seem pointless. If first his Agent as censor and then another person knew the contents there seemed little point to the exercise. What could he say? He hadn't seen Hortense since a brief visit home before leaving for the West Indies.

Originally they had met at the house of a cousin several years earlier, and each time he'd returned on leave he had become more aware of her devotion to him. He'd always been flattered by her attentions, especially as she'd grown, developing into a very attractive young woman in the process, with her hazel-coloured eyes that sparkled when he spoke to her. So, gradually, she'd won his affections. Everyone expected that one day they would marry, but time was passing and no one could say how long it would be before he finally returned home.

Henri tried to sketch her face on the paper before him, the eyes, the long dark hair which framed her fresh young face and her graceful neck. He was not an artist and nothing about the drawing seemed right; he began to wonder just what he did remember, it had been so long since he'd seen her. Now he had no idea what to write about, other than to repeat the news already sent to his father. How could he express his deeper feelings knowing that they were to be read by others? If only Hortense could read! In spite of this her liveliness of spirit had charmed him and captivated him eventually, but unlike many of his comrades-in-arms he had never received a letter either from her, or from his parents. The time to write of flirtatious love was past, he needed to talk of his emotions, of his doubts and frustrations, but it was pointless. He doubted if she would even understand. He looked out pensively at the falling snow, at the scurrying people, and never did start the letter.

When Brigadier General Francois Charles Joseph D'Henin reached Chesterfield after a long hard march from Portsmouth in the middle of winter, he was appalled to find himself apparently in the back of beyond. The place seemed to consist only of a cluster of dull, small buildings that showed few signs of prosperity. He had been recognised instantly by Philip Jager, Boyer's servant who had not been transferred, and Jager took him directly to John Bower's office.

The Transport Board's Agent was more than a little over-whelmed by the number of prisoners arriving together and by the importance of yet another General in their midst. Unable to find anywhere suitable to offer the Brigadier as accommodation in such inclement weather, he decided to risk his wife's wrath again and take General D'Henin home with him. The man's retinue he placed in various local hostelries. Strangely at that first meeting, John Bower and General D'Henin seemed to find an instant rapport, in contrast to the immediate dislike he had felt on meeting Boyer. He was nevertheless cautious, aware that the two Generals and their men had fought together on San Domingo and may well have been close friends.

Mrs Bower was not pleased to have yet another French prisoner foisted upon her, even if he was a Brigadier General. It was especially inconvenient as she already had a visitor from Scotland staying in the house. Nevertheless, as Mayor, it would look good if her husband was seen to be capable of mixing with the cream of the French Army, even if he was a prisoner, and so she decided to make him feel at home.

'I'm sorry,' she said to her friend Eleanor Dickson, who was the guest, a few days later. 'I do hope this hasn't spoilt the time you have had with us. Another man in the house does mean more work.'

'On the contrary, my dear, it has brightened things up a little. There's nothing to go outside for in this weather,' Eleanor replied, quite unconcerned. 'Besides, as soon as the weather improves I must go back to Scotland.'

'I shall miss you, Eleanor,' Isobella Bower said. 'You will come back when you can, won't you?'

'Of course! If only to see if the French General attracts the eye of one of your daughters.'

'Oh! Please don't say that, Eleanor. I don't want their heads turning, or their hearts breaking.'

Eleanor Jane Dickson laughed out loud. 'He does seem to be quite an attractive man, Isabella, but I think your girls a little too young for him.'

Mrs Bower looked at her guest and shook her head. 'Really, you'd think at your age you would have better things to do than think of romance.'

'My dear,' Eleanor laughed again, 'I might not be in the first flush of youth but I'm not dead yet. The family wouldn't begrudge me a happy thought now and then.' At this moment she was at the point of getting to grips with an inheritance which had further enhanced her life. She was attractive and well-off, and was beginning to find travelling quite enjoyable. She had only been having a bit of fun at Isabella's expense, trying to tease her, and she was sorry that if by doing so it had made her friend worry about her girls. Besides, what Eleanor had seen of the French General was pleasing and the thought that he might hear of her jest made her feel foolish and this disturbed her a little. Whenever their paths crossed he'd been extremely courteous and helpful and, more than once, his grey eyes laughingly met hers across the table when conversation became confused due to the language problem.

Eleanor always enjoyed her twice-yearly visits to Chesterfield, more so now that she was comfortably off and could extend her normally short holidays. However, winter visits were never as enjoyable as those in the summer months when she could take a carriage for a day out to the pretty town of Matlock, to Chatsworth, or even to Buxton to take the waters there for a couple of days.

'I'm sorry, Isabella,' she said contritely, 'I only meant to tease. The poor man will think ill of me if he knows I've used him so!'

'You always were a torment, Eleanor! For one moment I had begun to believe you—I should have known better.' Isabella was always sad to see her friend depart, as without her, life at Spital Lodge could be quite dull. As she continued to bustle about in her kitchen instructing the girl who came in to help, she looked towards the window and noted the darkening sky outside. 'I don't like the look of the weather,' she remarked, 'I think we're in for more snow.'

'Oh, dear! I do hope not,' Eleanor exclaimed, going to see for herself. 'If I am to leave for Scotland next week it could delay everything, and I have important business to attend to at home.'

'It may be all or nothing. What else can we expect in February?'

Within half an hour the view from the window changed dramatically as the flurrying snow began to fall in earnest. 'Poor John will be caught in it,' Isabella pointed out. 'It looks quite nasty out there—we could end up housebound by the look of it. I really don't know how you cope in Scotland with so much snow, it's often bad enough down here.'

Eleanor smiled, 'Yes, but somehow, with every new fall life just slows down for a while. One feels no compulsion to do anything other than eat and sleep, and I do love the isolation sometimes.'

'It's a good job the girls are back already,' Isabella said, shaking her head and ignoring her friend's enthusiasm for the extreme. 'Perhaps tonight, after tea, we can play cards or you could play the piano for us?' A sudden noise intervened and someone banged their feet against the doorstep. This was followed by a knock on the door. 'I do believe the General is back. Very sensible of him too!'

After stamping the rest of the snow from this boots, Charles D'Henin entered the house by the back door rather than trail the wet all the way through from the front of the house. He'd attempted to brush the snow from his coat but hadn't made a good job of it. Both women watched with some amusement as he stood in the kitchen, his eyebrows and moustache half concealed by white flakes, he had the appearance of a decorated tree.

'Bonsoir Mesdames,' he said, removing first his hat and then his coat as the ladies responded gracefully. He was quite aware of the spectacle he made and enjoyed the pleasure he felt on being welcomed into such domestic orderliness after the long trudge from town. Tidiness was something he appreciated, it was one thing he admired about the English. He'd found the ships of the Royal Navy cleaner and better disciplined than those of his own country's, the sailors he saw were also smarter and more inclined to orderly behaviour, due perhaps from being constantly at sea and not being land-based, simply awaiting action, like the French.

Eleanor hastened forward to take the hat from him so that she could put it where it would dry without dripping on the floor. Examining it as she brushed the snow off over the sink, it did not appear quite as faded in its wet condition as it had done earlier in the day. She was intrigued by thoughts of the foreign climes it had endured, the seas it had crossed, and the hot sun which had faded it so much. Although she had feigned disinterest in the General, she had felt a little flutter of pleasurable excitement over his coming in as he had. She quelled the feeling as being just another of her fanciful ideas and hung the hat and the coat she took from him near the range to dry.

Thanking Eleanor for her attention, and nodding with a smile at Isabella, Charles then went straight to his room. His visit to town had been to ensure that all was well with his immediate associates and particularly his black servant Paul who had accompanied him from San Domingo. Assessing the weather and the threatening snow he had decided to return to Spital Lodge immediately in case it became a problem. He now stood at his window looking across to the town, much as Henri had done before him in the same room, and with similar thoughts, that Napoleon was an ambitious man and would probably renew his attempts to conquer Europe, as well as England. It could be a long war!

Plodding through the hindering snow, John Bower returned to his house more than a little exasperated and certainly not good company.

To be greeted on his arrival with the suggestion of an evening of cards and music together with five women after dinner certainly met with no enthusiasm on his part. Like the General, he too escaped to his room, the study, to avoid the hubbub of family life. However, he felt rather guilty as time went on, his wife had not only been persuaded to agree to housing the general but she then considered it churlish for the man to eat alone in the kitchen. Thus it was Isabella who suggested the General might join the family for his evening meal. This might have been prompted by the evidence that neither Lucy, Thalia nor Elizabeth appeared enamoured in a flirtatious way with General D'Henin. His being a confident, pleasant but private older man seemed a barrier sufficient to deter the younger ladies of the house. As for Eleanor, he had certain reservations in that direction for one never could quite tell if her buoyant demeanour was a front for something deeper. At least if the weather didn't prevent it there would be one less woman in the house within the week.

Whilst Eleanor played the piano and Thalia sang, John relaxed and went over several problems in his mind, but when the music did stop he paid due attention as was expected of him.

The General, who had retired to his room, listened as the sounds of laughter came through the floorboards. He smiled, counting his blessings to be so comfortably housed. He had no particular dislike of the English and certainly no desire to kill any, yet he knew that if and when he returned to France that was exactly what he would be required to do. He too relaxed, the world outside was white-over and the innocent pleasure taking place below amused him. Yes, he could have joined them but declined simply because he felt uncomfortable, smiling like an idiot because he was unable to communicate without John Bower having to translate everything for him. He simply allowed the music to lull him into a deeper state of contentment; tomorrow he would endeavour to find ways in which the prisoners could usefully employ themselves, thereby improving their lot and keeping them out of mischief.

Chapter 5   1804
Settling In

All that was left of the snow a week later were slushy patches of mud and the occasional small drift against boundary walls and hedgerows. Heavy layers of snow had built up insidiously and, just when it looked as though there would be no more, another fall would come, inconveniencing farmers and traders alike. Then the snow turned to cold incessant rain making travel even more difficult, and yet more prisoners arrived in both small and large batches, all of them cold and wearied by the long journey north, their clothing totally inadequate in such weather.

Amongst the new arrivals was General Jean Lapoype and his retinue, together with three ships' surgeons. With Boyer gone Henri felt more at ease and slowly integrated himself amongst others of similar rank to himself, although he was still cautious about his remarks about Boyer, as several of the newcomers had been captured with the man on board the *Franchise,* off Brest. The officers and their aides began to gather in an organised fashion, choosing the Assembly Rooms in *The Angel* as being the most appropriate place to meet.

One day in the Market Square Henri heard a well-dressed businessman remark, 'Half the damned French Army seems to be here!'

Rumours were rife over which ships had actually been taken and where. One officer capable of translating the newspapers would tell them one day of news of the war, only to re-assess the situation the following week when announcements were made to the contrary. The businessman in the Square was partly right; half of Napoleon's Fleet seemed to have been captured if newspaper reports were correct. Henri took it all in his stride, and waited for official reports. What a state France was in, to be humiliated at sea; but let England watch out if Bonaparte chose to invade England, as planned!

Much to Henri's disappointment and anger, in the middle of February, General Boyer returned unexpectedly from Bath where Boyer reckoned he'd been for the benefit of his health. By this time, however, Henri had established himself comfortably within the now much larger French contingency, many of whom openly did admit to disliking the General.

Deciding that perhaps John Bower had been too busy or unable to find him work, Henri finally decided to place a notice in the town's coffee room to the effect that he was available to give lessons in the French Language. Prior to this he hadn't broadcast to his comrades the fact that he could speak more than an odd sentence of English, but by hard study and practise his capability had grown considerably, giving him confidence. By mid-March though, he had almost abandoned any hope of receiving a reply to his notice and began to wonder just what else he could do to earn money.

It therefore came as a pleasant surprise on his return from a walk one day to find a note from the Agent that had been pushed under his bedroom door, asking to see him regarding a position in a school.

This news put Henri in a state of panic—he could hardly present himself as a prospective tutor in a large establishment, wearing his shabby and faded uniform! There was nothing else for it, he would have to sacrifice his last two pieces of gold in order to procure a suitable outfit as soon as possible. He had postponed the purchase of such luxuries in case they weren't needed.

He explained his situation as best he could to Mrs Parsons, who suggested he went immediately to a friend who had a tailoring business in Packer's Row where, apparently, her husband had regularly bought his own clothing. She also told him to mention her name in the hope that Henri's custom would be found acceptable.

The business premises of Richard Bland were quite extensive in size and stock, as he was a tradesman in all kinds of drapery and finer things as well as offering a tailoring service. Yes, he could supply Henri with all he needed, two shirts, worsted socks, a pair of breeches and a jacket sufficient for his needs, not perhaps of the best quality but good enough. Breeches and jacket both required some alteration, but these could be made available by the following day for an extra shilling, which offer Henri reluctantly had to accept.

Now satisfied that he would be able to present himself to a prospective client in appropriate garb, he then went to the Church Lane office, hoping to find the Agent there.

The Mayor of Chesterfield sat behind a desk heavily laden with books, papers and pens. 'I see you are busy, Monsieur,' Henri greeted him on entering the office.

'More than a little my friend,' John Bower replied in English, his mind already nearly addled by the vast amount of work before him, and having little desire to work it harder. 'You received the letter then?'

'Yes, and thank you. Today I have used the last of my money to buy garments in which to go to the school. Tomorrow they will be ready to collect.'

'Good man! And your spoken English is very much improved too!'

'I have nothing else to do with my time. I try to read English, I hear your people when they talk in the Square and in the Ale Houses, and I go to the book-shops also. But it is you that has made all these things possible, Monsieur!'

'I'm pleased to be able to help. I'm sorry however to tell you that General Boyer has apparently sent a letter to Lord Eardly denying rumours that he complained about his treatment here. The *Derby Mercury* printed a copy of the letter and Boyer gives us a good word for our hospitality. Fortunately he doesn't realise that the men themselves wanted rid of him. How do the men feel about his return?'

Henri frowned. 'Many senior officers here try to prevent his grossièreté, his boorish behaviour, but the lower ranks they have nothing to do with him. I am able not to see him when there are so many of us!'

'My, your English has improved, you're dong very well!' John repeated encouragingly. 'Yes, there are many of your countrymen here now, over 120 to be precise, so that we can guarantee seeing at least one or two walking about every day.

'I am reading in the *Mercury* that General Rochambeau is here in your town, but I have not seen him?'

'Bah!' John exclaimed. 'Rumours and more rumours—though the next issue usually corrects them. I really could not do with Boyer and Rochambeau here together. Rochambeau denies his misdeeds in San Domingo and accuses English officers for these offences, but there are too many eye-witnesses to his own conduct for us to believe him. As far as I know he is currently in Ashbourne. I know we are not without our own miscreants but the evidence is stacked against him in this case.'

'You are good to us. Sadly there are some men who feel it their duty to France to cause you no peace.' He looked at the large pile of papers before the Mayor. 'But you are busy, Monsieur, I will leave soon.'

'Ah, but wait! The school! A relative of my wife runs a school for girls here in the town. She saw your advertisement and asked me for advice as she would like someone to teach French on two afternoons per week to her students. The girls are well-behaved daughters of local businessmen and should cause you little trouble.'

'I speak correct French, but my English is not so good, do you think a school too ambitious?'

'You can but try—Miss Bradley will no doubt let you know if you are not suitable!' John Bower said, handing a piece of paper with Miss Bradley's address and a sketch of how to find her, on it. 'Tomorrow should be convenient and, by then, you will have collected your clothes.'

'I am most thankful!' Henri bowed courteously. 'I go now and leave you to work.'

After collecting his purchases early the following morning, Henri proceeded to dress himself before the mirror in his room. He was pleased with his choices which, although not of the finest of materials, made him look tidy and smart, pleased too that his prudence had at least allowed him to purchase all he needed. The fact that he looked quite presentable added greatly to his confidence. He was, after all, a relatively young man and his reflected image seemed not a bad one. It had been some time since he'd been able to see himself smartly dressed and he smiled mockingly at the sight before him, even his sense of humour was beginning to return. Perhaps a little added weight would enhance the image and although the deep colouring from the San Domingo sunshine had long since faded from his face, he was still not a bad looking fellow. He nodded with satisfaction and went below stairs to see what Mrs Parsons' reaction would be, before setting off to find the school.

Miss Judith Bradley's School for Girls was situated in a large house where the proprietress actually lived. It was not quite as Henri had expected, there were no large grounds or gardens surrounding the sturdy brick dwelling yet, on being asked to enter, it seemed that the interior was remarkably extensive.

He was taken by an assistant to a small office cum sitting room and introduced to the principal, Miss Bradley, who welcomed him with a firm, decisive handshake and a business-like smile, which he readily returned. He was again thankful that he'd had the presence of mind and his gold pieces to suitably attire himself for, had he arrived in his shabby uniform, Miss Bradley would probably not have regarded him with as much respect as she did.

When John Bower had mentioned to her that he knew of a respectable Frenchman willing to instruct pupils in his native tongue, without desiring an exorbitant fee in exchange, Judith remembered the notice she had seen in the local coffee lounge. She had then begun to consider the situation; her pupils were growing up in a challenging world, most being daughters of businessmen in the area who wanted to raise their offspring to a higher social status. Chesterfield was a good market town but slow to progress further. Expansion was essential for any town, but many chose to move away rather than increase their investment in the area, and when these families did move up in the world their daughters also entered a more exacting society. At present there were few entrepreneurs in the town, yet if she, Miss Bradley, could see the need to expand why couldn't they? This sense would come, she believed, but perhaps not for several years yet. In the meantime, she would offer her students an opportunity to learn French from a native of that country which would surely enhance their prospects. Besides, the additional income each new pupil attracted by the offer would bring, should not only pay the tutor's fees but also help to offset the increasing costs the war was bringing to all, including her school. Certain industries benefited from wars, others suffered due to shortages of imported materials, whilst added taxes overall meant the poorer people could only buy things essential to their needs.

Addressing Henri, she began, 'I understand from Mr Bower, that you speak a little English—sufficient to control the girls in your care?'

'Yes, Mademoiselle, and I am trying to improve it. My French is, how you say—of good quality!'

'Have you taught before?' she asked, trying to assess his manner and aptitude for the post as much as anything.

'No, I am an Officer of the French Army, an aide-de-camp to a General, and read and write good French. I think you will not be sorry to have me!' He realised that he was more nervous before this confident woman than he would be in the presence of his superior officer!

Miss Bradley was equally as nervous as Henri; after all, she'd had little opportunity to converse with any of the prisoners in town. 'Mr and Mrs Bower speak well of you,' she said, 'I cannot pay a lot of money for your services, and only sufficient for two afternoons per week. If the girls progress well, and their fathers are impressed, I may be able to increase the work and, of course, your remuneration. Is that in order?' She let him consider this information thinking that she may have spoken too fast for him to fully understand her meaning. She was well aware that her own efficiency and manner often seemed to make men feel uncomfortable in her presence, but she ran a successful school of which she felt extremely proud.

It didn't particularly matter to Henri that he'd not understood every word; he simply needed the money and was willing to go along with her requirements. 'Yes, Mademoiselle, I think I understand.'

'Good, then I will show you around the school and introduce you to my pupils and the other tutors. Could you begin tomorrow?'

He tried not to appear too eager. 'Yes, I think that will be in order but I must always attend the weekly Roll Call.' Nodding her acceptance she led him through the house which he found extremely clean but sparsely furnished. The girls were polite, some barely concealing their curiosity whilst others giggled behind raised hands. 'Bonjour Mesdemoiselles,' he said, bending his head courteously to each new group. He was secretly elated by his new-found independence; this was his opportunity to live a useful and respected existence until he was either exchanged or the war ended. With the tour of the school completed, he thanked Miss Bradley and left after reassuring her that he would return the following afternoon.

Watching Henri walk away from the house, Miss Bradley was pleased with her decision and hoped the arrangement would be mutually advantageous to both of them. She had herself arrived in Chesterfield from Ashbourne on the Staffordshire border several years before, and knew that settling into a new town wasn't easy. For the French prisoners it would be even harder. Chesterfield might be larger than Ashbourne but she missed the elegance of her birthplace: the old almshouses, its Elizabethan Grammar School and the prettiness of it all. A place visited for centuries by artists and the cultured to see the beautiful monuments in the church. Even Dr Johnson and James Boswell favoured Ashbourne. Miss Bradley left the window and returned to the more pressing needs of the school, the main priority in her life.

Henri had taken to walking on a regular basis in the mornings, one particular route passed a small farm situated between Brampton and Walton, well within the limits of his Parole. Quite often on finer days an elderly man stood by the gate, a dog patiently waiting by his side. As Henri passed by he usually acknowledged the man with a clear, 'Good Morning!' and lifted his hat in respect. Never once did the old man do more than keep his eyes on the ground and grunt, or mumble something to himself. Henri persisted with the greeting, accepting the lack of response until it became part of a routine, a habit formed.

Towards the end of May, on a bright, warm Spring morning, Henri set out for his usual ramble, this time attired in the lighter clothing which he'd purchased to wear at Miss Bradley's School. The hedgerows were now thick with foliage, the grass a lush bright green and birds twittered excitedly in nearby trees. This put him in a happy frame of mind, seeing all around with an appreciative eye.

There, up ahead, the old man stood by his gate, the dog watching expectantly for someone to pass by and perhaps pat his head. In this happy mood, Henri decided to break his habit and stop. 'Good Morning Sir,' he said, waiting, determined to engage the old man in conversation.

'Mawnin,' came a begrudging reply, which took Henri completely by surprise.

Tentatively bending, Henri spoke to the dog. 'Good dog!' To which the animal attempted to lick his face. Henri was always wary of dogs knowing that so many animals in Europe suffered from rabies.

'Down, there!' the old man gruffly reprimanded his companion.

Having made such progress, Henri looked directly at the man, saying, 'A good day is it not?'

'If you say so,' came the reluctant reply, sounding as if this had been forced from deep within the older man's throat.

'I do!' Henri replied, and, realising the conversation was at an end, patted the dog again and went on his way. 'Good Day, Sir!' The usual mumble was received in return.

Henri wondered if the fact that he was without his uniform on this occasion had to some degree broken the ice? This improved exchange followed the same pattern for several days, the dialogue changing little, but the dog, a black and white collie, began to yap excitedly whenever Henri was spotted approaching the farm. Gradually the man added the odd word here and there to his reply, and Henri smiled to himself as he left. The old gentleman had now become a daily challenge and in inclement weather he quite missed the daily encounter. Strangely, it seemed to give Henri a sense of purpose. He was determined to befriend him if possible.

George Silcock on the other hand had no such intentions! However, Henri's persistent attention to the dog left him with no alternative and he found himself slowly being coerced into conversation. He also found that as the stranger was, to him, now dressed more like a civilised human being than a French soldier it was increasingly difficult to be deliberately rude. He was not an ignorant or spiteful man, but the loss of his son at the hands of the French had embittered him. Coming to a decision and being stubborn he resolved to miss going out at his normal time.

'What, not going to the gate this morning?' his wife Elizabeth asked, having noticed lately with some delight, that her husband's walk there had begun to stir him from his lethargy. Betsy the Collie meanwhile, sat impatiently waiting by the door for her daily run to the gate. 'What's he like, this Frenchman of yours?' his wife persisted, trying to prompt her husband into action. After all it had not been this particular Frenchman who had wounded their son, nor perhaps any one of the others now in the town; besides these men were also separated from their loved ones and she hoped that someone had taken pity on her own son and looked after him before he died. Anger and bitterness only bred hatred and there was surely enough of that in the world these days.

'How do I know! And he's not my Frenchman!' a grumpy George retorted.

'I do hope you're not rude to him,' Elizabeth persisted. 'The poor fellow can't enjoy being here. The tales I've heard about the state of some of them upsets me. If they're wrong 'uns, well then they deserve it, if not, they don't.'

Betsy, now at the door, yipped loudly as if in agreement.

With a familiar grumble George made for the door. 'Gerron you silly bitch,' he growled, opening the door to allow the dog to race ahead. Approaching the gate himself George slowed down, now unsure how to greet the man who he could see in the distance, heading as usual towards the farm.

The summer months of 1804 saw the repatriation of Captain Querangal of the *Duquesne*, his retinue and several other ships' surgeons back to France, exchanged no doubt for some of England's high ranking and much needed officers. Consequently there was a restlessness amongst some of the remaining prisoners who wondered whether to make a run for it but, cautioned by General D'Henin, his own men reluctantly agreed to bide their time. General Boyer gained no more admiration than before as he paraded the town in gentleman's clothing and was as abusive and foul-mouthed as before.

At Spital Lodge Isabella Bower awaited another visit from her Scottish friend with great expectation. Eleanor was visiting London first and would bring news of the latest fashions and gossip directly from the Capital. In her letter to the Bowers she deliberately omitted to say that she had added a smattering of French to her vocabulary; to admit to such an investment would have sent alarm bells ringing if Isabella had known about it.

As for Henri the summer passed pleasantly enough; Miss Bradley saw fit to keep him on at the school and his English was sufficiently polished now to enable him to hold a reasonable conversation with almost everyone. He was also fitter than he had been for a long time, this he put down to his regular walking regime which still took him past the farm in Brampton.

In October the unexpected transfer of General Boyer to Montgomery in Wales also pleased Henri, who before long heard that Boyer and Rochambeau were keeping their captors busy with their difficult behaviour.

Late autumn brought fresh, cold breezes and Henri dreaded the long winter months ahead. Also, when the weather was foul, with rain or heavy winds the old man naturally failed to stand by the gate. This disappointed Henri, though when it happened he understood, because he'd begun to notice as the leaves fell from the trees and the days became greyer and shorter so the old man appeared to wilt, almost as a consequence.

At first, old George, though Henri didn't know his name at this time, missed an odd day, whilst on others he would say, 'T'is me legs,' or 'T'is me chest,' until Henri eventually wondered if there was anything not wrong with the man. But he had learned a lot from old George with his slower country ways and farming talk, and a mutual respect had developed. However, George never mentioned his dead son and certainly not the events taking place elsewhere between England and France. Theirs was an oasis of peace, isolated from hostilities.

Towards the end of November George failed to appear at the gate for several days and Henri was resigned to the fact that he would have to wait until Spring to talk to him again. He would have liked to have knocked on the farmhouse door to ask after him, but was wary of approaching the house without being invited. He glanced towards the building in passing, but could see no sign of life so walked on, pondering the circumstances of George's absence.

A week later, to his relief and with some pleasure, ahead in the distance he saw the familiar figure by the gate. He was surprised at his own feelings and quickened his step to close the distance between them. However, the closer he got to the gate he realised that the figure was not that of the old man but of an old woman, huddled beneath a closely-drawn shawl.

'Good morning, Madame,' he said. 'Is the old gentleman not well?' She shook her head. 'Oh, dear,' Henri hesitated before continuing, 'is there anything I can do to help?'

Tears appeared in her careworn eyes and ran down her lined cheeks. 'He died yesterday morn. I thought you ought to know.' The voice was weak with emotion, and he needed to lean close to hear.

This news disturbed Henri who had begun to look forward to their daily meeting. 'I am very sorry, I shall miss him!' he said with a genuine feeling of loss. The old lady looked forlorn and frail as she leaned against the gate for support. Seeing her plight and thinking she might collapse, he looked anxiously towards the house, seeking help.

A figure appeared in the doorway as if watching in case something happened. 'Help! Please help!' Henri cried out, beckoning the person forward. 'She is ill,' he called lamely to the then hurrying figure who he saw was a much younger woman, presumably the old lady's daughter.

'I told her not to come out in this weather but she insisted,' the woman complained as she placed an arm protectively around the huddled old lady's shoulders. 'Come back with me into the warmth, mother! You've done what he would have wanted,' then she turned to go, supporting her mother-in-law carefully.

'Can I please help?' Henri asked. He was still bewildered by the turn of events. 'Can you manage?' The younger woman turned back and he was startled by the fierce, penetrating look she gave him. He didn't know why but he could see that she didn't like him. Or was it because of what he was?

'I can manage!' The tone was sharp and unfriendly, and Henri drew back as if stung. Seeing him flinch the woman relented a little, her tone softening slightly. 'We can manage. Thank you for talking to George, he would have wanted you to know what had happened.'

Henri nodded—it was obviously time to leave. 'Thank you, Mademoiselle,' he said, walking away. Some distance from the gate he halted and turned to watch the pair making their way slowly up the path to the house, and was sadly aware that any help he might now offer would probably be refused point blank. He walked on in deep contemplation; the incident had shaken him and taken all pleasure out of the day.

Now bereft of purpose in taking this particular route he considered changing it, but the following morning he found himself once again heading in the same direction, almost hoping the previous day's incident had only been in his imagination.

He had almost passed the gate when he heard the dog yapping excitedly as she bounced along the path. 'Hello, Betsy!' he said fondly, bending to pat her black and white head. 'You don't forget me?' He teased the animal playfully for a minute or two. 'I think you miss him too,' he said, as if expecting an answer. He was so pre-occupied that he didn't see the younger woman arrive, nor did he realise he was being closely watched. He rose, intending to move on and found himself confronted by the same pair of penetrating eyes that had so upset him the day before. 'Good Morning, Mademoiselle,' he uttered sombrely.

She made no attempt to move but seemed to be scrutinising every detail about him, a fact which did not please him. Then quietly she said, 'My mother-in-law says I was rude to you yesterday and that I should apologise.'

While she was speaking, Henri in his turn examined her. It was difficult to judge her age. She was careworn and, without the protective shawl of the day before, he could see how painfully thin she was, which if anything accentuated her piercing blue eyes. With a bit more flesh on her face she would no doubt be an attractive woman, he thought, and suddenly realised that she awaited some sort of reply. No apology had actually followed the explanation.

'How is the lady?' he finally asked. 'Was she the gentleman's wife, I think?' Your mother?'

'No, she is not my mother but mother by marriage, and George was her husband. She is not ill but in great despair over his death. It will take time for her to recover.' She paused as if not wanting to go on. 'I am sorry if I was rude!' The latter was hastily spoken and she averted her eyes as she apologised.

He wasn't sure if she actually meant it. 'Please to tell Madame I am sad about her husband.' Henri offered. 'Can I be of help?'

'No…no…you are…' her voice trailed off.

'I am just a prisoner here, Madame, not to be liked?' His frankness shocked her and she averted her eyes once more.

'You and your husband will take care of the lady, but if I can help, I can ask permission to come,' he offered, extending his hand in friendship.

'You will not come!' she cried out bitterly. 'We don't want you here! Good day!' She seized the dog by the collar and dragged the whining animal back to the house.

Henri stood for a moment stunned by the bitterness with which his offer had been rejected. What had he done to deserve such treatment, such rudeness? Then he recalled how the old man had reacted to his advances when he had persisted in trying to draw him out. Perhaps there were many others who felt the same way, but fortunately few had made their feelings known so strongly.

He walked away, quite distressed by what had occurred and on returning home told Mrs Parsons what had happened.

'Do you mean the small farm before you reach the wood?' she asked, trying to puzzle out exactly where Henri meant. 'Is it set back just off the road?'

'Yes, an old man—he used to talk to me at the gate, with a dog. Now he is dead! The younger lady she is full of bitter…' he hesitated, searching for the right word.

'Bitterness…'

'I offered to help but she is so rude.'

'George Silcock! So George is dead is he—always was abrupt that one, but there was no harm in him. It wasn't your fault. He was a broken man after his son died.' She stopped suddenly as if to think whether to go on.

'There is more, perhaps?'

Mrs Parsons sighed. 'It's a wonder that he spoke to you at all. It was a sad business,' she saw Henri's eyebrows lift enquiringly, waiting. 'You may as well know. Just before peace was declared last time with your country, young William Silcock was badly wounded somewhere abroad. Just another two days and peace was declared but it was too late, he died of his wounds and never came back.'

Listening, Henri went cold, for he may have clumsily forced the old man to speak to him, enjoying the challenge but not knowing the heartbreak he'd re-kindled. Yet it had not been done deliberately, and he himself had gained much from their acquaintance. He also recalled John Bower offering him a choice of accommodation on arriving in the town, and of one, a farmer, having lost a son in the war. They had needed to take in a lodger to make ends meet. Had it, indeed, been the same farm? 'I looked forward happily to the meeting,' he murmured, 'but tell, have many in Chesterfield died in the war?'

'Only him, as far as I know—why do you ask?'

'No reason—but the younger woman, so much bitterness. It is her husband?'

'Yes! And now they must run the place alone without their men—I don't know how they will manage with the few cows and poultry they've got, and the place is so neglected.' Letting the matter drop, Mrs Parsons reminded him that it was almost time to go to Miss Bradley's School.

The meeting with the young woman at the farm haunted Henri, but what could he do? She had made it plain enough that he wasn't welcome, yet as a Frenchman he felt partly responsible for the death of her husband. Now though, as a consequence of their bitter encounter Henri decided to avoid the farm altogether.

The long wintery days of December were upon them once more and Miss Bradley's school prepared to close for the Christmas break, which would leave Henri with time on his hands. It was just over a year since his arrival in the town and war still raged violently throughout Europe with no end in sight.

The bitter cold and damp affected his chest and Henri's constant coughing caused him difficulties in the classroom. He was grateful that Miss Bradley tolerated this, but it seemed that it was going to be an annual problem which he would have to endure; after all there were many of his comrades in a far worse condition, thanks to the war.

Chapter 6   1805
Triumphs and Tribulations

The year eighteen hundred and five proved to be a momentous one, although Henri could not have foreseen it. The war was spreading its evil tentacles over land and sea and seemed set to run on a never-ending course. Parole was intended as a means of controlling captured officers and men at a standard dependant on their rank; a holding place for many until exchanges could be made for their English equivalent in French hands. However, many seamen, servants and foreigners captured alongside the French were also allowed parole, and there were mixed feelings amongst these prisoners as to their commitment to it. Whereas some believed it to be a pledge to honour, others had no scruples regarding escape or sabotage, and discontent grew amongst the latter. General D'Henin felt it his duty to caution his own men to be patient; escape from England was almost impossible and if caught the prisoners were taken to Norman Cross, near Peterborough, a notoriously harsh and miserable prison. Attempt to escape also brought suspicion on the rest of those still on parole, guilty or not, and privileges would be curtailed as a result.

Meanwhile, Henri added to his work as tutor at the school by instructing the wives and older daughters of businessmen in French, at their homes and elsewhere. He was now better off in comparison to many of his comrades in the town but went to great lengths to conceal this fact. It was also to his credit that he didn't gamble as others did. His employment as a teacher suited him well and he was beginning to wonder if he would really want to return to a theatre of war with all its horrors. If that order came, however, he knew he would have little choice.

When Spring finally returned and the weather enticed him to extend his rambles, he occasionally passed the small farm at Brampton and saw the increasing neglect which was evident even from a distance. He couldn't dismiss the thought of the pain within the house and the bitterness of the younger woman that caused her to spurn his offer of help.

The entries in his notebooks were becoming fuller; he was enjoying recording what his fellow countrymen and others were doing, and as an observer and listener he gradually became aware of a growing restlessness amongst certain groups. Young Aides were keen to return to France to fight for the now 'Emperor' Napoleon. Captains and Masters of captured merchant vessels flying the French flag didn't see parole in the same light as Military men, nor did life on land suit their natures. One such man, George Caillaud, a wine merchant of Bordeaux and Captain of the ship *Les Amis*, took his chance and one day simply absconded.

Whatever his suspicions, and for security reasons, Henri only recorded this and similar instances after the deed had actually taken place, as if anything happened to him and the diary fell into the wrong hands the outcome could be disastrous.

Despite the heightened security caused by these defections it nevertheless came as a shock to Henri when, at the end of April, Pierre Alexis Victor Legay D'Arcy, Lieutenant Colonel and Aide-de-Camp to General D'Henin escaped successfully and was never caught. This added to the unrest and discontent amongst the prisoners, and he knew it wouldn't be long before others would try to escape as well.

Perhaps it was the unfortunate and untimely death of General Lapoype's nephew and Aide, Henri Lapoype, at the young age of twenty-four in June which added to the feverish excitement of those disposed to escaping. He had died on a Saturday night and, by the time he was buried beneath the handsome brass chandeliers in the Church of St Mary and All Saints on Monday, news had spread, and a great concourse of spectators attended to watch the funeral and say prayers, filling all the boxed pews and overflowing outside into the churchyard.

To men used to battle, death was not unusual, the sadness in this case came because there was no conflict, yet God had taken the young man anyway. It made them all feel vulnerable, there was no hiding from the call of God! These thoughts aroused a strong feeling in Henri who had almost abandoned his religion, yet deep in his heart there still lurked a belief in something and someone greater than himself. If this lingered from his childhood teachings then the revolution had not erased it completely.

It may have been this sense of vulnerability and awakening which drove Henri to do something quite unexpected. He bought from one of the other prisoners two pairs of pegged gloves. Knitted using only one needle, just one of the many items prisoners made to raise much needed income. To have bought a straw bonnet or finely crafted model ship from them would have given the wrong idea to the receiver of his gift, something he had no intention of doing. It was to be a gift simply to ease his and his country's conscience.

Several days after purchasing these neat and serviceable gloves he set out as usual on his morning ramble. He was surprisingly nervous, more so than when preparing for battle where he might need to kill, or be killed or maimed. His intentions today were for a more unfathomable purpose.

Reaching the gate to old George's farm, Henri walked up the short pathway to the house. As he approached the door, the tension within him caused the muscles at the back of his neck to ache and he strove to relax. There was no answer to his first knock which made him suspect that perhaps the house was empty of inhabitants after the long winter months. He had no way of knowing if the two women still lived there and began to feel a little foolish. He knocked again, but not even Betsy reacted to the noise. What was he to do next? Slowly making his way round to the back of the property the neglect became more obvious and he could see that it had now been abandoned to mother nature. He was disappointed for had he been allowed to assist them the previous autumn it was possible that something could have been done to avoid this. He hated waste, reacting just as he had when the Army razed and ravaged the lands through which it marched; it was such a squandering of effort and resources.

The door to what was obviously a chicken shed was open; but no hens sheltered beneath the broken and exposed beams; strangely however, in the adjacent abandoned garden, fresh growth flourished in spite of the neglect. It was a dismal sight, even worse than he'd expected. Perhaps it need not have been had he had his way. However, he should not be off the highway!

Quickly re-tracing his steps he closed the gate behind him and hurried away. What business was it of his anyway? Yet try as he might he could not put from his mind what the old man would think if he could see what had become of the farm, and what use were the gloves to Henri now?

As the year wore on, perhaps inspired by Legay D'Arcy's successful escape and the always present threat that Napoleon might invade, Henri heard disquieting rumours of plots, some so wild as to be improbable; others less extreme but not without possibility, given the opportunity.

Apparently it had been discovered that along the river Hipper, towards Walton, the ironworks there made cannon and cannonballs for use by England's Army and Navy. Cannons and munitions that were vital if England was to win the war against France.

Henri had in fact seen the Griffin Works, heard the heavy hammers beating and shaping the iron ingots, but never guessed just what was being made there.

Who had made this discovery was a mystery. Had a worker been so drunk in an Inn that he unwittingly disclosed details, or bragged over his work, or left some clue which a perceptive prisoner had followed up? Every so often Henri put two and two together himself and realised that a plot might be afoot to sabotage the factory despite it being heavily guarded by the Militia. Perhaps this alone had aroused the suspicions of a prisoner walking nearby who had then decided to dig deeper into the reason why? In any case the plot thickened and instead of raiding the factory and confronting the Militia an idea was put forward to sink one of the barges laden with cannon and balls, thus blocking Chesterfield's narrow canal.

So, that was what Henri had previously witnessed being loaded into the long narrow craft—and what had so quickly lowered the vessel deeper into the water! The weight of a barge so laden would have been enormous. Sinking such a vessel would probably only block the canal for a few days or so, and the trouble rebounding on the prisoners would not make the effort worthwhile, yet the idea gave those involved something to work on. It did, however, give Henri much food for thought also, as he knew that the canal must lead eventually to a port on the coast where the cannon would be transhipped into larger vessels, all then to sail away to English depots for use by their troops.

Nevertheless, an order was given by Senior French officers that no sabotage was to be attempted, they were to obey parole or life would be made very unpleasant for all French prisoners on English soil as a result. This order was not well received but reluctantly understood and obeyed. One such act would not in itself cause sufficient hindrance to make a worthwhile difference, the outcome however would inevitably outweigh the worth of the deed.

The consensus of opinion was that if a man did escape, the consequences should only fall upon the head of that man alone, unless helped by others, and they would have to stand by the outcome. It was very difficult for men who were allowed the freedom as parolees to sit back and do nothing, and the longer the war went on the more restless some became. Were they destined to die on this foreign island, as had Lapoype's nephew? Frustration, however, is insidious! It was contrary to men's nature not to attempt to resist their captors, it also took a very strong minded individual to suppress the emotions controlled by a promise to obey the parole terms.

Within three weeks of young Lapoype's death, Lieutenant Laurent Choissy of the frigate *Franchise,* upon which General Boyer had been travelling towards Brest when captured, absconded. Two weeks later Gerin Rose of the *Alfronteur* followed. Each time Henri heard of an escape attempt he secretly prayed that with the deed done, it should succeed.

Gerin Rose's attempt to walk to nearby Sheffield was unfortunately terminated after only a few miles when he was spotted by a sharp-eyed observer. As a result he was sent to the dreaded and notorious prison at Norman Cross. So, had Lieutenant Choissy made it? To a man they waited and after a couple of weeks it was concluded that all was well; but later it was disclosed that in fact he had been re-captured in London.

Because of these failures, and due to the heat of the very hot summer month of August, there were no further attempts to escape. Henri, on the other hand, had more time to spare on his hands than usual due to the school's summer break, and as Miss Bradley only paid him for the hours he actually worked he found himself unusually short of money. He therefore took to wandering and exploring every alleyway and thoroughfare allowed to him, noting the ancient bowling green on which a very different game was played to the one in France. He even read the inscriptions on the tombstones in the churchyard. Some days he would go down to the river and watch the children splashing about in the Hipper, wondering if he would ever have any of his own. Eventually the afternoon sun became unbearable and drove him back into the shadows of the narrow streets. He discovered the coolest place was actually inside the Parish Church of All Saints where he could sit in one of the many boxed pews to meditate or read. His presence there seemed to offend no-one and he sometimes dozed off in the tranquillity of it all.

During one such moment he was awakened by the sound of his native tongue being spoken, and was surprised to see Charles D'Henin in the company of a fashionably attired lady. They appeared to be oblivious to everything around them, leaving Henri with a dilemma; did he disturb them by moving from his seat or remain there quietly as if in contemplation and thought?

The couple passed Henri's pew and separated to walk on either side of the tall stove in the Nave, their footsteps ringing on the stone-flagged floor. Who was this handsome well-dressed lady, Henri wondered, and soon realised that whoever she was she struggled with the language of her companion. In spite of this difficulty the pair seemed to manage to communicate happily and quite well, eventually moving beyond the ornately carved black-oak Jacobean pulpit which had interested the woman. They then left the lofty Nave with its fine arches to view the alabaster tombs beyond.

Perhaps at this point Henri should have taken the opportunity to leave, but his curiosity was aroused, for it seemed that they were as much engrossed in each other as they were with what they saw.

When they re-appeared there was something softly sentimental in their faces, a pleasant normality which affected him deeply. They stood beneath one of the large elegant brass chandeliers, looking up. Henri was fascinated by this charade for when communications broke down the woman's eyes widened, questioning, as she gazed into the face of the General, who responded with a gentle shrug of his shoulders and a tender smile. Slowly the pair came nearer, oblivious to anyone else who might be in the church.

It was too late now for Henri to move and open the pew door as this would immediately alert them to his presence and reveal the fact that he'd been there for some time. He bent his head lower to further conceal himself and closed his eyes until they passed by.

Several times he glanced at his pocket watch, the last remaining thing of value from his past. Time was getting on and he realised that the couple had lingered deliberately, so content were they to share each other's company.

Thinking for a moment on what he had seen, Henri felt cheated by life; even when he and Hortense first began their association there had not been such rapport as he'd witnessed today. He and she had enjoyed a fulfilment that had never reached the depths of his emotions. He regretted this and felt a little guilty that he had not cared sufficiently enough to ask her to marry him, but something about the affair had been incomplete. A movement near the church entrance brought him back to the present day.

Finally the General left, somewhat reluctantly, leaving his companion hovering by the door, a gentle smile playing on her lips, and Henri knew that he'd witnessed something rather special. After a while he saw the smile fade to be replaced by a look almost of sadness before she composed herself and left the church.

Having allowed sufficient time for Charles to disappear into the town, Eleanor Dickson sought distraction in shops near the church. Tomorrow she would be leaving Chesterfield to return to Scotland. This time, however, the draw of the purple heather on rugged hills and the shimmering waters of the lochs and burns held little attraction. She knew she was falling deeply in love with Charles D'Henin, and also that by choosing to care for a foreigner, one of England's enemies, she would upset many people. Yet she was no fool, there was a war on and if the General was transferred back to France he would fight against her own countrymen. Where would this leave her, or the two of them? She must return home, take stock of her life and try to put Charles from her mind. Perhaps when she returned in the New Year he would be gone? This thought so dismayed her that she felt like returning to Spital Lodge immediately to finish packing, but she hadn't the heart to do so!

Although Henri had taken advantage of being hidden to watch the pair without being seen, he was unaware that he too had been observed. It was only when he rose to open the creaking door of the pew and turned to leave that he saw a figure seated two pews behind him. What this person must have thought of his spying, for that's how it must have appeared, caused him some embarrassment. He left the church in a hurry, seeking to lose himself quickly in the crowd beyond the graveyard as both Charles D'Henin and Eleanor Dickson had done before him.

Eleanor Dickson's visits to Chesterfield became more frequent and, although nothing particular happened to arouse his suspicions, this began to puzzle John Bower. Eleanor was extremely lively these days, in fact she was almost blooming. He did wonder if their very attractive visitor had found herself a man in Scotland but he didn't pry and always left the women to get on with things. Perhaps had he known of the growing attachment Eleanor felt for General D'Henin he might not have been so welcoming to her.

The mere fact that she'd taken the trouble to learn French should have been a warning! As always she was a charming, generous woman at pains to help others; John had seen it merely as a kind gesture on her part, or a challenge to her undoubted intelligence. He was himself out of the house most of the day when she was there and, as it was quite a sizeable property, it gave guests the freedom to exist without getting in each other's way. He wasn't aware of certain amblings in the surrounding gardens or highways, nor of the exchange of familiar glances.

As for Charles D'Henin he was a charming man adhering strictly to parole rules, never breaking curfew, and seeking official permission if for example, he went to visit Sir Windsor Hunlock of Wingerworth Hall. John was well aware that Hunlock had moved a boundary marker to the other side of his property to allow French officers to visit him without breaking the rules; to this John Bower had turned a blind eye, as he called it, providing Sir Hunlock acted as security for their presence at his home. After all, what difference did a few hundred yards make if it kept everyone happy?

By early September the atmosphere amongst the parolees had changed. Whether this was brought about by the prospect of spending yet another long, cold winter beneath grey English skies, or maybe the fact that Pierre Lagay, General D'Henin's Aide-de-Camp had still evaded capture after four and a half months. Consequently, when the General's second ADC, Camille Lavaud, also ran with apparent success, then, one by one, eight others also chose to decamp. As all but one of these escapees were Captains or Masters of Merchant vessels perhaps they considered it wasn't their war at all, and had no qualms at breaking parole.

As autumn approached and the curfew bell began to ring at five in the afternoon again, three more Captains, Monsieurs Désgranches, Sauvage, and Tappie took their chances along with the Master of the *Achille*, André Hughes.

When the news reached the town in November of the English victory over the French Navy at Trafalgar, at which Napoleon's sea power was virtually destroyed, there was great rejoicing. To the prisoners this crushing defeat was a serious blow, and they were comforted only by the accompanying news that Lord Horatio Nelson had been killed during the battle on October 21st, by a sniper on a mast of the French Man o' War *Redoubtable*. Tricorne hats flew jubilantly through the air and great cheers were heard from Napoleon's men in Chesterfield, much to the anger of the townspeople.

In spite of the blow of Nelson's death, considered by many English sailors to have been too great a price to pay for the victory, there were signs of continuing jubilation taking place. The people of Chesterfield roasted whole sheep and oxen in honour of the occasion, whilst the parolees retreated behind closed doors, dismayed at their own country's setback.

To Henri the sea battle at Trafalgar was an indication that the war would continue its wearisome journey, claiming the best of men on both sides as it went. He too remained indoors during the festivities, the school being closed so that the pupils could join in the celebrations; therefore he missed one of the happiest days Chesterfield had seen since the declaration of the short-lived peace only three years before.

When the excitement died down and the prisoners once more began to parade in the streets, the weather had turned; the cold days drew to an early close and apparently subdued further ambitions to escape. Nevertheless, two more attempts were made, one of which was by a midshipman named Petit of the frigate *Franchise*. He was soon captured and taken to Wakefield Gaol where he ran from the guards who were to transfer him to Chatham. He was caught again in London and taken directly to a prison hulk on the River Medway where, Henri knew, the man would rue the day he'd ever tried to escape. With little or no knowledge of the English language it was usually only a matter of time before the game was up for the escapees—if only the prisoners could see it.

By the end of November, however, plans were afoot of which Henri was completely ignorant. This final attempt to escape in 1805 was by far the most audacious and serious, as a local man was involved. Unknown to everyone, André Hughes and Jean Basil, both Masters of merchant vessels, were secretly collaborating with Thomas Whildon, a local hatter, to escape. Whildon of Chesterfield was either a weak man, a traitor willing to betray his country for money, or simply greedy, but he decided to help the pair. How the three of them met, Henri could only surmise, but it was probably in an ale house, yet sufficient exchange had to have taken place despite the language difficulties in order to pull it off! The Frenchmen paid Whildon fourteen shillings plus his expenses for him to procure a post-chaise to take them to London where he had also found them lodgings, and even bought a passage on a boat for them to go to Holland. Their journey, however, came to an abrupt end when they arrived in the Capital where the pair were caught and taken to Chatham, while Whildon soon languished in Wakefield gaol to await trial the following Spring for his duplicity. He could not have been unaware of the placards posted in the Market Square specifying the limits prescribed for prisoners on parole, or of the consequences for anyone found assisting the parolees to disobey.

In all, twelve prisoners chose to abscond in 1805, of these, seven were either successful or their fate was not recorded and, of the merchant seamen who were caught, several were later allowed to return to France.

Two of General D'Henin's aides had also decamped against his wishes and whilst he officially deplored their act, he secretly applauded their determination. Publicly he forbade any further attempts at escape and felt it his duty to set an example to those remaining on parole.

Having taken the initiative to make himself useful by teaching at Miss Bradley's school, Henri now felt obliged to consider helping those prisoners less fortunate than himself. It had been suggested that if any enterprising Frenchman was willing to operate and run a commercial outlet through which the men could sell their handiwork, this would serve to augment their income and give them an occupation through the long and boring winter evenings.

Arrangements were made to obtain suitable straw, this was then dyed or plaited and could be made into attractive bonnets or fancy boxes. Meat bones could be made into trinkets and model ships, whilst other men used their skills at woodworking. Even ornamental hair-working produced items much admired and sought after. These, together with the making of woollen gloves and silk weaving, encouraged a man named 'Bourlemont' (or little Boney) to open a dépôt in Chesterfield for British wines and an outlet for these 'cottage' industries. The more elaborate and finely-modelled ships were disposed of by the running of lotteries which also raised much needed funds. This was a great satisfaction to Henri, knowing that hands thus creatively occupied made living as a parolee much more bearable.

During the evenings after school, Henri wrote in his journal of the progress the men made but he also began to paint, small simple pictures at first until his skill improved. Helped by instruction from the Painting Master at the school in exchange for French lessons, he progressed painfully slowly, hoping that by summer he would be able to sit outside and copy images of the local landscapes to illustrate his now expanding notes.

With the worsening of the weather he was unfortunately plagued once more with his chest problems which were made worse by the cold air. Many nights he had difficulty sleeping due to his constant coughing which left him tired and drawn. He tried various remedies and a linctus which Mrs Parsons put his way, but to no avail, the damage done on San Domingo was irreparable and he prayed for an early arrival of Spring.

Talking with General D'Henin one day in the assembly room at *The Angel*, he was dismayed to be told that as a result of the fever and his lasting respiratory difficulties in bad weather he stood little chance of an early exchange to France, and that in all probability his career in the Army was at an end. This was not spoken of lightly, with malice or unkindness, nevertheless it left Henri in a quandary as to his future, immediate or otherwise.

As time passed, through his private tutoring and following several visits to Spital Lodge, Henri began to integrate himself more with certain business families in the town. He was not, of course, invited to partake in social functions, perhaps this was expecting too much. If it hadn't been for the school he would have been forced back into the company of his sometimes frustrated and insular fellow countrymen.

Chapter 7   1806
A Chance Meeting

After a dull and uninspiring Christmas in Scotland, Eleanor Dickson waited impatiently for the first weeks of the New Year to pass with mixed feelings. Should she go to Chesterfield as arranged at the end of January, or cancel her normal visit this time and sample the delights of London instead? She had received several letters from Isabella since August informing her of the happenings at Spital Lodge, with only occasional references to Charles D'Henin; mainly about his welfare, but Eleanor sensed her friend Isabella was reluctant to answer questions or regale her with too much news regarding him. Had she, Eleanor, made her interest in Charles too obvious? After all, she had tried hard to make the Bowers think that her associating with the man was only in order to practise her French, but could not know how effective her efforts had been.

Eleanor was actually afraid of the depths of her mixed emotions on the subject, yet in spite of telling herself that such feelings would pass, she acknowledged that she could not just enjoy Charles' company and leave it at that. With her finances now secure she had no need to risk everything by entering into marriage, but on seeing him again would she be able to suppress the emotions stirring within her?

When she'd left Chesterfield at the end of her summer visit it had been her intention to put him from her mind, hoping that time and separation would cool her growing desires. She was, after all, a mature woman, independent and confident, yet she found all her thoughts constantly drifting back to Charles D'Henin. The nightly dreams in which he constantly appeared uninvited left her no peace.

It was becoming obvious that she must do one of two things, either stay away from the Bower residence whilst ever the General was there, or be prepared to risk going and face any pain she might suffer as a result. That he found her attractive was not in doubt. He had been attentive and kind, almost tender whenever they had managed to be alone together, but he was out of his native surroundings and vulnerable, sensitive even in his forced circumstances. Would she eventually find the 'General' in him not to her liking and would she be prepared to go to France if this question ever arose?

Twice since her return he had sent her a small billet doux, and even though his words were simply expressed she still found them hard to read. They were sent merely to assure her that he hadn't forgotten her and were made deliberately circumspect, as John Bower had to read them first. He had made the foolish mistake earlier in his stay of writing to General Boyer under an assumed name and had been caught out and reprimanded. This he had done in the hope that no one would connect him with Boyer. Eleanor knew that he would be extremely disappointed if she stayed away, yet once there and near him again she would find it difficult to leave.

On the other hand the tender feelings which Charles D'Henin felt towards Eleanor were not of a transient nature. A bachelor he had always remained because he'd never before been sufficiently attracted to any woman, at least not enough to change that situation. His career had been an adequate fulfilment and the constant travel and years of war in truth hadn't encouraged him to consider a family life.

Now, nearing middle age, and with the horrors and disgust of San Domingo behind him he quite liked the peace that parole offered him. He had never been a religious man but the spirituality, which battle and the brutality of men had crushed, was beginning to resurface. Earlier he had allowed the constant English drizzle and damp to get him down and as a result of this and his attendant melancholy he'd been sent to Harrogate in an attempt to improve his health. On returning, he occasionally accompanied John Bower and his family to the Parish Church for the morning service, and at first this had been an antidote to boredom, but now it was becoming a form of solace. He'd even written to General Boyer again expressing his thoughts on this, in the hope that the man would regret and repent of his earlier wickedness, and cease the outlandish behaviour with which he and Rochambeau harassed the authorities. All such behaviour sooner or later found its way into the newspapers with due criticism, which John translated for Charles.

As the weeks passed and Eleanor's hoped-for visit drew nearer, Charles waited eagerly, expectantly even, hoping the response he'd seen in her lively eyes and womanly ways had not been pure imagination. He was in truth almost as much in love with her as she was with him, but it brought with it responsibilities. Her security, safety and comfort must take priority over his feelings which, if necessary, he must suppress for her sake. He cursed the fact that he was making such slow progress in learning English, for there was so much he wanted to say and write but could not. Meanwhile he certainly didn't want the Bower family, kind though they might be, to interpret his thoughts about her!

Time passed slowly. On a daily basis he joined other officers in the upstairs room of *The Angel* in their efforts to organize relief and provide advice to those prisoners who were struggling to survive. The long drawn-out evenings after curfew wearied him and tried his patience, and it was a strain not to ask Isabella Bower when her friend was coming without arousing her curiosity.

Eleanor had a weakness, she always followed the promptings of her mind. Deny this she might, although her close friends often wondered if one day she wouldn't rue the day when she didn't restrain her impulses. Finally she confronted her deep feelings and, true to her nature, found herself travelling not to London but to Chesterfield, in order to prove to herself that she was strong enough to face Charles D'Henin and the possible consequences of their meeting.

As the hired carriage trundled up the short drive to Spital Lodge, Eleanor glanced wistfully up at the window of Charles' room. As far as she knew he still lodged there, yet these were uncertain times, but there, framed within the casement of his window, he stood watching the carriage's progress and was gazing down at her!

Due to the fact that Isabella now stood in the doorway awaiting her, Eleanor could only smile to acknowledge him. She wondered if he had been waiting for her arrival?

All Charles had been told was that Eleanor was due to arrive by coach from Sheffield that afternoon. During the morning he had intended joining his brother officers as usual at *The Angel* but was unable to curb his impatience until evening to see if she had made the journey. Now that he knew she had, he was loath to remain quietly in his room and was tempted to throw caution to the wind and dash downstairs to greet her.

After a while, when the excited chatter below had subsided considerably and steps had been heard ascending the stairs, Charles left his room and paused on the landing. The door of the room used by Eleanor on her visits was slightly ajar and as he hesitated, Charles coughed lightly, hoping to draw her attention.

Knowing that John Bower was at his office and that there were no other men in the house, Eleanor realised that Charles must be near her. She was nervous, and whereas her instinct was to rush out to greet him, womanly intuition warned her that he might not be as keen to see her as she was to see him. Deliberately taking her time she finally went to the door and opened it wider as if ready to go down. He had his back to her and stood looking through the small window to the garden below.

'Bonjour, Mon General,' she called softly, attracting his attention.

He turned slowly as if taken by surprise. 'Ah, Madame Eleanor!' he smiled, waiting for her reaction with his head slightly inclined, inviting a warmer welcome. As she approached he took her hand and pressed it to his lips. 'Welcome home!' he said quietly, hesitatingly, suppressing his desire to hold her close, but all the time aware that there were people not far below, people who hopefully knew nothing of their mutual attraction.

Eleanor could not still the excitement which coursed through her as his lips touched her fingers. She closed her eyes; how was she ever going to conceal the feelings which she knew he would see in her eyes? She should never have returned here, but it was too late now for regrets.

He waited patiently, her hand still held in his firm grasp. It was a warm protective hand, the feel of which roused strong emotions in her. Slowly she raised her eyes to his and saw a questioning love there.

There was a sound from below and Isabella's voice called out suddenly, breaking the spell. 'Have you got everything you need, Eleanor?'

'Yes! Yes, thank you. I'll be down in a minute,' Eleanor called shakily back, perhaps a little too quickly.

'Are you alright, you sound strained?' Isabella queried.

Eleanor laughed, 'No, no! I have just bumped into General D'Henin, that is all. You know how difficult conversation can be sometimes, but I won't be long!' She gave a flirtatious wink at Charles and smiled conspiratorially at him before making her way downstairs. Charles watched her go, content now to simply have her under the same roof and near him once more.

The clandestine affair between Eleanor and Charles did not of course continue for more than a few days before concealment became impossible.

'Are you blind not to see it?' Isabella mocked her husband as he extinguished the lamp before climbing into bed a couple of nights later. 'You mark my words, I can tell when a woman is in love and Eleanor Dickson is either a cruel teaser or Charles D'Henin has captured her affections.'

'All I know is that Eleanor flirts harmlessly with everyone,' John replied, shocked at her remark. 'I'm sure she is sensible enough not to get involved with him. Besides, he may simply see her as an amusing companion.' John Bower sometimes despaired of the frivolity which overtook his household when Eleanor came to stay.

'You watch carefully, this is something very different!' His wife chuckled, 'There is definitely something in the air!'

'Oh, God! That would be yet another problem!' John replied with a sigh. 'The Transport Board have already complained over all the escapes, but what am I to do? I can't be in every house with each prisoner all day long, can I? The Militia should be more alert! With nearly two hundred men in the town walking free, what do they expect? Some are clever enough to plot and scheme and they're certainly not going to tell anyone. Do the authorities never consider that the prisoners' lack of English will not stop them if they want to go? It's just a great pity the men don't appreciate the leniency of their situation. We do our best, which I hear is not quite the case for our men in French prisons, yet they take advantage of the privilege of parole!' He sighed again, and in spite of the darkness in the room, Isabella could well imagine the worried frown which would be on his face. 'The Board regard my regime too lax and friendly, but what else can I do if they don't support me and lock them up!'

'You've been a very understanding Agent, John. Maybe a few of the clever men do get away, but the ordinary ones just get caught and are sent to Norman Cross or the hulks. I've heard terrible things about those places, and they say the death rate is very high at Norman Cross.'

'They're thinking of sending a Government Officer to take over my responsibilities altogether,' he went on, 'and I must admit the job is a lot bigger than I expected it to be. We thought the war would be over by now, but it's spreading throughout Europe. Countries are being ravaged by Napoleon's troops and rumour has it that he intends to invade England as well!'

'Really!' Isabella protested, 'The man must be power mad. How do you reconcile a nice person like Charles with that Napoleon. Which brings me back to Eleanor and the General.'

'Oh, just go to sleep, woman,' John pleaded, 'I have a lot of work to do tomorrow.' Then, much to his wife's irritation and within minutes judging by his breathing, he was soon asleep, leaving Isabella to fume at the ease by which he left his problems behind once his head touched the pillow.

Sleep didn't come easy to Isabella though! She pondered over what she'd witnessed between her friend and the General, and even her girls had begun to make comments to her over what was transpiring before them.

For all Eleanor's determination to control her feelings for Charles she was well aware that she wasn't making a very good job of it. Besides, Charles D'Henin wasn't being helpful, with his frequent touching and playful seizure of her hand when he thought no one was looking. Could he really not be aware of the delicious tingling sensation which coursed through her when he did this? She suspected not, or he would surely have avoided tempting fate by causing such flushes on her face, which she couldn't always conceal.

Charles D'Henin of course knew well the affect these fleeting contacts had on her and took great pleasure in his actions. It was, however, a poor substitute for being able to show his true feelings and he longed to declare these to her.

When this could no longer be denied, and their secret was too hard to conceal, Eleanor announced that she and Charles wished to marry. It was Isabella who strangely appeared the most taken aback by the news. The girls of course applauded excitedly and with enthusiasm, whilst John Bower shook his head in dismay over what now confronted the two people standing before him.

He was the first to respond directly. 'Do you really know what you're doing?' he asked Eleanor, as if talking to a troublesome client in his office. He seemed to forget Charles who was watching all of them with bemused eyes. 'You do know that any marriage in England would not be recognised in France, don't you?'

'I shall consult my Solicitor, John,' she replied with a wicked smile. 'I'm not a fool, and Charles wants to talk to you on the matter if you would be kind enough to hear what he has to say. However, my mind is made up!' Then, in a gentler tone she added, 'We are grateful to you and Isabella for your hospitality, all we need is your support, and blessing.'

Looking from one to the other and seeing the glowing faces of the pair, John wondered how he could have missed the signs of the growing liaison between them. Eleanor's face was a picture of happiness, whilst Charles watched her with a look of pride and mild wonder.

Throughout the discussion, Isabella had sat as if stunned. In spite of her hints and guesswork she really hadn't considered that such a big move might be afoot. To see her now so taken aback, her eyes darting between the lovers and her hand still clasping the fork now suspended above the plate, took the sting out of John Bower's argument and he had to admit that the atmosphere between them all was decidedly familial. There would be problems and perhaps heartaches too, that he could see, and yet the pair were ideally matched—if only circumstances were different.

General D'Henin had slowly become almost a member of the family; John enjoyed his company and it was stimulating to be no longer the only man in a household of women. When Charles had first arrived in the town he had been in a poor physical and mental state and John had been genuinely concerned for him. During the two years of his sojourn at Spital Lodge there had been a considerable change, which, on reflection was possibly helped by the regular visits made by Eleanor. Yes, Isabella had been right as usual in her judgement and he had been blind not to see it. Eleanor's presence, although exasperating sometimes certainly lifted their spirits, particularly in the drab winter months. He could readily understand her being attracted to Charles who was kindness itself and was highly courteous and polite. The fact that he was a Frenchman was no detriment as far as John was concerned, it was the disturbing fact that England was at war with the French that worried him. For instance, how might people react towards Eleanor as the news leaked out? Furthermore, where would they live? What would happen if Charles was exchanged and sent home during the hostilities; inevitably he would have to fight for France again. John doubted if Eleanor would heed his warning of potential trouble, she was a very headstrong woman who knew her own mind. To her credit she was also a shrewd and honest one who probed deeply into things which would be of little interest to others of her sex. Yes, he would talk plainly to Charles, man to man, although he realised there was little he could say that would change things if the couple were determined to go ahead with the union.

Beyond the closed doors of John Bower's study the deeper sound of the men's voices could be heard, although not loud enough to be understood by a frustrated Eleanor as she hovered on the stairs, hoping to hear what was being said. Even when she could make out an occasional English word it was followed by rapid French and thus meant nothing to her. Although nervous over the situation she knew that Charles loved her and would hardly let John persuade him against their getting married. She went up to her room endeavouring to be patient.

Charles was trying to explain to John that he had become a more piously natured man since his religious conversion whilst being in Chesterfield. He had abstained from ways which he'd previously enjoyed and planned to take Eleanor, whom he loved, back to France with him. There he would if necessary renew his marriage vows if the law required it of them. He also agreed to a Bond of £500, quite a considerable amount, as a sign of good faith. John Bower could find no fault in the man and only sincerity in his offer, so suggested that they be married by License to avoid the publicity the Banns would cause. To all this Charles readily agreed, and also to the appointment of an independent Attorney at Law to officiate in the security of the Bond.

When at last the study door opened and she heard their voices in the hall below, Eleanor could have cried with relief at the composed and amicable nature of their manner.

Henri on the other hand was feeling particularly low as the month of February drew to a close. The rain seemed to fall incessantly or else a chilling mist hung in the air, adding to his misery. On his occasional invitations to Spital Lodge the General's growing happiness brought out the basic human longing in Henri, the need for close companionship. He was not jealous of the couple, merely envious of the kind of normality which was denied to himself. This situation was highlighted even further when later on a fellow prisoner, one Jean Baptiste Delachy married a local girl called Mary Bradley, in March.

Meanwhile, Henri read the newspapers with great interest of the case of Thomas Whildon, the hatter, who had resided in the Market Place and had aided and abetted two of the earlier escapees. John Bower, as Agent, had been summoned to Wakefield as a witness in the case where Whildon had subsequently been found guilty of conspiracy. The Transport Board now judged that Agent Bower had been too easy-going with the prisoners and intended replacing him with Navy Lieutenants in the future. John, once again Mayor of Chesterfield, was in many ways relieved to have the responsibility taken off his shoulders.

Henri received this information with mixed feelings. How the Board could have expected any one man to take responsibility for so many had seemed to him to be an impossibility anyway, especially if they were intent on mischief or absconding. Henri's own chances of repatriation now looked less likely as he would apparently be of little use to the French Army due to his precarious state of health, but there were many moments when he too began to feel that his promise to obey the restraints of parole was too harsh a penalty to pay for his comparative freedom. The situation was ludicrous and against a man's instinct when, in the middle of a conflict he should be living a near normal life. Sometimes anger swept through him against Napoleon, but never once did he deny his love for France, nor strangely did he hold it against the people of Chesterfield for his restricted life.

The tragedy of war raged on and on, with nations constantly changing allegiances involving England and the whole of Europe, but usually France was the manipulative instigator. As Henri read of these things from his unique position, he often shook his head in disbelief. It would be years, perhaps generations before stability could be restored on the continent and the identity of the victors lay far ahead in the future.

When the date of the marriage between General D'Henin and Eleanor Dickson became known to him it only served to re-enforce Henri's feelings of melancholy and loneliness. He no longer thought about Hortense, it was as if she never existed. Few other people were told of the forthcoming marriage at the Parish Church, and in order to avoid prejudice and any unpleasantness, a special license had been purchased, thus avoiding the public reading of the Banns. Only a small group of close friends accompanied the couple to the service on the fourth of May. Amongst those who did attend were, of course, the Bower family, and several officers including Charles' friend Commander Duveyrier, and Henri.

The ceremony was short and simple, but sufficient to bind the pair of willing lovers in the state of matrimony. If either had any doubts or fears for their future, they concealed such beneath the devotion which appeared so obviously on their faces.

When Henri sat in his room later that evening, long after the Frenchman's Bell had rung, he penned a letter to his father partly to inform him of his situation and also to ask him to advise Hortense to forget him. He was no longer the man she had known, life and experiences had changed him. Not only was it unfair to them both to waste the best years of their lives hoping for a future that might not now be, but also because, in his heart, he knew that his love had been replaced by a feeling only of friendship. After six years Hortense would have changed too from a girl to a mature woman with whom he would by now have little in common. She might even by this time have already given up on him and married. Time and distance led to disenchantment, and the past object of his desires might no longer appeal to him. He didn't enjoy being deprived of the warm company of a woman, he had simply learned to live with the situation, yet he was lonely and often longed for that which he couldn't have.

Having a little time on his hands to spare before curfew one day, Henri went again to *The Falcon Inn* to meet and talk with several other officers, and to browse through the newspapers in the Reading Room there to see how the war was progressing. In spite of the commodious size of the heavily beamed rooms at the Inn they were nevertheless warm and comfortable, the thick drapes at the window kept out the draughts and roaring fires blazed in the large fireplaces. He had learned during his time in Chesterfield to frequent the Inn as a place in which to keep warm whilst usefully occupying his time for the simple cost of a drink or two, which he could now afford from his tutoring fees.

The reception of the news was mixed depending on which side one supported. To the French today's report was encouraging for it announced that Napoleon had recently invaded and was subduing Prussia. However it looked now as if their Emperor wished to further his conquests over all of Europe, thus prolonging the war.

After nearly three years in captivity, Henri's appetite for war and military service had almost disappeared and he much enjoyed his role as tutor. He looked up from the newspaper to the clock standing against the wall, noting with a start that he was alone and that curfew was due in fifteen minutes! He rose reluctantly from his seat and donned the thick heavy coat which he'd hung on the stand by the window and left to brave the elements.

The contrasting keen November air struck him the moment he stepped outside and he caught his breath. Fortunately it wasn't far from the Inn to Glumangate and he had ample time to cross the Market Square and walk to Mrs Parsons' house.

As he entered Glumangate the figure of a woman came hurrying towards him on her way towards the Square. As they drew almost level, Henri was struck by the familiarity of her features and he hesitated, smiled and raised his hat instinctively before realising that she was probably a complete stranger. He made to walk on but was then surprised when the woman also paused and then nervously spoke to him.

'Excuse me, Sir,' she said, 'I hope you don't mind but I have often seen you and never dared speak.' Realising how forward this must sound, and the startled look on his face confirmed this, she was overcome by embarrassment. 'What must you think of me?' she asked. 'You don't recognise me, do you?'

Scrutinising her face, Henri was perplexed. Certainly she was unknown to him yet her eyes had something about them which puzzled him. 'I am sorry, Madame, I regret I do not recall meeting you before,' he said politely.

The woman's eyes clouded over, her brow furrowed. 'Perhaps I should not have approached you—however, for some long time now I have wished to talk to you. I need to apologise for my rudeness when you offered to help at the farm where I lived.' She saw a glimmer of enlightenment cross his face as he became aware of who she was. 'I have regretted my sharpness,' she went on, 'but never dared to speak to you until today. To pass you would have been a further insult if you had recognised me and I had not spoken out!'

Suddenly the church clock started to chime the hour of five and Henri was in danger of breaking the curfew. He began to panic, 'You must please excuse me, Madame, but the bell goes and I am not yet home!' He raised his hat and hurriedly said, 'I must go, but there was no need for your apologies!' With that he walked swiftly on his way bemused by this strange encounter. There were many questions he would like to have asked, about the older lady and about the demise of the farm, but there had been no time to linger. The woman's eyes were the only feature he'd really remembered in a face then pale and thin. The same blue eyes were now in pleasant and rounder features, no longer fierce with anger.

Henri was pleased she'd had the courage to confront him, and also to note that life was obviously being kinder to her. He smiled to himself as he entered Mrs Parsons' house, wondering if he ought not to have lingered a little longer after the lady had made such an effort. What difference would an extra two minutes have made?

More than once during the long evening he mused on the encounter which, had it taken place two years before, would have been of greater comfort to his soul than it was now. He still had one of the two pairs of knitted gloves he'd bought for the women at the farm as a peace offering, the other pair he'd given to Mrs Parsons as a little 'Thank you' gift. He went to the heavy five-drawered chest and took the remaining pair out. What a pity he'd not had them with him today.

Now, without his earlier desperation for money, Henri was perhaps embarrassingly comfortable compared with some of his follow officers, so much so that Mrs Parsons' table saw a greater variety of eatables than would otherwise have been possible. He dressed moderately in the English fashion, as many prisoners did when their old uniforms disintegrated if they had earned sufficient to be able to replace them. One enterprising man made bird-cages and trained linnets in order to supplement his income.

'I want to buy a caged linnet,' Henri informed Mrs Parsons one evening as they sat eating dinner. 'A little company in the evenings would please me, no?'

Getting used to his strange ways and requests by now, Mrs Parsons' eyes widened enquiringly. She had become quite fond of her French lodger who never ceased to provide her with little treats. She had discovered that beneath his good-looking countenance there lay a gentleness which, if he chose to show it, was remarkably touching. Yet she knew from such incidents as the snails that he could be stubborn, and could also be difficult to divert when he'd made up his mind to an action. Her house was clearly not the place it had been before his arrival, but she took it in her stride. She'd long since stopped protesting at the sight of his bedding thrust through the open window on a nice day, left to hang there apparently for an 'airing' as he put it. She often smiled at his fastidious personal cleanliness and his punctuality. Supper it seemed needed to be placed on the table by six in winter and eight in summer. Henri had brought a sense of purpose into her life. Now it was to be a linnet!

'A linnet!' she cried, in a manner that Henri had come to know as a half-hearted protest.

'Not a snail Madame, merely a beautiful little bird. In a cage of course!' He smiled defiantly at her.

'Poor thing, how would you like to be in a cage?' she retorted.

Henri laughed. 'Madame, I am in an English cage, am I not? Your house is my cage after curfew!'

'No mess, mind! And you feed and clean it!' Mrs Parsons said, although inwardly she couldn't help smiling. She really should stop giving in to him so much! She guiltily hoped that Napoleon Bonaparte would take his time in losing the war, as she knew he eventually must, because her life would be very different when Henri left her.

'The bird is trained, trained to go back in his cage when told to!' Henri explained. Then, with a saucy grin, he cajoled, 'I will not have to pay his rent, will I?'

Mrs Parsons returned his smile with a frown. 'No snails! And no frogs, mind you! And cover his cage when he's too noisy!'

The following day, after mustering in the Square, Henri bought an extremely well-made cage already occupied by a lively chirping linnet. Several prisoners had trained such birds which they taught to take food from their owner's mouths, or to perch on their shoulders until a small bell in its cage was rung to attract it back inside. Other prisoners took dogs and trained them as companions, but Henri didn't think Mrs Parsons would appreciate a dog in her proud little home.

Ruth Silcock was no longer the embittered, waif-like scarecrow who had spoken so harshly to Henri at the farm gate when first they met. She was so dramatically changed now that Henri hadn't initially realised who the polite young woman was.

On returning to the farmhouse that day two years previously, her shoulders rigid with anger and her eyes ablaze, Ruth had slammed the door shut behind her.

'What did you say to the man?' Elizabeth Silcock asked her daughter-in-law, suspecting that she had been rude again instead of offering her apologies, 'or did you make it worse? You look as mad as a cat!'

Ruth turned, her eyes unable to disguise the pain she felt. 'He offered to help us! I told him about George and that we could do without any assistance from a Frenchman! I don't think he'll bother us again now, thank goodness!'

'Oh, Ruthie, it's not his fault,' the old woman scolded. 'The pain of losing William has left you lonely and bitter of course, but you've got to stop hating and try to forgive. I have lost my son and now my husband but I feel no anger, only a great sadness. It is hate and greed that causes wars. Try not to let it spoil the rest of your life. You're in danger of becoming a harpy!'

This uncharacteristic reprimand by Elizabeth took Ruth by surprise and she sat down wearily. The emptiness which losing William had created was driving her mad and she stared broodingly at her mother-in-law.

'Think about it girl! And just look at yourself, you're like death warmed up!' Never before had Elizabeth spoken so harshly to Ruth, but looking at the pale, wan face before her, and knowing of the anguish locked deep in the young woman's heart, she felt obliged to speak out. 'It's as if we're both waiting to die!'

'Is that so bad?' Ruth cried out in despair. 'We're stuck here unable to work the farm and when you're gone, what of my life then?'

The distress in this outburst made Elizabeth sigh. She had her own losses to cope with and she suspected that her own time on earth might only be of short duration now. The pains inside her were getting worse, not better, but she hadn't wanted to alarm George by telling him. It was as well he'd gone first in the end. All that was left for her now was to set Ruth free and on the road to happiness, even if it meant hurting her in the process. Never before had she been so annoyed by the futile wasting of a young life, and she owed it to her son to shake Ruth into adopting a more positive outlook for her future before she was left alone in the world.

Softening her tone and suppressing the pain which her agitation had aggravated, Elizabeth spoke, 'You must know that we have to leave here before the winter sets in. I want to fetch an auctioneer in to value and sell anything worth selling, the tools, the hens, everything.'

Ruth was horrified by this remark. 'Oh! But why? Why so suddenly? Where will we go?'

'I think you should also know,' Elizabeth whispered, 'I think my end is coming. Most of the time I'm in pain and I know the signs!' She saw Ruth's jaw drop with this shock, and there was genuine concern on her face. 'I didn't want George to know and thank goodness he never did. But we have to go, and go soon. And you have to start living again!'

'Oh, Ma,' Ruth cried out. 'Why didn't you tell me? I wouldn't have told George. What are we to do?' Her eyes, brimming with tears now searched the wrinkled, tired face of her mother-in-law. 'I have been so obsessed with my own problems that I didn't know, didn't even suspect. What must you think of me?'

'You had too much grief locked up inside, I couldn't add to that, not whilst I had George. But I cannot go on, and you must prepare yourself for a change in life. Go and tidy yourself up then go to town and ask John Bower to come out, he will know what to do!'

By the end of 1806 the town had got used to the familiar sight of seamen wearing large looped gold earrings, military men with drooping moustaches and Legion of Honour ribbons, and the trained poodles carrying walking sticks in their mouths, as they all paraded along the High Street.

Just occasionally the town's merry lads goaded the Frenchmen, both sides having nothing better to do than retaliate at the other's expense. One such episode did, however, get out of hand with the result that six French prisoners were taken to the local gaol before being transferred to Norman Cross—where they no doubt soon regretted their hasty actions. The local lads meanwhile nursed their bruises and laid low until the atmosphere improved.

As the years passed and men on parole came and went, a kind of truce was established until having foreigners in the town became an everyday, even acceptable situation. A constant trickle of prisoners arrived, taken captive as far away as Calabria in Italy and Maida on the eastern shore of the Red Sea in the Yemen. When a death occurred of a prisoner from ill-health or as a result of wounds incurred in a battle prior to his capture, these deaths made Henri feel very vulnerable indeed.

Ruth's hatred of the French and her distress subsided as she gradually got on with her life. Deep down, though, she was aware that as she got older her chances of having children diminished with each succeeding year. Forgive the circumstances that caused her loneliness she might, forget she could not, and the longing was always there deep inside.

The combined income from Henri's work at Miss Bradley's school, together with private requests for his skills gave him a great deal of satisfaction. The Generals and other officers with monies in France were able to have Bank Orders sent over to England, but the lower ranks were compelled to manage and take advantage of any work that came their way. At least one man found occupation by digging coal in the nearby Hady pit. Aware of his own good fortune, Henri often purchased lottery tickets whenever other men's excellent pieces of handiwork were on offer; not because he believed in gambling but it was a way of helping out those less fortunate than himself. Thus it came as a very pleasant surprise, when in one such draw he became the proud owner of a beautifully-crafted model of a sixty-four gun 'Man o' War', complete with rigging made of finely woven hair. He took it home and wondered if he would ever get the opportunity to present it to his ageing father.

As yet another Christmas approached and the D'Henin's prepared for the birth of their first child in the following Spring, Henri accepted an invitation to attend a service with them on Christmas Day in the Parish Church.

Once seated amongst the group in John Bower's family box-pew, crowded though it was, Henri experienced a sense of oneness with normality he'd not felt for many years. To hear the music of the organ was sweet joy to his ears and he vowed to attend church more often, if only to savour the uplift the powerful instrument brought to him.

The obvious happiness he observed in the D'Henin's pleased him. Eleanor's face glowed with an inner joy, whilst General D'Henin held her hand with great pride. When all was over and the congregation moved towards the door, Henri became aware that standing in the porch was the woman who had accosted him in Glumangate a few weeks before. If she was aware of his presence she didn't show it; the shelter of the private boxes would have prevented her from seeing him—unless she had been upstairs in the gallery.

The peace he'd felt during the rather long service still held him in its spell, and taking this opportunity he deliberately made it his duty to approach her.

'Good Morning, Madame,' he said quietly. 'I trust you are well?'

It was obvious from her startled response that she had in fact been oblivious to his presence. 'Oh!' she replied unguardedly. 'Why—yes! Thank you, sir!'

Having gone this far, Henri was now at a loss for something else to say. His mind raced as her clear blue eyes watched, waiting for him to say or do something. 'The day we met, in the street,' he said, searching for ideas. 'I had to leave to get to my lodgings before the curfew. I would have asked questions about the farm but there was not time enough, then one day I passed it, and it was empty!'

Ruth nodded sadly. 'Perhaps if I had not been rude and had accepted your help, the farm might have survived,' she admitted more to herself than Henri. 'We couldn't manage alone, not the two of us, and mother wasn't well!'

He was almost afraid to ask if the older woman still lived. 'How is Madame?' he ventured as gently as he could.

'She is dead!' Ruth replied. 'She was already very ill, although I didn't realise it at the time. It was then better to move somewhere where she could be more comfortable, until her end came. I believe she was relieved to move.'

'I am sorry to hear such news,' Henri averted his eyes from the face before him, a face suddenly downcast and sad. 'And you?' he asked gently, 'are you being taken care of?' He had surprised himself with the question for she was not his responsibility and yet, in a way, he felt she was.

'I have somewhere to live and work to do,' Ruth informed him. 'But it is not the same without the family.' A look of resignation replaced the sadness and Henri sensed the loneliness which lay beneath the surface.

'I remember the old man with affection,' Henri pressed on; he was happy to talk rather than return to Mrs Parsons' so soon. 'In the early days the walks gave me a purpose, and talking to him gave me comfort.'

This frank admission caused Ruth to recall the way both she and George had at times behaved towards the foreigners who had been forced into their world. She was not totally without feelings and knew now that Henri had meant no harm. 'Again I am being impolite,' she said, 'I haven't asked how you are managing here, away from your family? You must think me most uncaring.'

Henri sighed. 'The time passes slowly, and this war seems never-ending. I sometimes wonder how I came to be here. It is very strange, very unreal. But I teach my language to those who want to learn, and the work pays my bills and passes the time.' His voice had dropped and began to trail off as the effort to contemplate his lot disturbed him.

To Ruth this added revelation bit deep for she'd never considered that he could have been lonely or in want of comfort. He was after all a soldier, and a soldier marches and fights, a mere killing machine, and yet…her William had been a man, a soldier, but a husband too! Her eyes misted over and her mouth trembled at the memory. 'I'm sorry,' she replied humbly. 'Why do we have to have wars?'

Seeing her distress, Henri felt embarrassed. What could he say that would be of help? He was, or his country was, partly responsible for her problems. 'Madame,' he said softly, 'if I could have it any other way, I would. But I cannot. Our world is in chaos.' He felt that there was nothing more that he could add and his presence was only making matters worse. 'I am late,' he lied, 'I wish you well. I must go now!' He smiled kindly and bowed his head. As he walked away from the church he wondered what would become of her, and indeed what would become of all of them in the end.

Ruth watched Henri leave with sadness in her heart, and then she sat down on the stone bench at the side of the porch. She had seen something of her own predicament in him, an emptiness. Perhaps he too spent hours alone, simply wishing to be sent home and frustrated by the longing to get on with his life. She knew others too had sadness and suffering but they seemed to hide it far better than she did.

The church was, by now, almost empty and the sound of shoes echoing on the stone flagged floor reminded her that it was time to return to her duties in the large house where she worked.

Rose Hill, known originally as the Mansion house, was one of the first Georgian residences to be built of red brick in Chesterfield. A fine two and a half storey building, the lower half covered by a rich green and flourishing ivy, stood proudly on the edge of town looking out over the valley to the River Hipper below. To have obtained work there for the owner, Milnes Lowndes, Ruth felt was a privilege. It gave her security and protection even though the work was hard and the hours long. Not long after leaving the farm in which the family had been tenants for generations, her mother-in-law had died leaving Ruth barely able to pay the rent on a tiny terraced property in Silk Mill Yard. It was then as if God had been looking after her, for out of the blue the Parish Clerk had recommended her to the occupant of Rose Hill, a wealthy parishioner who was suddenly in need of a housekeeper.

Christmas day at Rose Hill was usually a quiet time, there being no young children to scamper round the many rooms or demand attention. It was a large commodious house, too large for the small number of people who lived there, but it was work for Ruth and she had a small attic bedroom to herself. She also had an adjacent sitting room overlooking the valley and the tree-covered hills beyond the river. This compensated to some degree for having to leave the farm, and was certainly an improvement on the small terraced property that had no views to back or front and opened directly onto the narrow street, with a shared yard and midden to the rear.

Apart from the hipped roof and its distinctive balustrades beneath the five second-storey windows, Rose Hill was of plain design and yet was one of the two more elegant properties in the town.

A church-going man himself, Milnes Lowndes gave his staff the opportunity to attend morning service if they wanted, providing their duties were performed and completed when requested. However, Christmas Day was considered more a day of rest than a feast day.

Little did Henri know that whenever he left the south-western exit of Swine Square, which was separated from the Market Place by a cluster of old buildings, that he could have been seen from the house further up the hill to his right. Nor would he have been aware of the lonely figure in the attic room looking down on West Bars and the road leading to Brampton Moor. The distance separating the pair was sufficient to conceal their identities one from another, consequently it was some time before Henri and Ruth met again.

Chapter 8   1807
Great Changes

*O*nce again, the damp cold weather of winter depressed all and sundry, and Henri's cough returned as usual, so, when not needed at the school, he joined the other officers at the *Angel* or *Falcon* for the warmth and company therein. He avoided attending the church during the really bad weather in case his affliction irritated others in the congregation—the chilly air in there only made matters worse. He did often wonder if the young woman from the farm would be there and for that reason he was disappointed at staying away.

When Easter drew near and signs of Spring returned, he took his chance one morning to attend, if only to hear the music of the powerful organ again. On entering the church he found himself looking around with the thought that he might catch a glimpse of her. It struck him then that he had no idea what her name was, she was simply the young woman from the farm. He later realised that he'd continued searching to such an extent that he had totally lost interest in the service. It was only the deep reverberating opening music of an anthem from the organ which stirred him, surging through his mind. It began to re-awaken his otherwise long-controlled and abandoned desires to live a normal life. There were prisoners, he acknowledged, who quietly found outlets for their needs amongst the lower orders of the town but Henri had no desire to go down that particular route.

The glorious music made him both sad and excited at the same time, filling his mind with ideas. Should he break parole and make a run for it? His English was now good enough for him to pass as someone other than a Frenchman, yet where would he go and how could he reach France?

His eyes scanned the balcony opposite once more, but to no avail, nor could he see the lady in any of the box-pews below, so when the organ finally ceased playing, Henri felt quite drained of emotion. He would have remained in his seat simply contemplating his lot if a sudden urge hadn't persuaded him to go downstairs to the church entrance before everyone left, in case she had escaped his notice.

He stood in the porch waiting and apparently absorbed by the inscriptions on the memorial plaques on its walls, but frequently glancing at the congregation streaming out from the body of the church. He was surprised by the strength of his resolve to find her, so much so that he'd no idea how he would approach her if she appeared.

Ruth, however, had seen Henri from her position on the back row of the gallery, and had watched him fidgeting restlessly, realising he had been scanning the congregation but not the reason why. She'd had every intention of passing the time of day with him, given the chance, but as he'd dashed away immediately the service finished she had abandoned her plan, and took her time in descending the wooden stairs to the floor below. She too had paid far less attention than normal to the lengthy sermon preached by the Reverend Bossley; her mind had been elsewhere, thus it had been easy to study Henri without drawing attention to herself. Nobody would have guessed that he was a prisoner, he dressed in the English style, and she was pleased that he had neither moustache nor hooped earrings like many of his countrymen.

When Ruth eventually reached the porch, Henri quickly approached her. 'Good Day, Madame,' he said, bowing slightly. 'May I ask if you are well?'

Ruth smiled at him, she was pleased to find him still at the church. 'I am well enough, thank you,' she replied, lowering her eyes from his intense gaze. 'I thought perhaps that you had already left!'

'You saw me?' Henri was puzzled as to where she'd been sitting and hoped she had been unaware of his inattention to the service.

'You were almost in front of me in the Gallery—I could not miss seeing you!' she chided gently. 'But you seemed distracted, then hurried away before I had chance to speak.'

'It was the music that disturbed me. The singing also reminded me of my childhood in church before the revolution. The hymns I miss, but I am not now very interested in religion as such.'

Ruth shook her head. 'That is a pity—it gives me great comfort to come here every week.'

This informative remark did not go unnoticed by Henri, who thought that he might now find himself making his way to the church on a Sunday more often. 'May I escort you?' he offered, realising that she was unaccompanied. 'I have time to spare, I was thinking of taking a walk to enjoy the sunlight.' He was hoping his suggestion wouldn't alarm her and was pleased when she was agreeable.

'I haven't far to go but I would like that very much.'

They left the porch and took the path through the graveyard, saying very little to each other. Once away from the bustle of the departing congregation they slowed down. 'Where do you live?' Ruth asked.

'Glumangate, with Madame Parsons. Do you know it?'

'Why yes, we have to pass across the top of Glumangate to get to where I live, it is on the way.'

'Please excuse me,' Henri turned hesitatingly, 'I am afraid I know not your name?'

'Ruth!' she responded quietly. 'Ruth Silcock.'

'I am Henri Pichon, a French prisoner in your town,' he said with respect and courtesy, as if introducing himself for the first time. 'I am pleased to speak with you. I have wondered many times how you managed the farm alone.'

'We couldn't.' Ruth was quite aware that he was going to a lot of trouble trying to be friendly and her mother-in-law had been right, none of it was his fault. 'There had been too much neglect for us to deal with, it was inevitable that we should have to leave. Even with your help I think it would have been too late.'

'Such a pity, but now you live here, in the town? Does this make you happy?'

A wry smile crossed Ruth's face. 'I am comfortable enough and fortunate to have work and a place to live. Very fortunate.' Ruth then fell silent, wondering what to say next.

Leaving Holywell Street the pair strolled along Saltergate towards Glumangate at a leisurely pace. This semblance of normality pleased Henri and he was reluctant to reach their destination.

'Madame,' he asked by way of making conversation, 'Do you go alone to the church each week?'

'Well, yes,' she replied, 'you see I have no one now. I wasn't born in the town, so I have no family here. Like you I am a stranger,' she paused, 'why do you ask?'

'I do not intend any harm,' he assured her, 'I think, maybe, we can sit together another time? Churches are cold places for one alone.' As she didn't answer immediately, Henri wondered if he had expressed his thoughts badly or whether she might think him too forward. He waited patiently as they walked on.

'Do you have any children?' Ruth asked a little shyly, changing the subject. 'It must be hard to be away from them for so long!'

Henri laughed. 'Unfortunately, Madame, I have no children. I have not a wife either!'

As if satisfied by his answer Ruth replied, 'If you think it would be appropriate, then I would be happy to sit with you some Sundays!' She had lowered her voice, nervously surprised by her forthrightness.

Looking now towards her he spoke quietly, 'I thank you—it would please me to sit with a friend.' Putting two and two together he realised that if he had been a man with a wife and children then she would have declined the invitation. 'I would not like to make you uncomfortable in front of people,' he added respectfully, 'I would understand if you have fear, but you would honour me to sit together in the church.'

They had almost reached Glumangate and Ruth wondered if he would bid her farewell at this point or ask to walk a little further with her, and was gratified when he did so.

'Do you mind if we walk more in the fresh air?' he asked. 'I do not wish to go to my house yet, the days are too long on my own.' He turned again to look directly at Ruth, noticing that they were almost the same height and also for the first time, how pleasant she looked with the sun shining on her face.

'I haven't far to go myself, but yes, a little walk would be pleasant,' she agreed. Although the air was quite fresh, the sun's rays brightened the morning and it was indeed too fine a day to retreat indoors. Within a short distance the elegant mansion of Rose Hill came into view on their left and Ruth halted before a gate in its garden wall. 'This is where I live.' She saw Henri's eyes widen with surprise and laughed, 'I work here, but I have only two rooms—up there,' she pointed to the attic level. 'My rooms are on the other side, looking out across to the hills.'

'So near to Glumangate! It is a beautiful house and away from the old buildings.'

'How do you pass the time?' Ruth asked. 'So many of your countrymen wander around the streets aimlessly.'

'Having too much time to do nothing is frustrating. It makes the mind slow and sick. We try to help each other. I am lucky I teach my language at Mademoiselle Bradley's school, and when I can I teach private people!'

Although Henri's spoken English was good, just occasionally he mixed words around so that together with his natural accent Ruth found him intriguing to listen to. There were times when she felt tempted to correct him or finish a sentence off, but knew this would not do, as it could easily seem to be a criticism. She admired the fact that he'd taken the time and trouble to learn English, when so many other prisoners seemed not to think it worthwhile to do so.

They were now well beyond Rose Hill and stopped on the brow of the hill to look down on the wide expanse of fields stretching out to form a basin to the west of the parish. Here and there, scattered farm buildings could be seen and also signs of quarries and factory chimneys along the lanes and roads that crossed through Brampton Moor.

Ruth had fallen silent as if distracted and Henri wondered if there was anything amiss. She seemed almost to have forgotten that he was there, then, following her gaze he saw a smoking chimney on what he realised was the very farm she'd been forced to leave. From this distance no sign of neglect or abandonment could be seen, but the smoke would remind Ruth that someone else now lived where she had once been so happy.

Without speaking, Henri stood patiently by her side leaving her to her thoughts and memories for a few minutes. Instead, he examined the same view with interest. He almost envied her having these deep emotional memories, sad though they were, because such feelings had so far been denied him. How long would it be before he could even hope to start building a future of such importance?

When finally she stirred, Henri asked gently, 'Why do you not return to where you came from? Would it not be better there?'

Realising that he'd been watching her, and was obviously concerned, Ruth replied, all the while pensively looking towards her old home. 'Too many years have passed, I'm not a young girl anymore and I have work and lodgings here. If I returned to Belper I should be forced to work in a mill or live with relatives who would hardly know me now.' She plucked a bud from a bush nearby and rolled it slowly round in her fingers, lost for a moment in her past life.

The trees were still bare but showing tightly closed buds awaiting the warmth of Spring to make them open into life. Henri felt that Ruth too needed the warmth of something to lift her spirits. He did not feel excluded by her distraction, but was pleased when finally the mood left her and she asked, 'Do you miss France? Is it like this where you lived?'

He was relieved that their conversation had resumed although he'd been quite content to just savour the close companionship of being with a woman of such an undemanding nature. Of course he longed to see the familiar sights of his home, of the broad, lively, unpredictable River Loire, spanned by the old stone bridge; and of the troglodyte cave dwellings cut into the cliffs. Yet he knew contentment at this moment such as he'd not felt since leaving France.

'Yes,' he sighed, 'I miss my home but for so many years I have been away. I was first in Egypt, then San Domingo, always with the Army. In France I was born in a town where there is little smoke and the river is very wide.'

'What will you do when the war is over?' Ruth asked, hearing the longing in his voice.

Henri shrugged his shoulders. 'I am a soldier but I begin to dislike to fight. I like this teaching. Perhaps I will do this, who knows?'

'Do you think the war will be over soon?'

'All over Europe people fight, changing sides, and many lives destroyed. I do not know but I think not soon!' He turned away and coughed as the breeze blowing across the valley met them and, despite the sun, he knew they had stood too long in their exposed position. 'Do you wish to walk or return home?' he asked, coughing again.

The chill in the air belied the beauty of the sunshine, causing Henri to cough repeatedly. 'Forgive me, it is from the cold air. Perhaps I had better go inside.' This was not what he wished to do but he realised that to stay outdoors would be foolish. 'Next Sunday I will go to the church. I would be happy to sit with you please?' He coughed again as they began to re-trace their steps.

Seeing him in distress, Ruth slowed her pace. 'You should not be out here,' she advised and waited until his cough abated. 'I have enjoyed talking to you, and yes, I will sit with you in church next week!' Further conversation only seemed to aggravate Henri's condition so they walked back towards Rose Hill in silence. 'Goodbye,' she said, holding out her hand and smiling warmly at him, 'until next Sunday!'

Releasing her hand, Henri watched as she closed the gate behind her, then hurried home just as another bout of coughing shook him. 'Dear God,' he cried out loud, 'am I to die here, so far away from France?' He was close to tears with frustration.

For some reason unknown to Henri, Ruth did not appear at church the following Sunday and he sat alone on the hard wooden pew wondering if she was sick or had decided to avoid him. Without her company he began to doubt his own motives for attending the church at all. He had spent the week awaiting their meeting with pleasant anticipation, and now he was deeply disappointed. There was nothing to be done except return the following week in the hope that Ruth would keep her promise to come, if not he would be left once more without optimism.

Henri's coughing had gradually abated as the weather improved, leaving him quite tired but he decided to walk past Rose Hill on the off-chance that it might reveal some clue to Ruth's non-appearance. There was of course nothing there that he could see to indicate the reason, so he walked on. He went further than planned until finally he found himself quite near the old farm where there was now evidence of good husbandry. A few cows grazed contentedly near the house, and he could clearly see a child beyond the hedgerow, playing by the door.

Had Ruth seen these changes, he wondered, or had she been unable to approach the farm to confront what she might find there? He too had been forced to face up to his own problems when associating with Boyer during the General's brief sojourns in Chesterfield, and so had eventually been able to come to terms with the disturbing experiences he'd faced in San Domingo. He hoped she might also find real peace of mind one day.

In the mangle and drying room at Rose Hill, Ruth folded the laundered linen sheets and fed them through the machine. She felt guilty, and didn't know quite why she'd made trivial excuses to herself for not attending church that day. She'd seen the difficulty Henri was having with his chest when they were together the previous Sunday and this had perturbed her. He was a sick man. He was also French and a prisoner at that. What would people think if she took to walking with him, no matter how innocent their friendship might be? Would her employer, Milnes Lowndes, dismiss her? Ruth found it hard to even consider the other possibility; that she was beginning to welcome and enjoy the company of another man. This, she felt would be betraying William, yet, had he too been in a strange place without comfort or care to ease his passing?

By the time Ruth had finished the washing she was annoyed and ashamed of herself and bitterly regretted letting Henri down, but it was too late to do anything about it.

For differing reasons the following week seemed a very long one for both Henri and Ruth. Henri had lost heart, and hope. Ruth simply lived with a guilty conscience.

So, with little anticipation, Henri entered the church early the following Sunday and made his way upstairs to the gallery, seating himself where he'd previously been so that Ruth, if she came, could either join him or sit discretely somewhere else. The church slowly began to fill up and he knew that it wouldn't be long before others crowded in alongside him—and he could hardly object to them doing so.

Then, to his undisguised delight, Ruth slipped quietly in beside him. She would have had to be blind not to see how pleased he was at her arrival, and she responded with a shy smile. Due to the number of people close by it was impossible to explain her absence of the week before, as had they been overheard tongues would soon have wagged. So, to make amends she gently touched his arm and whispered, 'I'm sorry I didn't come last week!' Perhaps the gesture had been a mistake for he appeared to stiffen at her touch and she quickly withdrew the hand. What must he be thinking? She flushed and busied herself arranging her skirt neatly.

It had been purely an act of sincere contrition on Ruth's part, to touch him. Henri knew that but the warmth he felt in response almost choked him and he fought to check his emotions. At that moment the desire to hold her hand, to touch her in response was so strong he could hardly contain himself, such was his need for close human contact. His intentions had originally been just to assist her, and help her to overcome the pain of loss caused by his country. Of course he wanted her in his arms as a man wants a woman, otherwise why had he spent the whole of the previous week in a state of misery? But it had to be more than simply that, and she had been hurt far too much for him to be careless at this moment.

He bent his head and whispered back. 'I missed you!' The soft tone of his voice did not, however, fully disguise the emotion he felt and Ruth realised just how sensitive and vulnerable he was.

She touched his arm again. 'Hush,' she said softly, 'the service is about to begin.' This time however she did not remove her hand.

Suddenly, the church no longer felt cold, the old yellow stone walls seemed brighter than before and the organ music sounded somehow more mellow. Henri swallowed hard and breathed deeply, a sensation of peace swept over him and he risked turning to look directly at Ruth. She appeared prettier somehow, not beautiful but serene, and the pallor of anguish was no longer there.

During the months that followed, Ruth and Henri met frequently in the church on Sundays before proceeding to walk together about the surrounding areas which lay within his parole restrictions. Although Henri had taken many of these walks before, they now took on a new meaning for, where she could, Ruth was able to explain much of the town's history, or to later find answers to his questions. He was delighted to discover that Ruth was able to both read and write and he began to teach her a little of his own language. Whatever her feelings for him were, she kept these locked within and he in turn felt he could not pry, being content instead to enjoy the companionship and happiness they shared. Those few hours each week helped to restore and sustain them both.

Quite soon, when the weather was still cool, Henri gave Ruth the gloves which he'd originally intended she should have, and explained what had happened when he'd called at the farm to hand them over, only to discover the place deserted.

The shadows that had darkened Ruth's mind slowly disappeared as Henri contrived ways of talking about the past to help ease her memories and lessen the pain. He wanted her to confront her problems as he had done his, thereby gaining happiness once more. There was of course always the danger that in doing so she would grow in confidence and no longer need him. That was a risk he was prepared to take, the only true gift he was able to give.

With the sun on their faces and the song of the birds around them, their walks became an essential part of Henri's life, his one real pleasure. On one such hot, halcyon day, when not a breeze disturbed the leaves on the trees, Henri asked Ruth if she would mind pausing at the top of Glumangate while he went home to fetch something.

Waiting patiently, she was intrigued as to what he had in mind, for there had been an air of mystery in his voice and manner before he left her. So far neither had been to the other's dwelling place and Ruth wondered what they would do when the summer ended and the biting cold of winter arrived. Pushing these worrying thoughts from her mind she continued to wait, but not for long as Henri soon returned carrying a strangely shaped parcel. The people of Chesterfield had long since become accustomed to the Frenchmen and their odd ways; parading the streets with their trained poodles, and the monkey on a lead brought all the way from San Domingo. Today, Henri was carrying a large object in a cloth bag drawn together at the top with a ribbon, making it quite impossible to discern the contents from the outside.

'Come,' he smiled at her, 'all will be seen later!' This, of course, only fascinated Ruth the more.

They continued walking and nothing was explained, nor were questions asked, over his strange behaviour, although it was obvious the contents of his bag seemed to be both light and, perhaps, delicate. Ruth's curiosity almost got the better of her but this wasn't to be satisfied until they were beyond the houses where, on a Sunday, few passers-by would observe them.

He stopped. 'I have this made for you,' he said shyly and then opening the bag withdrew a beautiful straw bonnet decorated with pale blue ribbons. Ruth gasped with amazement. 'To protect those beautiful eyes from the sun!' Saying this, he gently removed the rather sombre hat Ruth always wore when attending church and placed the bonnet on her head with a sigh of satisfaction. 'On a hot day it is perfect.'

'Please,' she laughingly begged, 'let me look at it, I can hardly admire it when I can't see it.' Henri released the ribbons and removed the bonnet for her.

'Such extravagance,' Ruth remonstrated, 'and so wonderful. Is it for me to keep?' Her eyes danced wildly with an excitement and joy that Henri had never seen in her before.

He laughed. 'Well it is too small for me! Besides, who else would I buy a bonnet for?'

As she examined the gift she was aware that he was studying her carefully. He was gratified by the pleasure it had given her, for it was as much a token of gratitude for the companionship they shared as for a recognition that the hat she habitually wore had seen better days. Besides, it was now too hot to wear such a warm item and it did little justice to the Ruth he was getting to know. She let him place the straw bonnet back on her head and as he tied the ribbons beneath her chin he tenderly touched her cheek with his fingers.

'What do I do with this?' Ruth asked shaking her old hat, although still very conscious of the feel of his soft touch on her face.

'Here,' he said, 'put it in here.' He opened the bag for her, his pulse racing from the feel of her skin. He was tormented by the fact that she was so near and yet seemingly unobtainable.

'Frenchmen seem to make such pretty things,' she remarked, appreciating the craftsmanship she'd seen in the bonnet's construction. 'Who made the bag?'

'I did!' he confessed, almost with pride.

The stitching was as neat as any woman's handiwork and Ruth knew the care he would have taken in making it. 'Thank you,' she whispered, 'it must have taken you a long time. You are too kind.'

'Too kind?' He was puzzled by this. 'Why too kind?'

Ruth smiled at him almost as if he were a child. 'It's just another way of saying that you are very, very kind!'

Having now understood, he sought to answer her. 'A soldier has to repair his uniform, and when there is nothing to do a man must keep busy, just as sailors do.' He could see by the way she moved her head that the gift pleased her, and from the delighted smile on her lips that he had reached the heart of the girl that still lived within her. He was more than satisfied by what he had done, especially as it had given him the chance to see a deeper aspect of Ruth's feelings. They strolled on but it was becoming harder with each meeting for Henri to say 'Au revoir'.

Several Sundays later the day dawned wet and miserable, Henri was disappointed as he would have no alternative but to take Ruth straight home after church. He thought hard over this until finally, taking courage, he addressed Mrs Parsons over breakfast with a nervousness which puzzled her for a moment.

Then Mrs Parsons realised by his manner that he was about to ask a favour of her. In the four years he'd lived in her house she had grown to understand Henri's ways, so she said nothing but waited, wondering how long it would be before he broached the problem besetting him. Nor was she entirely surprised by what he asked.

'Madame,' he still called her that, 'it is very wet today!' Then he paused.

'It is indeed,' she replied in her usual manner when expecting a request.

'Too wet to walk,' he paused again.

'It is?'

'I have a friend with who I walk!' Mrs Parsons of course knew of this, firstly from his behaviour after meeting Ruth, and more accurately from the gossips who took delight in informing her of almost everything he did.

She nodded. 'Yes, you're right it is too wet to walk today,' she remarked non-committally, giving him no encouragement at all. She was enjoying the game they were playing.

'I do wonder if I might bring my friend to eat? I will give the money for meat and cakes!'

She appeared to consider his request before replying. 'Well now, this Frenchman, does he eat snails?' she finally asked with raised eyebrows and a wry smile.

Something about the question told Henri that he was now the butt of one of Madame's little charades, and he suspected that she must already know about Ruth. 'I have a very good lady who goes walks with me, that is all, but it is wet today.'

Seeing the earnest pleading in his eyes, his landlady softened, as she usually did. She simply liked him to remember who was in charge.

'Yes, I suppose so,' she agreed. For weeks now she had been speculating over the accounts given by gossips of their meetings, both in church and out. She was just a little concerned that if he took up with a woman he might leave and she would be alone again, but of course there was always the possibility that he could be returned to France anyway, with little notice being given beforehand by the authorities. 'But no jiggery-pokery, mind!' She chuckled to herself at the complete bewilderment on his face at this last comment.

That particular Sunday Service, which Henri barely heard, took longer than usual. It wasn't pleasant sitting in damp clothes and he was more conscious than ever of his situation. He glanced sideways at Ruth, who he noted wore the old hat again to fend off the rain. She appeared oblivious to the occasional glances which came their way and he feared that their friendship might be compromising her reputation in the town. Afterwards they ran through the heavy rain from the church porch to a nearby archway where they paused to catch their breath. Up to this point Henri hadn't mentioned the invitation to Ruth in case someone overheard, causing further speculation.

Henri chose this moment to make his offer. 'Madame Parsons asks if you would like to come back for something to eat, because the weather is so wet?' He was quite unsure how Ruth would react to the suggestion.

She was, of course more than pleased to accept as she'd had visions of spending a lonely afternoon just staring though her window at the appalling weather. 'How kind of her. Yes, I would like to come.'

Before they continued, Henri hesitated and asked, 'Tell me, what is jigerypoki?' Ruth giggled. 'Only Madame said we could have dinner, but no snails, no frogs and no jigerypoki. Is this an English animal?'

Trying hard to suppress her amusement, Ruth found it hard to reply. 'I think what she meant is that we must behave and be very circumspect.' Seeing that he still looked puzzled, she said 'I would not use the word, if I was you!'

When they arrived at the small terraced property, Henri tapped on the door and after opening it called out, 'Madame, please I have a friend to meet you?'

More than eager to meet the woman who had made such a difference to her lodger's life, Mrs Parsons hurried into the small sitting room cum front entrance. 'Come in, my dear,' she said, eyeing Ruth inquisitively. 'Give me your wet things.'

'This is Madame Parsons—Madame, this is Madame Silcock, Ruth.' Henri introduced the two women in a polite, almost old fashioned manner. There were times such as these when Ruth could see a different side to him and the formality of the Army Officer, which immediately reminded her of his true situation. She could even more understand and appreciate the frustrations which must result from his position, and of course the danger of her becoming too fond of him. 'May I fetch the linnet?' he asked. 'Then I have all my friends together.'

'No mess mind!' Mrs Parsons called automatically, as was her way.

Ruth smiled to herself, she could almost hear the woman saying, 'No snails, no frogs, no jiggery-pokery and no mess!' It was all she could do to stifle her amusement.

The twinkle in her eyes did not pass without notice, but Mrs Parsons simply assumed that Ruth was a woman of a happy disposition. 'Sit down my dear, won't you?' she offered. 'Aren't you Elizabeth Silcock's daughter-in-law?'

Ruth was startled. 'Why, yes, did Henri tell you?'

'No, but I saw you with Elizabeth sometimes, before she died. That was a sad business, a sad business all round,' she saw a shadow cross Ruth's face. 'Now you take care not to hurt that good man upstairs,' she hastened to add before Henri returned.

'I won't,' Ruth found herself replying without thinking. The elderly woman's words had been as unexpected as they were pointed. 'He is a very good friend!' And would be more if you weren't so blind Mrs Parsons thought.

Henri reappeared with the cage in which a bell hung from its apex inside. The little occupant chirped and fluttered, anticipating that the door to the cage was going to be opened. 'When I let him out he goes in again at the sound of the bell,' Henri explained.

'Yes, the Frenchman's bell at eight o'clock,' Mrs Parsons reminded him sternly.

'Madame, he is fortunate and could fly away when I take him outside if he wanted! I cannot!' There was no resentment in Henri's voice but she knew from living with him, that given a chance he too might probably fly away—back to France. Just as long as Ruth Silcock understood what she was about, befriending her Frenchman, or hearts would be broken without a doubt. She watched the pair with experienced eyes, surmising it was probably already too late to prevent heartache.

Henri knew it too, having seen it happen before, time after time amongst his friends. The Army had the power to make a man or break him, and rarely kept him long in one place. He had never liked seeing the results of officers' and men's wives following their men like some kind of baggage, camp followers, in situations which showed some men for what they were, often brutish, never really wanting the entrapment and responsibility of a camp wife. Where danger was about a soldier had to be free to act as a soldier should and not have to think of protecting his wife from attack or crudity.

'Don't let that bird out in here,' Mrs Parsons protested as Ruth put a finger to the wooden bars of the cage. 'We don't want feathers all over!'

In spite of Mrs Parsons' brusque ways, Ruth had been told by Henri that the lady had a warm, kind heart if one took the trouble to nurture it.

'Put the cage on the table over there if you're not taking it back upstairs!' Mrs Parsons didn't care if it was male or female, they all looked alike to her. 'Why don't you show Ruth the boat you won?'

Henri hesitated, feeling a reluctance to introduce a warlike topic into this special occasion, but then realised that to reject Mrs Parsons' suggestion would be embarrassing, so went to his room to collect the other of his two treasured possessions.

After he'd gone, Mrs Parsons noticed that Ruth's face had lost some of its colour and that she now had a perturbed look. 'What is it dear, did I say something I shouldn't?' she asked.

Ruth tried to smile but found it difficult to explain her alarm. 'You have done nothing,' she said trying to reassure her host, 'it's just that my husband, William, died from wounds whilst on board a ship.'

'Oh, dear, I didn't know how it had happened,' Mrs Parsons said, keeping her voice down so that Henri wouldn't hear. 'I'm sorry, I wish now I hadn't asked him to bring the boat down. Does he know much about your husband, how he died?'

Ruth's voice was husky, 'No, we haven't talked about it. I think he feels guilty because he is French. Please, don't tell him, I don't want to spoil today for him. I know it wasn't his fault, although at first I did blame him.'

'Oh, how unthinking of me! But you know your husband may have killed a Frenchman or two, that's war!' She heard Henri's footsteps on the stairs. 'Perhaps you really ought to tell him more about William?'

Returning, Henri placed the model carefully on the table. It was a sixty-four-gun French Man o' war, the top deck gun ports were open and the cannon positioned as if ready to fire. Henri looked guardedly at Ruth, having noted her pallor as he entered the room.

'It's very skilfully made,' Mrs Parsons remarked, admiring the model and trying to divert Ruth's mind away from her morbid thoughts.

However, like so many people who had never been near the sea, Ruth had not seen anything larger than a canal barge, except in a painting in the drawing room at Rose Hill. Nor had she any idea of the difference between an English vessel and a French one.

'It would have sixty-four guns, on different decks,' he explained 'we can only see some of them.' Ruth's colour had returned and she seemed enthralled as he pulled one of the two toggles attached to thin cords at the stern. When he did this all the cannon disappeared through the gun ports. 'Now pull the other toggle,' he suggested, and the guns, which had been retracted into the gun flats, reappeared, making Ruth gasp in amazement. 'The man makes a mould out of straw in which to form the body of the ship,' he added, not knowing if he was boring her.

'Have you sailed on one of these?' she asked, her eyes filled with wonder.

'Something like it, but fortunately not with the guns firing.'

This appeared to please Ruth who, having seen cannon barrels being moved from the factory at Brampton in the past, knew just how big and heavy they were; sixty-four of them on one ship seemed almost unbelievable. 'It's hard to understand why a ship with so many cannons doesn't sink,' she remarked as she examined the fine ropes and rigging made from human hair, and wondered at the delicate tracery and fittings cut from bone. She had nothing but admiration for men who could fashion such works of art, even prisoners here in Chesterfield. 'How can a man remember all these details?'

'In Toulon and other ports where a sailor learns, can be seen larger models than this and if he looks closely at all the parts he can learn how his ship works before going to sea.' Henri tried to explain in the hope that the two women could understand him.

'Well,' Mrs Parsons said finally, slightly bemused by his attempt to explain, 'dinner is almost ready.'

'Let me help,' Ruth offered, following her hostess into the kitchen.

Henri reminisced as he gazed on his beautiful replica of a ship of the line, remembering the warm spray of the Caribbean Sea, and compared that time with the cold, lashing waves of the Atlantic, all of which seemed so long ago.

The first visit to Glumangate passed off well; it was a relief to know that in the winter he and Ruth would have a refuge, as Mrs Parsons made it clear they could meet and be welcome there. A more serious consequence of the visit was that Henri acknowledged to himself the depths of his true feelings for Ruth. Had these been feelings only of desire and passion he would have risked everything; instead his growing respect for her and his need of her friendship was more important than simple gratification.

He had watched the affection grow between General D'Henin and Eleanor Dickson which eventually resulted in the birth of their beautiful daughter, and he was often tempted to throw caution to the wind in order to obtain such happiness for himself. The General's rank and circumstances were, however, entirely different to his own humble status in life and because of this, he deliberately avoided any real physical contact with Ruth, except for the most simple, in case he ruined everything. This reserve on his part was understood and appreciated by Ruth who was not unaware of his torment but obviously did not want to be drawn into a probably futile love affair, nor did she want to lose the most important person in her life. She loved him the more for not taking advantage of her vulnerability and asking for what she could not agree to.

The following Sunday was as perfect as any August day could be, enabling Henri and Ruth to walk together once more. This time though, Ruth soon became aware of a restlessness in Henri that hadn't been there previously. Had the visit to Glumangate stretched their friendship too far? When suddenly he stopped walking his nervous frustration was obvious.

'What is it, Henri?' she asked, concerned that he was unusually quiet. 'Today you are preoccupied, are you not well, is something the matter?'

'I am not ill, nor is it anything you have done!' His voice was strained. 'I walk and walk and walk,' he complained, 'the same roads, the same distance, for four years now! There is a world beyond these hills that I am not allowed to see, sometimes I ask, who am I, what is to become of me?' His clenched hands were almost white, his face a picture of hopelessness, his eyes deeply troubled. He was tired of walking, trying simply to keep fit, trying to fight off his depression.

Not knowing what answer or comfort she could give, Ruth could only try to placate him and offer words of encouragement. 'You are a very patient man, Henri, and I can understand how terrible it must be for you to be trapped in this small backwater. But you're not in a dark prison somewhere, and at least you are alive!'

There was a gentle reprimand in her voice and he knew that she was chiding him. He knew also that he deserved it. After all, he had an income, he was safe, but was this all that his life was about? 'You are true,' he lamented, 'and I am sorry that I do not fight off these bad feelings of uncontent which come over me. I try hard. If only I could get back to France!'

Ruth wondered if he was actually thinking of escape. 'You probably wouldn't get very far,' she cried in panic, 'then you would be shut up somewhere and things would be worse for you than they are now!' He was silent and she knew by his lack of response that these same thoughts weren't far from his mind. 'Please,' she urged, 'think carefully about what might happen.'

'I have, Ruth, over and over again. Do I break my word and try to escape, or...,' he watched her, testing for her reaction, 'or am I a coward for not trying?' He was plainly agitated. 'When each winter comes I think I am going to die anyway.'

At this, Ruth spoke more firmly to him. 'You are not a coward for keeping your word!' Suddenly she too was tired of walking. They walked so much from fear of what people would think if they stopped, unless there were sufficient people around for it not to matter. 'Please, do you think we could find somewhere to rest, the heat is tiring me and I am fed up of caring what people think? I want simply to sit beside you and talk. Last Sunday I enjoyed the peace and lack of complications, but with Mrs Parsons being present I couldn't talk openly.'

'Was it a mistake, to take you there?' he asked, alarmed by her words.

'No, not at all, but it made me see things differently. I wanted to tell you about my husband, William, and about my life.' Until she explained her feelings there would remain a gap in her relationship with Henri. William was someone they had skirted around and she wanted to talk about him, not to do so would be as if she was ashamed of him and had wiped the memory of him from her mind.

Henri took note of where they were. Today they had taken a different route, this time crossing the River Rother by Spital Bridge and then continuing towards Upper Hady. It had been when passing the lane leading to Spital Lodge where General D'Henin lived that Henri's spirits had sunk to their lowest. He had nothing but respect for the General. He was well liked and had settled as a happy family man in the Lodge, though Henri sometimes wondered if he wasn't simply pleased to be out of the war; he was also mystified as to why the General had not been exchanged back to France by this time.

'Can you manage to get to the top of the hill?' Henri asked. 'There we could rest and look towards another horizon.' Ruth agreed and was content to walk quietly up the hill, pondering how best to tell him about William. When he saw a likely spot, Henri paused. 'Is this not a good place to sit?' he ventured, seeing that she was hot and perhaps weary.

'You are used to marching,' she complained, 'I'm afraid the hot weather doesn't suit me.' She settled herself on the grass just as a horse and cart trundled past a few yards away.

'Tell me about yourself,' he urged as he sat down beside her. 'What do you see yourself doing for the rest of your life? We have walked every path imaginable round here, going round in circles. The winter will come soon and I shall be parading in my small room from the hour of five every night. If I thought the war to go on much longer I really would like to run.'

Where should she start? What could she say that would be of any help to him. She had existed for so long with her own private misery occasioned by William's death. 'You have been very kind to me,' she whispered, 'but I am unable to help you very much in return. Without you I would still be locked in a world of my own, with no means to break free. You have had the patience to open my eyes to all about me, and have given me hope for a better future, yet I cannot do the same for you. If you feel that you must go, all I ask is that you do not tell me. I would give nothing away but I wouldn't want to

146

betray my country, or William!' There! She'd said his name at last without even thinking. Whatever Henri did she would wish him luck but she could not be party to his defection. If, however, he chose to run she would be bereft of a dear, dear friend.

Henri was instantly contrite. 'I am sorry. I have no right to talk to you about running away. If France wanted me enough they would have tried to exchange me. I am not important enough to be asked for, nor am I fit enough to fight again. I must push these thoughts out.' He turned his face away. 'I apologise, I see I have distressed you, this has not been my intention.'

From where they sat the outskirts and buildings of the town below seemed smaller than they actually were, and the hill they'd climbed led on to yet another blocking out the horizon Henri had envisaged in his thoughts. Had they been able to walk another mile to the east the view would indeed have been vast.

Watching him as he studied the town below, Ruth had no idea of his thoughts yet she could sense his ambition was to venture further afield. 'You have travelled to so many places, it must make you want to move on. I have never been further than Derby,' she said wistfully.

'Perhaps one day...' His voice trailed off. He had nearly added, I could take you, but quickly realised the futility of it all.

'I wanted to ask you about Egypt. You said that you had been there. What was it like?' Ruth had little concept of lands beyond the shores of England.

'Hot, very hot and sandy.' The memory of yet another of France's atrocities returned to him. 'We took the ancient city of Alexandria.' He refrained from admitting that the French could have simply occupied the city without then sacking it but he was too ashamed to admit it.

'I ask because my husband William was wounded in Egypt.' She hesitated, 'But he died on a ship coming back to England and was buried at sea. Maybe his wound became infected.'

'For this I am sorry.' Henri fought off the desire to take her hand to comfort her, as he feared his action might be misunderstood. 'It must have been terrible for you to lose someone when you were so young. How long had he been your husband?'

Henri had lost his despondency and had become the under-standing friend he had always been, and Ruth saw that by helping her he was in fact forgetting his own problems. 'We were together three years, the last two of which he was away fighting.' Surprisingly she was no longer afraid to speak of her husband, the pain had turned to a fond remembrance. She would never forget him but the festering wound had healed at last, leaving only fond memories as a reminder. 'He was a good man and a good husband. I would not like to think of him suffering alone and without comfort.'

'A man gets used to pain,' Henri lied. He'd seen suffering beyond her imagination but he couldn't tell her of it. 'If he was a farmer why did he join the Army? Was he forced to do so?'

'Only by circumstance. When lands were being enclosed and fenced in by Law they took away the grazing land from the poorer people, and the smaller farms became merely homesteads. They weren't big enough to sustain a family and William knew of no other occupation. He joined the Army in order to give money to his parents.' Seeing Henri's interest gave Ruth the encouragement to continue. 'There wasn't enough land to feed a family, and we couldn't graze the animals for free anymore.'

'Was the farm so small? Could it not have been extended?'

'William's family didn't own the farm, they only paid rent and the landowner wouldn't let us have more land at a reasonable price.'

'If you came from some other town, how did you meet William?' Henri asked, eager to learn more about Ruth herself, and this, in turn, helped her to continue.

'I was born in Belper, a small town where they spin cotton. It's not far from a much larger town called Derby. One day I went with a girlfriend to a Feast Day there and met up with my friend's brother who lived in the town. He had joined the Army recently and so had William. He introduced us and the four of us had a wonderful day at the feast. William came to see me several times before we got married, then when we did I moved to Chesterfield to live with his parents, and to help them while William was in the Army.

'You were very loyal to them, William would have been pleased about that,' Henri assured her. He was calm now and more like his usual self, asking, 'Where did you learn to read?'

'The local mill-owner Jedediah Strutt was very keen that the children in Belper learned the basics of reading, and at Chapel we studied the Bible. I found it easy and enjoyed reading. I had no other schooling except what I learned from books.'

'Then you have done wonderfully well, Ruth. I enjoy our walks and conversations, I only wish I could show you more of this world.

'Tell me about your home, is it very beautiful there?'

He laughed. 'To me, sitting here, the Loire Valley is very different. There is a very wide, fast river with beautiful towns and villages, which seem more beautiful now because I cannot be there. My parents worked for a local landowner who lived in a chateau, a castle. As a boy I was made to help the local Abbé with his garden, and he taught me to read and write and to speak a little English. I loved fishing as a boy and also watching the horses of the cavalry at the riding school there. The chateau and houses are made of white limestone rock that shines in the sun: it is very beautiful. Many people live in cave houses called troglodytes, houses hollowed from the rock face of the cliffs.' He saw Ruth's eyes widen in astonishment. 'These houses are very comfortable, good places to live.'

'Did you live in a cave?'

He smiled at her childlike reaction. 'No, but there are hundreds of these clean, honey coloured homes. Not ugly red brick, covered in soot.' Ruth flushed at this apparent criticism. 'I will try to paint a picture of Saumur so that you can see for yourself.'

'I would like that very much,' she replied happily, 'but why did you join the French Army?'

'Well, I could not join the English Army, could I?' He was being facetious now but Ruth was pleased to see his humour return. 'No, Napoleon decreed a mass conscription and when I was old enough I had no choice. I was fortunate that I could read and write so, with the influence of the Abbé, I was assigned to an officer in the dépôt who guided me. I know no other life—there has always been war.'

'But when the war stops what will become of all the generals and soldiers, they will need to do something?' Ruth offered.

'I somehow think that Napoleon likes making wars, and will always need men.'

'But if you are not well enough to fight, what will you do then?'

Reflecting on this point for a moment or two, Henri plucked a blade of grass which he chewed, then replied thoughtfully, 'Perhaps I teach or find work as a secretaire.' He spat the grass from his lips. The news was not good. Each new prisoner who came to Chesterfield brought stories of battles everywhere, the war was spreading and now there was trouble in Spain and talk of the Spanish joining with the English.

'I shall hate it if you go back before the war is over and you have to fight again,' Ruth stated flatly, and sighed. 'I would not like to lose another friend.'

'First I am a soldier,' he said softly, 'if I am sent back and Napoleon needs men then I have to fight, but I think I am not important enough or they would have tried to get me back by now.' He was able to talk to Ruth in a way that he couldn't with his fellow officers. He took the canteen he'd filled with cold sweetened coffee and offered it to her. 'Would you like to drink?'

'Yes please, and I managed to find some apples from the orchard, they're quite good.' She opened a linen bag to reveal several ripe windfalls which she had collected before leaving Rose Hill. As they sat together eating, another wagon passed by, the horse heaving and sweating from the long climb up the dusty hill. The man on the wagon raised his hat, hailing them as he went by.

That evening, with gentle strokes of a charcoal stick, Henri endeavoured to sketch for Ruth a picture of what Saumur looked like from across the River Loire. It wasn't easy to remember the finer details of exactly how many arches the white limestone bridge that spanned the broad river had. These were the same waters that he'd fished as a boy. Was it twelve or thirteen arches? He couldn't recall now, nor could he say for certain just how many turrets the imposing chateau on the lovely limestone hill above the town had, or their exact positions in relation to each other. He wasn't a very good artist, all he wanted to do was give Ruth an idea of what the place he loved looked like. He made a mental note to count the arches if ever he returned there.

When he'd finished he held the sketch at arms length and judged it not too bad, providing no one from Saumur examined it closely. He had tried also to draw the troglodyte dwellings in one of which an uncle still lived. This disturbed him for he could not convey to paper the way of life or pleasures these stone caves had provided for him. How he missed the vibrant diversity that was the Loire Valley! Would he ever…? Just what would he do if, as a sick man he was unable to rejoin the Army? Saumur was a cultured town, yet not a place where anyone might want to learn to speak English. Suddenly his self-confidence diminished. His education was not sufficient for him to teach anything else in Saumur, and the Army would probably have a surfeit of fit men and so not need him. No matter which way his thoughts went he acknowledged that he was not in charge of his own destiny.

The idyllic summer of 1807 finally drew to a close. Ended were their picnics by the river during sleepy warm days when they unknowingly made love with their eyes. It was once more time for Ruth to put the unflattering, dowdy old hat on against the cold and wet, and pack her precious bonnet safely in the drawstring bag until summer returned. It would return, but how things might be for them then, who could say?

Examining the rather sad felt hat, which now seemed even worse by comparison, she decided it was time to buy a better one.

Not all the enforced newcomers to Chesterfield were as likeable or as trustworthy as Henri and General D'Henin. In November that year yet another soldier of distinction and a member of the Legion of Honour, a Colonel Richemont was paroled and travelled to the town in the company of one Captain Méant.

Their journey from the Chatham hulks was a long one and the Colonel became ill after having travelled only as far as Athenstone in Warwickshire, where he had to remain while indisposed in the local Inn. Eventually, when able to do so, the pair left the Inn and finally arrived in Chesterfield where the new Agent advised them to take rooms at *The Falcon Inn*. This was a temporary measure until they could obtain suitable lodgings elsewhere.

Having spent three nights at *The Falcon*, Colonel Richemont managed to find accommodation more suited to his station. He returned to the Inn to pay his bill and collect his belongings, which included a strongbox containing silver plate, jewels and other items, also some paper money equivalent to almost a thousand pounds. All of which had been in his possession at the time of his capture. Once opened, much to Richemont's horror and dismay he found that someone must have used a false key and raided the box, removing the money and most of his valuables which in themselves were worth a further five hundred pounds.

What was he to do in a foreign country, with no authority of his own and expecting little or no sympathy from his captors? His rantings drew the attention of the Landlord, John Deakin, who on investigating the disturbance found the irate Frenchman almost apoplectic.

Seeing the nearly empty box and remembering how heavy it had seemed when lifted off the coach, he realised there had been a robbery. 'I'll send for Lieutenant Gawen the Commissary and Parole Agent! No-one here had a key to your room!' he said, but his words were lost amidst the Colonel's tirade in a foreign language which he couldn't understand. 'I'll fetch the Commissary,' he repeated, trying at the same time to apologise for the incident and indicating that he would go for help.

Turning from the apologetic and slightly fearful landlord who swore again that no one at the Inn had touched the box, Richemont beseeched Captain Méant for assistance as he entered the room.

'This is disgraceful, what am I to do to receive justice?'

The Captain shook his head, 'I'm afraid you can't trust anyone these days, Colonel. I suggest we find someone who speaks our language and get them to help.'

'And meantime what am I to do? I have to pay the bill here and future rents where I am to lodge. Be a good fellow, you have considerable property with you, can you see your way to loaning me a couple of hundred pounds, enough to temporarily pay my way?'

'I could,' his fellow traveller replied, 'but I would appreciate a signed paper to that effect, so that I can claim it back when you can afford it. In case you get transferred back to France, for instance.'

Fetching a suitable piece of notepaper from his own room, Méant counted out the loan with extreme care and made sure the Colonel signed the receipt.

'It's lucky that you haven't been similarly robbed,' Richemont said as he folded and pocketed the money. 'Perhaps the strongbox was too obvious a target!'

Meanwhile, his host, John Deakin, understanding only that the box had been broken into but not yet the value of the theft, sent his pot-boy to fetch Chesterfield's new Agent as a matter of urgency, and to bring someone with him who could speak French.

When Lieutenant Gawen arrived together with Joseph Gratton, a good French linguist who lived in the Market Place, together they did their best to calm the agitated Colonel. 'I will contact the Transport Board immediately,' Gawen explained, using Gratton to interpret. 'Everything possible will be done to apprehend the culprit, I can assure you! Do you think the box was broken into on the journey here? When did you last open it?'

Colonel Richemont thought for a moment. 'Not since leaving Athenstone,' he admitted, and realised that the goods could have been stolen earlier than he thought, perhaps as far back as a week ago. Turning to his friend the Captain, he asked, 'Is there any sign of anything of yours being tampered with?'

Méant shook his head, 'I keep my valuables about my person,' he offered, 'besides, we had separate rooms at the Inn.'

'Lieutenant Gawen says you are to be assured that we will find the culprit,' Joseph Gratton intervened, 'and will inform the Transport Board immediately.'

Leaving the victim and his friend deep in conversation, Gawen and Gratton left the Inn determined to get to the bottom of the matter.

The Colonel had little faith that the English would recover his possessions and was grateful that his friend had loaned him enough to tide him over the immediate future, until he could get funds sent out from France.

When informed of the robbery the Transport Board wasted no time before investigating the crime. Such incidents only inflamed relations and interfered with negotiations between France and England, thus hindering efforts to exchange prisoners or secure help for English citizens in Europe.

At the Inn in Athenstone the innkeeper was very co-operative and the servants having been examined were proved innocent of any involvement. The chambermaid, however, gave evidence that she suspected the Colonel's friend was responsible and stated several incidents to support her theory. There followed a thorough search of the Inn which led finally to the discovery of a well-concealed handkerchief containing a pocket book, with French paper money inside to the amount equivalent of £900, plus a variety of small objects.

The Agent accompanied by the innkeeper then proceeded to Chesterfield, and together with the Magistrate and two constables waited in Captain Méant's room for his return. Eventually he arrived and instantly recognised the innkeeper from Athenstone.

'You have business with me, I suppose?' he exclaimed, obviously shocked and surprised.

'Yes Captain,' the Agent stated simply. 'We are waiting for Colonel Richemont, so that he can formally identify what we have found.'

When the Colonel arrived, Méant was sitting pale-faced and nervous, flanked on either side by the constables, facing the door. Seeing his erstwhile companion and supposed friend thus constrained, the Colonel appeared shaken.

'Can you describe the items which you have lost, Sir?' The Board Agent asked, and found as expected that the book and other items secreted with it did indeed belong to Colonel Richemont.

Seeing that he had been found out, the culprit Méant confessed his guilt. 'I took all of it, the rest is hidden amongst my belongings here.' He waved his hand towards the cupboard where the Colonel's larger possessions had been concealed. Rising from his seat to show exactly where he'd placed the goods he then asked if he could have a drink as he was thirsty. Turning, he reached out for a bottle on the mantelpiece and repeatedly drank from it, the gentlemen present assuming that it was some cordial or other. Suddenly he attempted to seize a knife within his reach but was prevented from doing so by the constables. The colonel was stunned by this sudden turn of events and demanded to know why his friend had deceived him, but received no reply as the man appeared to be choking.

In a short space of time the effects of poisoning by laudanum became evident and the others in the room realised that he had taken this before their very eyes.

'Fetch a doctor immediately!' The Magistrate ordered, 'and find something to make him sick.'

The constables seized the struggling Méant and attempted to make him vomit, but to no avail. The strength and obstinacy of the man prevailed all attempts to make him regurgitate the poison but it wasn't long before the spasms of pain made them realise that it was probably already too late to save him.

In moments of calm between bouts of agony he showed signs of remorse. Then at one point he asked, 'Please, I need ink, pen and paper. I must make a will!'

The landlord hastened from the room and soon returned with the items requested. Meanwhile, Colonel Richemont although shocked at Méant's behaviour was becoming concerned at the intensity of the man's pain.

After completing the will Méant suddenly lunged for a knife which had lain unobserved by the rest of them, also on the mantelpiece, which he plunged several inches into his left breast.

'Damn the man!' The Agent shouted at the constables. 'Why didn't you keep a closer eye on him?'

'It's too late now,' the doctor said, as he tried in vain to stem the blood oozing from Méant's chest. 'All I can do is give him something to ease his condition. Even that will not help as the poison continues to do its work.'

'You mean he is going to die?' Colonel Richemont asked in disbelief. 'Is there nothing to be done?'

The doctor shook his head. 'Nothing! There will be several hours of agony for him before the end, but there is nothing else I can do!'

Having now recovered his possessions, Colonel Richemont decided he would remain in the room watching over the man with whom he had previously shared a good friendship. He said little, for that friendship had been sadly abused, yet he could not let a fellow countryman die amongst strangers in a foreign land. The man had a wife and six children in France all of whom would now be deprived of his protection, simply due to an act of greed. It was not as if the man was poor, he was wealthy enough and yet he'd risked everything for even more.

Eventually Captain Méant passed away, having committed the mortal sin of self-murder, and as a result he would be denied a Christian burial in consecrated land.

It was with little satisfaction that Colonel Richemont left Méant's lodgings, and with even less a few days later when the man's body was buried in a piece of derelict ground near the town. Such a waste of life! The two men had enjoyed a worthwhile companionship, one which was ruined in the end by avarice.

Strange to relate, later in the war Colonel Richemont escaped back to France, leaving large debts in the town behind him. He was a wealthy man and after peace was declared he was sued, but the tradesmen of Chesterfield never recovered their money. So much for 'A Man of Honour'.

The house was strangely quiet when Henri returned home after seeing Ruth back to Rose Hill one day in early December. There was no clattering of utensils from the kitchen so he called out, 'Madame, Hello?' to which there was no reply. He closed the outer door and went through to the kitchen, his curiosity aroused by the unusual quietness in that part of the house, as normally at this time in the afternoon Mrs Parsons would be preparing their evening meal. He wondered if she had gone into the small back-yard for some purpose or other; it certainly wouldn't be for wood or coal because only that morning he had brought in sufficient to last the whole day. As he stood looking through the kitchen window he heard a most peculiar noise. He waited several seconds before returning to the living room where, sure enough, he heard it again, only louder this time. He instantly recognised the sound of human breathing, but a heavier, deeper drawing of breath unlike snoring, so loud that it penetrated the floor of the room above, from Madame's room! He knew from its intensity that something serious had occurred and ran quickly up the stairs where, without knocking, he hastily pushed the door, which was slightly ajar, until it was fully open.

There on the floor beside her bed lay the old lady, apparently unable to move. Although she was conscious the gasping from deep within her chest told him that his friend was seriously ill. He took her hand in his and smiled comfortingly at her. 'I need to fetch a doctor,' he said, 'I'll be as quick as I can.' He gently released her and fetched a pillow from the bed placing it carefully beneath her head. 'You rest now,' he urged as she tried feebly to protest, 'I will be only one minute.'

Knowing already in his heart that Madame might be permanently at peace before long, he nevertheless hastened out into the street. First he knocked on the door of the adjacent house where a middle-aged woman responded to his urgent call. 'Please, will you go to Madame Parsons' bedroom? She is very ill—I will fetch a doctor.' Without any hesitation the woman hurriedly shut her door and rushed to the house to help, whilst Henri ran along Saltergate to where he knew another prisoner, an Army Doctor, was living. 'Is Monsieur Murat in?' he asked when the door finally opened. 'I need him quickly!'

He waited impatiently, thinking the man had no idea of the urgency of his request. Over the years several captured doctors and surgeons had been paroled in the town, some staying only a short while before being allowed back to France by the Transport Board. Often they offered their services to the community as well as helping their comrades when they were sick or had injuries that troubled them.

'Please, Sir,' he said in French when the doctor arrived, 'My landlady is very sick, will you look at her for me?'

'Of course, I'll get my bag, wait a minute will you?' The doctor dashed off to collect his things. More precious time lost, Henri thought as he waited yet again.

The doctor soon returned and by the time the two men entered the house in Glumangate the neighbour was awaiting them in great distress. 'I think she's dying,' she cried down the stairwell. 'Hurry up! Please!'

Kneeling down by Mrs Parsons' small, frail figure the doctor examined her as a matter of course, although he knew from her stentorian breathing that there was little chance of her lasting the night out. 'Help me lift her onto the bed,' he asked, 'all we can do is make her comfortable, but someone must stay with her, to reassure her. I'll come back tomorrow if she's still with us then.'

'I'll stay with her, she's been very good to me,' Henri offered, as they gently lifted Mrs Parsons from the floor and placed her on the bed. Henri then turned to the anxious neighbour and spoke in English, 'Please can I speak with you outside?' With the door closed behind them he continued, 'I am very sorry but we think that Madame is dying. I will stay with her until the end, do you wish to stay also?'

'No, it would be better if you spent the time with her, I know she's very fond of you. I'll be next door if you need me, just knock on the front bedroom wall.' Seeing how distressed Henri was she asked, 'Would you like me to bring you something to eat?'

'You are kind, Madame, then I will not have to leave her alone for long. Tell me, please, does Mrs Parsons have any family, or anyone I should tell? She never spoke of other family?'

The woman thought for a moment. 'Only the friends you have seen—she has no family, no children, and she kept herself very much to herself. Look, I'll go now and come back with something for you to eat when it's ready.'

'I thank you! I shall sit beside her and read.' After the woman left, Henri returned to the bedroom with some trepidation. It was getting gloomy so he lit the candles on the table beside her bed. 'This lady has looked after me and saved my sanity,' he told the doctor, again reverting to French.

The doctor nodded. 'If she dies during the night cover her face and leave her in peace, there will be nothing you can do until morning anyway. Are you sure you can manage?' Before Henri could reply Mrs Parsons struggled to speak, her low voice competing with the deep rasping of her chest. Henri took her hand to comfort her whilst the doctor brought a chair for him saying as he did, 'I'll leave you and Madame, if you cannot cope send for me but I think she will give you no trouble.' The man picked up his bag and prepared to leave.

'Thank you, Sir,' Henri said, 'I will see you tomorrow and pay you.'

The doctor waved his hand and shook his head. 'That she gave comfort to a French soldier is sufficient, Lieutenant.'

Left alone with Madame, Henri said softly in English, 'You are not well, Madame, but I will stay with you. Can I get you anything?' He wasn't even sure if she could hear him let alone understand what he was saying, so he sat alternately watching her and glancing round the room for something he could do. It was a very feminine room in a plain, austere sort of way, not at all as he'd expected, but then he'd no idea what had lain behind her door as she always kept it shut. After a while he released her hand as she was sleeping, left the room and went to fetch a book to read.

When he returned her eyes were half open and she struggled to speak. 'Hush, Madame, don't tire yourself,' he said softly.

Between wheezes and gasps and with great difficulty she struggled to form words which were barely audible and he thought she whispered, 'take care of Ruth'.

Henri looked at the face whose voice could seem sharp at times and then at others would be soft, and he smiled. 'I will Madame, I will,' then as suddenly as she'd started to speak she dozed off again, leaving Henri to his own thoughts.

Some time later the neighbour quietly reappeared carrying a basin covered with a linen cloth. 'It's the best I can do I'm afraid, but it's better than nothing,' she said, looking down at her friend now sleeping. 'Where shall I put it?' she asked Henri.

This act of kindness stirred Henri. 'Madame, my heart is full, I thank you.' He stood and gratefully took the offering.

"Tis nothin', now you eat. You'll need your strength.' She left, a little embarrassed by his florid gratitude. Strange people these French, she thought, as she closed the door.

Occasionally Henri walked up and down the room, small as it was, in order to stretch his legs. He'd seen death come to many over the years and was glad that Madame's was likely to be a peaceful passing. However, another worry was beginning to beset him. When Madame died where would he go, where would he find the comfort that the frail old lady had given him? He looked fondly at her, recalling the incident with the snails. He thought about his own mother who had left this world without him even knowing, and closed his eyes to pray. When he glanced again at his friend he realised that she too had left him.

Slowly, and with great sadness, he covered her face with the sheet, left the candle alight beside her and retired to his room. In these familiar surroundings he acknowledged that he was more in need of mental comfort than physical rest. As he stood there within the walls that had sheltered him for so long, he dreaded the arrival of dawn and the uncertainty it would bring. The sunrise was a mere three hours away so there was no point in disturbing anyone else, there was nothing now left for him to do but give Madame a decent burial. Only partly undressing he got onto the bed as he had done so many times in his career when awaiting urgent orders to march, and soon dozed off.

When the morning light eventually filtered through the badly-drawn curtains it woke the linnet which he'd omitted to cover during the night's disturbance, it was almost eight o'clock! Hurriedly washing and then dressing fully, Henri went next door to the neighbour to tell her of the death of his landlady and friend.

'I expected it,' she replied sadly. 'Don't you worry now, I'll go and fetch the undertaker for you.' She saw his tired and drawn face, he was obviously greatly upset. 'Get yourself something to eat. I'll go right now.'

'Your meal last night was a blessing, Madame. I cannot thank you enough. I will return the bowl when I have washed it.' He returned to the house, all was too quiet without Mrs Parsons' activities and he wasn't sure what to do next. The neighbour was right, so obeying her and his soldier's habit he instinctively ate whilst he had the chance and waited patiently.

Once the undertaker had been and Madame was safely installed in a plain wooden coffin in the sitting room, there was nothing more he could do so Henri left the house and made for the one person who would be able to help him.

John Bower had been early arriving at his Church Lane office that morning, and by the time Henri Pichon got there he was almost buried in his paperwork. He saw by the downcast expression on Henri's face that something was amiss, but as he was no longer Agent for the Transport Board he was a little mystified as to what had brought him there obviously seeking help.

After shaking hands Henri wasted no time before explaining the purpose of his visit. 'I have dreadful news, Madame Parsons died late last night.'

The news was not unexpected but it saddened John Bower. Several weeks previously Mrs P, as he called her, had been to his office saying that she had been feeling rather tired and out of sorts recently. 'At eighty it's to be expected, I suppose.' She'd said this in her usual manner. 'But I have a premonition that prompted me to come and see you.'

'I stayed with her until the end,' Henri continued, 'it was a peaceful going. The Madame next door fetched the coffin man this morning early.'

'What a shame. In these past four years you gave her something extra that she never had, a kind of son to care for. You knew that she was eighty years old, didn't you?'

'I would not have guessed! Without her I might not be here either. Beneath her abruptness she could be quite gentle.' Henri looked lost and forlorn sitting there. 'What do I do now? I must move I think, so I come to you, not because you were the Agent but you also have been a friend to me. Who will look after Madame's affairs for her?'

'Don't you worry, Henri, I will do everything as her appointed Attorney, and all that is required by her will and instructions as her executor. Stay in the house until everything is sorted out and don't do anything in haste. I might be able to help you.

'I am thankful for that. It has been a bad shock and I am tired. I have been up half the night. I must now go and explain to Miss Bradley at the school that today I am unable to teach.'

'Do that. Then go home and rest. I'll deal with everything else. There is no need for anyone to call at the house, but I'll fasten a note to the door directing anyone who does enquire to come direct to me here. Don't bother answering the door until you have rested, Mrs P. is going nowhere yet.'

'You were a good Agent, Mr Bower, both fair and considerate. It is a pity they replaced you.'

'I don't think they appreciated my difficulties or my efforts, lad. No matter, I've got enough work,' he said pointing to the piles of paperwork in front of him, 'without all the worries that job brought with it.'

'The prisoners are the ones to lose!' Henri commented. 'Men will run no matter who is in charge.'

John Bower smiled benevolently. 'If I've been the instrument in helping to make life easier for the remainder then that's reward enough. Now don't you worry, I'll solve your problem soon enough.'

Once Henri had informed Miss Bradley of the reason for his unfortunate absence from the school that day he returned home to Glumangate. As he passed the coffin in the sitting room on his way to the kitchen, he crossed himself and then gently patted its top panel. 'Sleep well,' he whispered, 'sleep well Madame. It is all in God's hands.'

After his long and eventful night, all Henri wanted to do now was sleep, and was thankful that John Bower had already placed a note on the house door, instructing enquirers to call at his office for information regarding the occupier.

Later that afternoon Henri rose and, although rested, he was constantly aware of the coffin in the room below, he missed the clatter of kitchen utensils and the sounds of other movements he'd taken for granted for so long. With a deep sigh and in order to pass the time Henri set about tidying things away and washing up.

At about four o'clock there was a light tapping on the front door which Henri ignored as John Bower had suggested. After several seconds the tapping started again, there was a further pause followed by yet another onset of tapping. Deciding that whoever waited there might not be able to read John Bower's note, Henri thought it best to respond. As he passed Madame's coffin he heard the murmur of voices from outside the house.

On opening the front door he was quite surprised to see John Bower and Ruth standing in the street as though they had been looking up at his bedroom window. 'I hope we didn't get you out of bed,' John said, 'can we come in?'

'Please, do,' a relieved Henri replied, moving back to allow them to enter. He was completely taken aback at seeing Ruth there looking so concerned.

When Ruth saw the coffin she whispered, 'I'm so sorry, Henri. Thank you for taking care of her.'

He nodded, still stunned by her visit and the speed at which fate had taken a hand in his life again. 'Would you like a drink?' he asked them both, unable to think what else to say. He even sounded like Madame who always asked any caller the same question. His eyes misted over. So far he'd managed to keep his emotions in check but Ruth's sudden appearance brought home to him how much he'd relied on both women's company. 'Come in the kitchen,' he said, barely able to conceal the tremor in his voice.

'I brought Mrs Silcock because I felt it wasn't right for her to come alone,' John Bower had taken his time before joining the conversation, mainly because he could see how shaken Henri had been by everything, and he sympathised with the young man who was always so friendly and well-mannered. Whether he'd had the officiousness that most officers had knocked out of him in San Domingo or not, he couldn't judge, he just hoped life had better things in store for Henri in the future. 'This lady was concerned for your welfare as much as anything.'

Henri looked directly at Ruth, his eyes conveying the gratitude he felt. She was all he had now. 'Thank you Madame!' he said humbly.

John Bower laughed. 'Call her Ruth in front of me, I'm well aware that you're good friends.' This brought a smile from both of them. 'I need to speak with you anyway, about the burial and concerning your lodgings.'

The kettle which Henri had left simmering on the hob was about to boil. 'I'll make tea,' Ruth said. 'I know where she kept it, so sit down, both of you.'

Henri was only too pleased to have the chore taken from him. His head was spinning and he needed to concentrate on what John Bower had to say.

'The burial will be at eleven o'clock tomorrow at the Parish Church and someone will come at ten-thirty to collect the coffin. I'll put another note on the door to tell neighbours and friends, word will soon get about.'

'Has she really no family?' Henri asked, 'Has she no-one at all?'

'No, she had none. At her age and with no children I'm afraid there's only a few friends, and I'm sorting everything out on her behalf. As to your living accommodation, I'll be able to let you know the details tomorrow afternoon.' He sipped the tea which Ruth had given him. 'Sugar! My word! Mrs P. didn't have much money but in spite of the cost she got her priorities right,' he ended with a chuckle.

'She kept it for special visitors,' Ruth informed him. 'I don't think she would mind today.'

'I must go through Mrs P's personal matters to see if there's anything to be dealt with. Bills and all that. I'll start upstairs, you two have a talk.'

When the Solicitor had gone Ruth sat beside Henri. 'I shall miss her,' she said.

'And I certainly will. I know she could be a strong-minded lady, but we got on, perhaps we were alike.' He played with the sugar tongs on the table and his fingers went white as he squeezed them too tightly. Rather than tell him to relax his grip, Ruth reached out and placed her hand gently on his.

'Don't,' she said kindly, 'you'll hurt yourself.'

This comforting touch triggered a release in Henri, and for the first time since he found Madame on the floor, he felt tears prick his eyes. 'I'm a little lost,' he choked. 'I never thought I would come to like Madame so much when first I came here.'

Ruth smiled. 'She liked it when you called her 'Madame', it made her feel special.'

Henri shook his head. 'I didn't know that!' Ruth's hand still covered his comfortingly and when John Bower returned with a few items that's how he found the pair, sitting quietly at the table, oblivious to his return.

He smiled and coughed. 'I've done up there, I'll look in the sitting room and in here, then we shall have to leave.'

Ruth withdrew her hand and placed it modestly in her lap, wondering what each of the two men might independently make of her action.

The following afternoon, when Mrs P's remains had been placed with those of her husband in the graveyard of the church, John Bower thanked the curate for conducting the burial and asked Henri to call at his office later, at three o'clock.

'Sit down, lad,' John said, pointing to a chair when Henri arrived. 'I couldn't speak earlier until I'd read out the Will Mrs P. left, as I must follow the law. You are aware that she had no relations but not that she owned the property in Glumangate? She left that in trust— I'm afraid I can't say to whom, but it was on condition that you should be allowed to use the house while you remain in Chesterfield. You've to pay me the same rent as you paid Mrs P., and you must not take in a lodger, let alone another prisoner.'

It took Henri a while to take in this news, news that he found to be almost unbelievable. He was speechless for a moment, and then asked, 'But why me?'

'There was no-one else and I think you brought a lot of comfort to her life in the four years you were together.'

'I cannot believe that she would think so high of me, I did nothing special. We had times when we did not agree!'

'Nobody ever got on much with Mrs P. Perhaps you treated her with fairness and respect.'

'I did try. But I might be here many years, who can tell?'

'It doesn't matter, that's what she wanted and the new owner quite likes the terms of the agreement. The rent is their unexpected bonus. The furniture will stay but you are not to sell it, or, and she was most specific about this, burn it when you run out of firewood.' John Bower smiled, watching the amazement and incredulity on Henri's face. 'I think, my man, that was her parting shot, intended especially for you.'

Henri grinned, 'No snails, no frogs, and no jigeripoki! Now no burning.' He couldn't help laughing out loud at this.

'I think you get the message. She was chuckling to herself when she dictated it. Oh, and just one more thing. She also asked that Ruth should take any clothes, jewellery and womanly fripperies from her bedroom, to sell if she doesn't want them. She quite took to Ruth and felt very protective towards her.'

163

'Madame was a good woman, I shall miss her!' Henri sighed and began to relax, his worries for the immediate future now over. He couldn't wait to tell Ruth. 'Does Ruth know?'

'Yes, as a benefactress she was present at the reading of the will. I will arrange to bring her to the house so that she can look through Mrs P's possessions. I'll send a note to her at Rose Hill. In fact, how about arranging things for Sunday after church? You can spend time with Ruth then, can't you, and my wife won't mind if I'm a little late back.'

'And the money for my rent?'

'Bring it to my office every week, Henri, and I will pass it on.'

'I am blessed!' Henri was quite moved as he shook hands with John Bower. 'I have good friends, and my eyes are open about the English; I do not like this war, Monsieur!'

'No, neither do I! I think Mrs P., in her own way, has tried to offer a token of peace.'

Until now, in bad weather, Ruth had been able to go back to the house with Henri on Sundays, thanks to the chaperoning presence of Mrs Parsons. This was now no longer possible, neither could Ruth make the weekly evening visit which Mrs P. had suggested so that they could play cards together. Suspecting their dilemma, when John Bower, Henri and Ruth returned from church the following Sunday, John tactfully left the couple alone sorting through Ruth's inheritance in the bedroom upstairs, whilst he made himself a cup of tea and relaxed, pondering on the quirk of fate which led him to this situation.

Upstairs Henri watched Ruth's delight as she unearthed small trinkets, none of which were of great monetary value but certainly luxuries nevertheless, and he saw the pleasure the bequest gave her. He also enjoyed the moments when she turned to show him what she found with such girl-like delight, as if it was important to her to share the discoveries with him. Henri helped carry the items downstairs for her to take away, knowing that she must leave with John. After they had left the house he felt depleted and alone.

With such dramatic changes in his circumstances, Henri was now more than ever left to his own devices. He'd been lonely before, but he found the emptiness of the house without Madame's occasional chatter and clatterings difficult to bear. Now, of course, without her ever-watchful eye it would be impossible for Ruth to visit unescorted again, for not only would people gossip but he doubted that he would be able to resist his fierce desire to take her in his arms. By placing her hand so comfortably on his the day before the funeral, and reassuring him with such a tender, loving look in her eyes, she was causing him to become tormented by desire. His frustration showed no sign of abating and he acknowledged it would be impossible for him to remain in the town with her so near. He would perforce even have to consider asking to be transferred to another parole town. What, he wondered, would she say if he asked her to marry him? What then would happen if he was suddenly sent back to France? Under no circumstances would he take Ruth back to his war-weary homeland; when the war ended then that would be a different matter and decisions like that could be made more easily.

Christmas was now fast approaching. This was going to be a difficult time for Henri who, without Ruth's companionship, had only the company of his fellow officers to fall back on. Although the house gave him greater space and freedom it now lacked human warmth, and as the Frenchman's Bell rang at five o'clock in winter and kept the other prisoners in their own lodgings so it confined Henri to his.

There were now fewer opportunities to speak privately to Ruth, certainly not on intimate matters, and he could not wait until the Spring when better weather would again allow them to wander freely outside. Henri was missing her more and more as the weeks dragged on. Almost nine months had elapsed since they had taken that first walk together and these walks had given him a purpose and reason for existing. After many hours of heartfelt deliberation, Henri finally came to the inevitable conclusion that something had to be done, and to this end he decided to discuss the situation firstly with John Bower. This he did one day when taking payment of his rent to John's office.

The preliminaries over, and the rent paid, Henri did not leave immediately but hesitatingly enquired, 'May I ask for help once again?'

'By all means. Is it about the house? Is something amiss?'

'No, Monsieur, it is regarding Ruth.' This statement instantly alerted John who listened intently as Henri continued. 'You know the situation for me as a prisoner, any day I could be sent back to France, and I would have no choice but to go! I could not take an English wife there and leave her alone if I have to fight. I might be killed!' He knew he wasn't making a very coherent explanation of his feelings, but then he hadn't declared these to Ruth either.

None of these sentiments came as a surprise to John Bower who fully appreciated Henri's excited state of mind and was aware of what he was implying. He was sympathetic but had to ask, 'Have you discussed this with Ruth then?'

'Why, no! That is what I wanted to talk to you about.'

'Do you intend to ask her to marry you?' John asked, sitting back in his chair. 'How do you think she feels about you?'

Henri shook his head. 'I dare not say to her my feelings if I have nothing to give her.'

'Then why ask me? What can I do for you?'

'Since Madame goes, Ruth cannot come to the house alone. It is bad weather, too wet and windy, and too cold to walk. I have no one special only Ruth. Monsieur, I need Ruth. I do not say anything because I do not want to lose her friendship but how else can we meet?' Henri paused in some confusion. 'And if we meet...I want her, you understand? But I do not want to hurt her.'

John Bower had trodden this path before, and was saddened over the effect his words might now have on Henri for whom he had considerable respect and liking. 'You know, I went through all this with Eleanor before she married Charles D'Henin. You realise that if you marry here it wouldn't be legal in France?'

'This I know. I would marry her again there!'

'There are women in other towns who've married French prisoners and whose husbands have been exchanged or sent back. These wives receive letters and money for a time, then eventually this stops and the women are left to fend for themselves, often with children to feed.'

'I would not do that, Monsieur. I would not see her hurt again.'

'And if you were killed?' Henri of course could not answer this, and John continued, 'Or, if you weren't sent back until the war ended, what would you do then?'

'That is why I come to you. If I continue to meet Ruth then the matter must be settled now, before it is too late. I am struggling to do what is right but it gets impossible.'

'Unless you know Ruth's feelings there is nothing I can advise. She will no doubt have considered all these possibilities as the months have gone by. I would not want her hurt again either, so you must seriously make up your mind whether you are prepared to fulfil any promises you make, or let her go her own way immediately.'

Henri sighed. 'I do not have much money but I can earn more. If I am sent back I would send money until the war is over and I can return, either to fetch her or to stay.'

'I'm sorry to repeat myself, but what if you are killed? Your government would hardly feel obliged to provide for her, would it?'

'Would she be able to live in the house, if I returned to France?'

'If the rent is paid, then yes, I think the owner would agree.' It seemed to John that the conversation was going round in circles. It was also taking up valuable time and Henri wasn't paying a fee for his advice. 'Look,' he said, 'if you both feel strongly about each other you'll have to take a chance, lad. You've always struck me as an honourable man, just make sure you mean to keep your word. Ruth Silcock is an honest and vulnerable woman who has seen enough misery.'

'I love her Monsieur! I have no intentions of harming her, or why would I come to ask your advice!' Henri was quite fired up by John Bowers implication that he might let Ruth down. 'When I give my word I keep it! I could have run very easily before now.'

Trying to lower the tone of their exchange John spoke quietly. 'Yes, Henri, I know—but in my job as a solicitor I see many well-intentioned people under pressure and with changes beyond their control it isn't always easy for them to comply with what originally appeared to be a wonderful idea. I've seen it happen many times. Look, if I can help you further when you've spoken to Ruth come back to me.'

'Thank you. I have no-one else to speak to who would answer plainly and honestly. As to how I can speak to Ruth on such matters in the street, it is impossible.'

Relenting and well aware that Henri was genuine in his loneliness and his desires, John capitulated. 'Let me make a suggestion. This Sunday, and this Sunday only, let me bring Ruth to the house quite openly. After a while I'll leave discreetly and that will give you both time to talk. She can leave through the back yard when it is dark. How does that sound?'

'Oh, Monsieur, I cannot thank you more. Who knows, Ruth may not want to be my wife. I will respect her wishes, please believe me.'

'Good! So I'll see you both after the service tomorrow then.'

Henri slept like a log that night and woke with a thrill of anticipation and excitement at the thought of having Ruth to himself later in the day. After his discussion with John Bower he'd gone shopping with the intention of buying a few delicacies that he thought Ruth would enjoy. Unfortunately he was not much of a cook but thought that the act of preparing a meal together would ease conversation and soften the way for what he hoped might follow. He marvelled to think that when Christmas actually came a year would have passed since he and Ruth had held their first real conversation. All manner of thoughts passed through his mind as he fussed around, making the house tidy and clean, and he wondered if Madame would have approved of his plan. Before leaving for church, Henri took extra care as he stood before the looking glass, his hand trembling as he adjusted his necktie; and was that a streak of grey amongst the strands of his dark brown sideburns? He pondered not so much on the reflected image before him but on the changes within himself that had occurred during the past year. His spirits were so much brighter now than after the week of sadness and worry since Madame's demise. Only one shadow cast a chill over his optimism. Did Ruth's feelings match his own?

As they sat together later in the upper gallery of the church, Ruth was quite intrigued by the barely-concealed excitement in Henri's demeanour. His hands resting on his lap clasped and unclasped repeatedly, and this fascinated her, for it appeared as if he wanted to reach towards her but then stopped and continued to fidget as before.

On the occasion when their eyes met, she also saw something other than his usual sober gaze, and he seemed unable to suppress a liveliness which made him appear younger. The previous afternoon she had received an unusual message from John Bower asking her to call at his office as soon as possible. This she did, and although John had not revealed Henri's true intentions, he explained that he considered Henri's position to be a sad one, and that as there would be little opportunity for the pair of them to meet during the Christmas period except at church, he would escort her to Glumangate after the service on Sunday. All Ruth knew was that she would not be going back to Rose Hill afterwards. She could hardly contain her curiosity!

'Would you like to come back to the house to eat?' Henri whispered as the introductory music on the organ died away, 'Monsieur Bower will accompany you.' His eyes held hers in anticipation, dreading a refusal.

'That will be a pleasure,' Ruth responded, apparently with no conception of the possible consequences.

Henri though, was not entirely convinced by this answer, as a twinkle lurked within her pale blue eyes. 'Have you been talking to Mr Bower?' he asked.

A wry smile crossed Ruth's face. 'I do admit it,' she replied, 'and I am still happy to come.'

With a deep contented sigh of relief Henri relaxed against the back of the pew. As the service slowly continued he found his concentration less and less on the preacher's words and more on the prospect of the coming afternoon. He almost sprang to his feet in unseemly haste when the service finally ended, until he saw that John Bower still remained seated below him as though in no hurry to leave.

When, an hour later, John Bower left the Glumangate house by the back door he wondered if his judgement had been impaired by his impetuous suggestion of today's meeting, and sincerely hoped he wouldn't live to regret having brought it about. The smell of food cooking at Glumangate had made him even more eager to be home to see what Spital Lodge had to offer.

With a cautious glance at the selection of items Henri had bought, Ruth had been relieved to find neither snails nor frogs amongst the root vegetables, and was pleasantly surprised at the thought he had put into providing for her comfort. As they worked together preparing and cooking the meal, she was amazed to find Henri quite adept at domestic tasks, due he explained, to the need to survive in the army during campaigns and also from his four years' residence with Madame.

In a time of national shortages, it helped to be living in a market town where farmers brought their freshly picked crops, or birds ready for sale—as with the chicken in the oven. Once selected, killed and gutted before his eyes, Henri had brought his prize home, plucked and cleaned it. Before leaving for church he had placed the bird in the oven to cook slowly in his absence. He'd paid a good price for it even if it was on the small size, as suited his pocket, but in comparison to the shortages experienced by many of the other prisoners on parole he was blessed indeed. He felt almost guilty in his indulgences, although he intended that what was left would feed him for further meals that week.

When at last it was time to eat, Ruth and Henri sat in their usual places opposite each other, leaving Madame's place empty at the head of the table. Their's was a comfortable friendship, although today Ruth could see that Henri was a little distracted.

Perhaps it had been remiss of Mrs Parsons, and she had not done it with ulterior motives in mind, or through spite, but over the months prior to her death she fondly described to Ruth a few of

Henri's little habits. How he tapped the table when his point of view had no effect on her, and the boyish look when he wanted to wheedle something out of her. Or, as now, rocking the fork back and forth between his fingers, quite unaware that Ruth could recognise it as a sign that he was about to announce something and was unsure of his ability to convey his meaning. Easy conversation had never been a problem between the two of them, even if it was only about their observations over the state of Europe. Only personal matters caused problems and there were times when she knew almost to a word what he was going to say; there were other times when she wanted to give him a push or guide him. Today was one of those days!

Deep in her heart Ruth suspected she knew what he was going to say. In the meantime she tried to suppress her own optimism and desire so that she might see if she had guessed correctly.

'We will not be able to meet like this again,' Henri finally came out with it as Ruth finished eating. 'Monsieur Bower will not accompany you again.'

'It was thoughtful of him to do so today. I think after what has happened he felt we had nowhere else to go in wintery weather.'

'You must not come alone here or there will be talking. I do not want bad gossip about you, Ruth. I have come to enjoy your company, and since Madame has gone I have no-one. Only the other prisoners...!' He was floundering a little now.

'I think,' Ruth said, looking directly at him, 'there is already speculation.' She realised the word puzzled him, and added, 'People are already beginning to talk.'

'Then we must put a stop to it,' he was quite adamant in her defence. 'You can always marry me!' It was not how he'd planned to tell Ruth he loved her, but there it was, he'd said it.

'Lieutenant Henri Pichon,' Ruth remonstrated, 'do you only wish to defend my honour or have you other reasons for asking me to marry you?'

With the colour rising in his cheeks, Henri strove to correct his clumsy proposal. 'You and I,' he said hesitatingly, 'well I...I have to come to love you! I want you as my wife, I am tired of saying "au revoir".' Never had Henri expected to find asking a woman to marry him to be such hard work. 'Madame,' he said very formally, 'will you become Madame Pichon?'

Ruth's face glowed as the question finally left Henri's lips. 'There will be many problems if I do marry you, a French prisoner,' she replied though with little genuine conviction.

He wasn't sure if Ruth was tormenting him or not, but at least she hadn't turned him down. 'There are many things to discuss, I know. I never intended to speak out so quickly but I can hope that you will say yes? Yes?'

Ruth nodded modestly knowing that he deserved a better answer than the flippant one she'd given. 'I would like that very much, although some aspects of this do worry me. If you go back to France you may not be able to return here, or to take me home with you. Also, I could not bear it if you too were killed during more fighting.'

The time had come for Henri to end the charade, time to leave the table and assure her that his intentions were in earnest. More importantly to show her just how much he needed her, how much he loved her. Rising, he held out a hand inviting her to come to him. 'Madame,' he said softly, 'Madame with the beautiful pale blue eyes, I want to marry you!' He drew her close, wrapping his arms firmly about her. She was everything he wanted and needed and, apart from eventually dying, he would never leave her or let her down.

'We could be married on Christmas Eve,' he whispered. 'There is enough time and then we need not be alone again.' He took her hand and lifted it to his lips in the French way. 'Please, what do you say?' He held his breath, waiting for her response, knowing that such a short wait until Christmas would seem an eternity.

'Henri Pichon,' Ruth coyly replied, 'I think Christmas will do very nicely.' She raised her head and let him kiss her. What did it matter if there should be problems ahead, life had already dealt her one bitter blow and now she was fortunate to have found another love, and could begin to live again. That, or lose Henri, which she could not bear to do.

Chapter 9   1808-1809
Unrest in the Town

*T*he year eighteen hundred and seven ended with yet a another marriage when Louis Pilchowski, a Polish officer captured at Calabria, near Naples, married Rachel Wood on New Year's Eve. For Henri and Ruth the coming year became the sweetest of the entire war, wrapped up with each other as they were. Whether it was because of their new relationship or otherwise, Henri acquired further respect amongst local people and he managed to find more teaching work so increasing his income. This was a great help in a time of general shortages in all commodities, the price of grain and other imported necessities rose annually, just as taxes increased to pay for the cost of the war itself.

In spite of the chaos that hostilities were causing throughout Europe and beyond, England's physical position was safe surrounded by sea as she was, and protected by her mighty Navy. By now Napoleon had abandoned all hope of invading and the English could sleep peacefully in their beds with her lands not ravaged, razed and plundered as was happening in much of Europe. The British Army's Regiments however, were being scattered in all directions and over many continents fighting for King and Country. Seemingly Britain was becoming like France in taking possession of other lands as if it was her right to do so.

Increasingly, though, England was being embroiled further into the European theatre of war, starting with Portugal and spreading into Spain. Slowly at first, some of the men captured by the British there arrived in Chesterfield to swell the numbers already on parole. A few of those who had been in the town for almost five years inevitably died, whilst several attempted to escape with varying degrees of success. By December, tensions within the town due to the everlasting conflict were running high, tensions which, if allowed to fester too long, would sour the comparatively easy relationship which existed between the citizens of Chesterfield and its prisoners.

For weeks Henri had been aware of the increased ill-feeling and general discontent rising amongst some of the prisoners. The weather was bleak with miserable misty days, and the Frenchman's Bell now rang at 5 o'clock, keeping all prisoners indoors for the rest of the evening. Those less fortunate than Henri had to manage on poor rations, their allowances could not be increased to combat the rising prices, and tempers were getting short. The war appeared to be lengthening and this further aggravated both sides; the prisoners' despair was equally matched by the resentment of certain townsfolk, particularly those burdened with trying to provide for their families on inadequate wages. The price of bread was almost beyond their means, and yet the prisoners seemed only to spend their time in a state of idleness, and were being paid to do so!

In early December Henri heard more disturbing rumours, particularly at Muster, which of course he was still compelled to attend, but on his own he was powerless and could not interfere without being disloyal to his countrymen.

Ruth despaired over Henri's humiliation at being forced to join the assembly in the Market Place. 'It's demeaning,' she remonstrated. 'Twice a week you have to stand there like cattle to be counted and paid, in this weather and with that chest of yours!'

'I knew the terms when I agreed to parole,' he said, trying to calm her. 'I would have been dead by now had I been in the hulks. What kind of prison is this, anyway, where I can sleep happily in a comfortable bed with my wife beside me? It is small price to pay.' He laughingly held her close. 'Either my arms are becoming shorter, Madame Pichon, or I feed you too well,' he teased.

'It's still not right!' Ruth wriggled, pulling away in protest, but he caught her again.

'I must go,' he cried, 'or I will be late and they will think I have run away to find another wife.'

When he returned to the house later in the day he was quite agitated. 'I do not like what I hear. There is such discontent that I fear at the slightest provocation there will be trouble. I dare not get involved to try and stop the men. I have tried to calm them down but if I warn anyone my people will treat me as a traitor.'

'You must do nothing, Henri, so stay out of it. You cannot win whatever you do.'

'To do nothing and stand back it traitorous as well!' Often when excited he still confused his English. 'But I tell you to stay indoors until I tell you it is alright to go out again.'

Seeing the depth of his concern, Ruth realised that he suspected trouble to be imminent so she agreed not to venture outside the house. 'But where will you be? Promise me you will be careful, won't you?' she pleaded.

'Yes, and tomorrow I am in school. Hopefully all will be over by the time I leave there.'

The following day whilst Henri was instructing pupils in his native language and Ruth busied herself about the house, tempers came to a boil on the streets of Chesterfield.

A number of trouble-makers in the town had for some time been taunting the prisoners with insults to which the French had retaliated verbally. Eventually this teasing eased, only to leave simmering resentment and malice on both sides. Today those French prisoners, with little else to do, finally decided to take revenge, and a group of them armed with bludgeons, at the first sign of trouble paraded through the streets, each with a white handkerchief tied to his arm as a sign of unity. This intimidation roused the fury of the town's hooligans who had never experienced a full-fledged battle, and clashes turned into an angry affray until the local Militia arrived. By this time several men on both sides were injured, some quite badly, while others were arrested and locked behind the heavily barred doors of the House of Correction until legal action could be taken against them.

When Henri arrived home he was relieved to hear that Ruth had obeyed him and remained in the house, quite safe from the troubles in the Market area. He, on the other hand, had heard a full report from a fellow officer who had closely observed the commotion and its aftermath.

As a result of the near riot, six of the prisoners involved were sent to Norman Cross to be kept in close confinement for the rest of the war. Ruth was greatly relieved that Henri had kept his word by refusing to become involved in the whole affair. Subsequently the town settled back into its more easy-going ways and what could have permanently soured relations between both sides was soon forgotten.

Many of the French Officers were Freemasons in their own country, although Henri was not. Even so, for him to be invited, in 1809, to join the Lodge newly created by the officers in Chesterfield, was an honour which he did not turn down. The 'Loge de L'Esperance' was the first of two Lodges formed in the town during the war and Henri knew his joining would further his standing within both communities, leading to openings for his teaching, and, if he was to be returned to France this would hopefully open doors for him there.

Ruth had her doubts, fearing that if Henri lifted his sights above his station she would not be thought good enough for him.

'Ridiculous!' he stated firmly. 'It may even open up new ways for us. I'm not ashamed of my wife, and it might make us more secure. A Freemason's wife would always be looked after if something happened to me.'

This had never occurred to Ruth. She had suffered small slights from some in marrying a French prisoner, but had held her head high even though the vindictive gossip passed on to her had hurt deeply. As always, though, once the curiosity value had worn off, and the nature of Chesterfield's inhabitants being what it was, people soon forgot to comment about her, and she began to enjoy being Mrs Pichon.

Occasionally, Henri invited fellow officers of good standing back to the house. At first Ruth was ill at ease in their company, especially as most of them could not speak English, although she was slowly beginning to master their language with Henri's gentle encourage-ment. He had begun romantically with small endearments as they made love in an evening and gradually increased her vocabulary until she could use phrases naturally, and without thinking.

Whereas some in the town still mocked and mimicked the Frenchmen's exchanges of embraces and even kisses in public streets when they met, Ruth responded to their courteous behaviour and the respect they showed her, more so because she understood Henri and some of his language. Her world was opening up and with her friend John Bower becoming Town Mayor again for the sixth time, she began to feel part of the town's society, humble though it was.

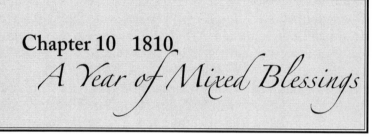

Chapter 10   1810
A Year of Mixed Blessings

The year began slowly, with Henri once more finding that his arms were too short to reach around his wife's normally slim waist.

In spite of John Bower having been replaced as Agent for the prisoners in the town, decamping seemed to be ever on the increase, and amongst the culprits was another of General D'Henin's servants.

By February, three more prisoners took 'French Leave', helped by a Matthew Burgin of Sheffield who procured a post-chaise to convey the trio from Chesterfield to Redcar. From there they journeyed on to Gateshead where they embarked on board a Danish vessel, and as nothing was ever heard from them again even by their friends, they were presumed drowned or successful.

In March Ruth became irate when an acquaintance named Elizabeth Bennett was badly let down after another prisoner, Louis Souplet, had banns read in the Parish Church but the marriage did not take place. He later ran, and Ruth was heard to say, 'Good riddance', when informed of his callousness.

She was excited however to learn in July that a friend, another Elizabeth, daughter of John Turner the Parish Clerk, was to marry Francois Marie Dupe. He had been a ship's purser captured on the sloop of war *Le Diligente* at Porto Rico. This marriage was much to the chagrin of the bride's father.

Another marriage like this meant that Ruth was no longer isolated in her position as the wife of a prisoner, as there were now six local women, including Eleanor D'Henin and the Parish Clerk's daughter, in the same position.

Much to Henri's disgust, on the day before Elizabeth Turner's marriage, Lieutenant Colonel Louis Richemont whose so-called friend had attempted to relieve him of his possessions before committing suicide, astounded fellow officers and townsfolk alike by decamping, leaving behind large debts. This cast a shadow over the whole proceedings and Henri felt ashamed to count Richemonte as a French Officer.

Meanwhile the war escalated and spread into the entire Iberian Peninsula of Spain and Portugal, where both England and France made gains and losses. This resulted in more prisoners arriving in the town, many of them captured from General DuPont's land forces in Spain. Some were in bad condition and their clothing very ragged indeed.

Barely a month later six more prisoners broke parole and as more details came to light, Henri followed their progress in the newspapers. It transpired that the six reached Folkestone on the Kentish coast without hindrance.

'It's almost like a novel,' Ruth commented as Henri related his latest finding on returning home.

'I do not condone their flight but the consequences of being caught are so great, I wish them luck,' he confided as he recalled what he had read, 'it appears a landlord named Richard Hambrook of the *Blue Anchor Inn* in Folkestone found them lodgings, with three more runners from Ashbourne. He then helped them obtain two boats and in these they crossed over to France.'

'They made it, then!' Ruth sounded almost relieved as she knew several of the men in person.

Henri shook his head, 'Nearly, they were re-captured by *HMS Cordelia* off the French coast and brought back.'

'Oh! What a shame! All that effort for nothing,' Ruth couldn't help but be sympathetic after the men had braved so much in order to obtain their freedom. 'What will happen to them now?'

'I suppose they will end up in the hulks, poor devils.'

When eventually the full report of the court proceedings from Maidstone was published the fate of the men became known. After re-landing in England the men were escorted under military guard to Canterbury to be examined, the result being that they were returned to Folkestone to be confronted with the men from whom they had purchased the boats for their escape. These men were also arrested and the prisoners were finally sent on to the hulks, just as Henri had predicted.

'That will be the end of them,' Henri said, shaking his head. 'If they remain there for long they may as well be dead.' He had no wish to elaborate on the conditions in the hulks, his own few days there had almost destroyed his will to survive. 'The escapees were identified by a witness who recognised the large deal box they took with them. Why on earth didn't they leave it behind?'

Several more prisoners arrived in the town, again captured in Spain, and some of these were accompanied by their wives and children. All were in a pathetic state and Henri particularly asked Ruth not to attempt to mix with these 'camp followers', knowing them to be of very low class and very coarse. 'You can send them cast-off clothing, by all means,' he suggested, seeing the disbelief on her face. 'Believe me it is not advisable to mix. It was their choice to live and travel in such an uncivilised manner.' Later Ruth saw for herself the coarseness of many of these wives in the Market Place, and had they been English she would not have chosen to mix with them either.

At the end of October Henri returned home frowning and in a strange mood. 'What's the matter?' she asked, worrying in case the news he had would spoil their happiness. 'You aren't being sent back, are you?' Her hand was shaking and she felt quite frightened.

'No,' Henri replied. He was disturbed having learned of a new arrival in town and told her of the officer, General Joseph Exelman, who had been one of Napoleon's favourite commanders in DuPont's land forces in Spain.

'Do you know him? Why does he upset you?' She had fears that as with Boyer, over whom Henri had once suffered a nightmare which had terrified her, this new arrival might invoke the same response.

'No,' he said shaking his head, 'but do I speak now as a Frenchman or an Englishman? General Exelman was taken at Bailen, two years ago. Sometimes we win, sometimes you win. He seems to think the war will go on for years. Apparently we dis-honoured ourselves again, this time it was at the town of Cordova. After we took it our men disgraced the Tricolore by devastating the town with debauchery and barbaric acts to such as a degree that when we left, Exelman doesn't know whether we were more burdened with hatred from the Spanish than with the riches stolen from them.' Henri banged the table with his fist in frustration. 'Why? Why?' His face was flushed with anger and bitter shame. 'They will hate us forever! Why must we always destroy?'

How could Ruth calm him down? It was better for him to get it out of his system but his deep distress continued unabated.

'After plundering Cordova they moved on to Bailen where DuPont wasted his force in skirmishes before becoming entrapped. With his men dying of hunger and thirst, and with Spanish peasants baying for their blood, just as it was in San Domingo, DuPont's men were surrounded and he surrendered to General Constanos. Since that defeat apparently, people are now beginning to think the French need not always win. They are fighting back!' Here, with his anger spent Henri sighed deeply. 'I have no wish to return to fight, to fight anyone, any more. Those same horses and the chasseurs riding them were all trained at my town of Saumur—it is such a waste!' There was little Ruth could say, all she could do was pray that he wouldn't have to return and perhaps be involved in Napoleon's reckless ambitions again.

Chapter 11 1811
A Sharp Reminder

A bitter blow was to fall upon Henri and John Bower during the eighth year of Chesterfield's part in the paroling of prisoners, for Charles D'Henin was ordered in February by the Transport Board to return to France. He went, taking Eleanor and their daughter Sarah Ann Hamilton D'Henin with him to Paris. He had been well liked and popular in Chesterfield with his pleasing address and manners; Spital Lodge seemed almost empty without the lively trio, and Henri was more than a little perturbed to see him go, wondering also if, after all this time, the powers that be were remembering their men and would arrange an exchange even for him.

Not long after D'Henin had gone back to Paris, General Joseph Exelman had no qualms in breaking his word by running. Together with Colonel Auguste de La Grange, and helped by a man named Jonas Lawton who acted as interpreter, they left the town for Mansfield concealed in a covered cart. The following morning they travelled on by a post-chaise from there and were pursued by a police officer who failed to stop them.

Despite the following excellent descriptions distributed nationwide for this pair, and offers of financial reward, they were never caught:

Joseph Exelman, age 36, 5' 11½" in height, stout, oval visage, fresh complexion, light brown hair, blue eyes, strong features.

Auguste de La Grange, Colonel, age 30, six feet tall, stout, round visage, fair complexion, brown hair, dark eyes, no marks in particular.

Their accomplice, Jonas Lawton, was a young assistant to a Chesterfield surgeon, John Elam, and he was rewarded for helping the two escape with a good position at a hospital in Paris. His brother, George Lawton of Sheffield, having already helped several other prisoners to escape was not so lucky and spent two years in Derby gaol for his treachery.

The year eighteen hundred and eleven also saw the last parole prisoners ever to arrive in Chesterfield. Those who were already there waited for the apparently never-ending war to finish. Several died, many ran, and a few others married. Always there were mixed feelings of hope, desperation and frustration, but this was not so for Henri who had many reasons now to count his blessings, life was no longer empty.

'Papa, look!' the child cried as it ran by the river in the sunshine. 'What is it?'

Bending, the man took the child's hand lovingly in his own while he peered into the weeds at the edge of the riverbank. He laughed softly, 'It's a frog; a frog.' The child poked with his stick until the creature leapt for freedom, thus making the boy jump excitedly from the outstretched hand which held him.

'A frog, a frog,' the child repeated, dancing with glee. At the age of three he was becoming sturdy, with rich dark brown hair in ringlets and the happy smile of a young innocent.

Watching him, Henri found his thoughts turning to the banks of the Loire and his own childhood there. He couldn't have been as young as Joseph at the time, as he would not have been allowed to play on the banks of such a powerful waterway as the Loire. Nevertheless, the smell of grass and water was tantalizingly poignant as Henri watched Joseph at play. How he loved him, his child, Ruth's child. Therein lay his happiness as it did with the boy's smaller little sister in the house with her mother.

So many times did he climb the stairs to the bedroom in Glumangate to peep first at one, then the other child when they were newly born, 'What are you doing?' she finally had to ask as he repeatedly left the sitting room during one of their evenings together.

'Just making sure they are still breathing,' Henri had to admit.

To Ruth these many attentions to her and the children were just a pleasing part of Henri's personality, and never had he given her cause to regret her decision to marry him. During the four years since their union they had put the war from their minds except on very rare occasions, and after dwelling in Chesterfield for eight years Henri couldn't imagine why Napoleon continued to squander the youth of his countrymen, neither did he see himself as a soldier, or of any further use to the Emperor.

Meanwhile in Europe men of all nationalities were still dying in their thousands in skirmishes and battles, whilst countries were being laid bare by starving, foraging troops who had no thought for the peasantry whose land they ravaged. Those countries whose lands were now battlegrounds saw devastation and starvation as being only two humiliations amongst countless others which they suffered.

Shortages and high taxes England might have, but at least she was safe in a world of turmoil. Suffice to say that if Napoleon won, England would never be the same again.

Chapter 12   1812
A Year of Turmoil

The year 1812 was not a good year! Winter gave way to Spring and, in May, the Prime Minister, Spencer Perceval, was shot dead in the lobby of the House of Commons in front of his friends and colleagues. In the same month America declared war on England due to her constant meddling in that nation's politics and interference with her trade. This lead to further shortages and price rises in England.

Summer followed, always the happiest time of year for Henri in his state of health, to be followed by Autumn bringing with it shorter days and casting long shadows from the trees on the tired grass of summer. Autumn also brings great changes, and nature cannot be halted—just as events in life are impossible to hold back. To Henri his inevitable autumn finally arrived.

While he watched his children playing peacefully and unaffected by the war, Napoleon's Grande Armée of a quarter of a million men was marching the 800 leagues towards Moscow. By the time they reached Smolensk, 75,000 had perished through typhus, dysentery and starvation, and only one tenth of this total had been lost in battle en route. Napoleon lost a further 30,000 men at the battle of Borodino and, with just 95,000 men remaining, finally entered Moscow on the 14th September. As a result of this heavy death toll Napoleon began to recruit men wherever he could to make up his losses.

It was, therefore, a terrible shock when, to Henri's dismay, he received instructions from the Transport Board that he was to be exchanged and returned to France within the week. There was nothing he could do other than tell Ruth immediately and endeavour to soften the blow.

Sending the children upstairs to play, he sat Ruth down and with his emotions in turmoil gave her the news causing her to sob uncontrollably.

Leaving Ruth distraught in Glumangate, Henri hastened to convey the news to John Bower in Church Lane. He was terribly downcast as he faced his friend, 'I am being exchanged,' he blurted out without formally greeting John, 'I have only three more days with my beloved family before I am to leave. Oh, Monsieur, it was always a possibility but I have frankly no desire to leave. The war could go on for years and my little angels will grow without me!'

'It was to be expected,' John Bower agreed. He was low in spirits himself. 'Nevertheless during the, what... ?, seven or eight years you've been in England you have enjoyed some normality with Ruth and the children. Surely the war must end one day, and these extra taxes and high prices will cease. Maybe there will come a time when we can get up in a morning full of optimism for the day ahead.'

'How can I leave them,' Henri cried, 'yet I cannot call myself a Frenchman if I refuse to return, I am a soldier after all.'

'You're not the only one, you know,' John sounded hollow and disgruntled. 'General D'Henin had his doubts when he left last year. I fear my house is an empty one without him, Eleanor and Sarah Ann, and now that my Isabella has passed on I sometimes wonder what life is all about. Without my three daughters I don't know what I'd do.'

'Oh, but I am selfish!' Henri cried, 'you have your own troubles. I am remiss in forgetting that Madame Bower has so recently died. My apologies.'

'The General took his family back to France,' John sighed, changing the subject. 'I don't know how wise a decision it was to take them but Eleanor wanted to go to Paris with him.'

'I couldn't take Ruth to France, I doubt that it would be safe. General D'Henin's rank will protect his family, I doubt if mine would. Besides, Ruth knows no-one there and I have no close family since my father died last year.' There was a glazed look on John Bower's face, and Henri realised that his grief still lingered. 'I must leave them here where they are safe,' he said, gently breaking into the elder man's reverie.

Looking up as if startled, John Bower attempted to gather his thoughts together. 'Yes, Ruth will be safe here,' he replied, 'providing you keep your word and send money to her.'

'I will,' Henri hastened to assure him. 'But I came not simply to say thank you for all you have done and to say goodbye. I wonder if you could act on my behalf for my family.'

'I do act for Ruth now. It will be my pleasure to see to both your affairs.'

Henri was a little puzzled by John's claim to act on Ruth's behalf for she had never mentioned this fact to him. Brushing this aside for the moment he went on. 'I have saved money from my teaching in case I was sent back, and now I want to leave all of it here for my family, in case I am killed. Napoleon needs all the men he can muster and he'll not let my bad chest hold him back. If I live, then when the war is over I will return; I would never abandon my children, or Ruth.'

'Then let us pray that the war ends soon! I wish you all the best of fortune and that God's hand will spare you.' There was already a sense of finality and conclusion in the room and John felt quite emotional at parting from Henri after so much had happened to bring about a form of friendship. He coughed to clear his throat, almost ashamed of the display of emotion that welled up inside him. This was a sad time for all concerned.

'There is another request I have to make,' Henri said, still a little unsure of himself. 'I would like to show my gratitude to the owner of the house, for allowing me to stay after Madame died, and for the fact that Ruth can continue to stay in it with the children. You did say it would be possible, some time ago?'

For several years John had wondered what he would say if this situation ever arose. He looked directly at Henri. 'You have already done that, lad.' Henri gazed at him in bewilderment. John shook his head, 'No, not me! You have given that person happiness and two beautiful children—Ruth has no worry about the house.' He smiled benevolently, hoping that Henri would not be too proud to accept the truth.

Henri gasped, hardly able to digest the implications of the words. 'You mean... it is Ruth's house?'

'Yes! Mrs P. wanted Ruth to have security. You could have been returned to France at any time and the house would then have been of little use to you. However, Ruth had no option but to accept and obey the will, and she was happy for you to live there. She had no idea at the time that you would ask her to marry you.'

Henri was still taken aback by all this information. He had always considered Ruth to be a clever manager of his money, as she'd always made it go further than he could have done. 'But the rent,

185

Monsieur, what of the rent?' There was no rancour or resentment in his voice, only amazement.

'When you needed that which you couldn't afford she used some of it, the rest she has saved for the future, so that you had no need to worry. You are a fortunate man in having Ruth for your wife.' There had always been the possibility in Mrs P's well-laid plan that Henri might resent Ruth's inheritance, and much as she trusted the lodger she considered it better to protect Ruth from the unknown. John watched as Henri considered Ruth's actions and was relieved to see that Mrs P's faith in her own decision had been well founded.

It took Henri several moments of contemplation before he replied, whilst John mused on his own misfortunes. 'Well, I am indeed a lucky man,' he said eventually, and there was a hint of pride in his voice. 'How could I go away and forget such a wife? If, God forbid, I am killed, then my angels will be in capable hands, but ...' the pride changed to fear, '...what if I never see them again?'

Seeing Henri's utter desolation, John felt helpless. He'd seen the anguish inflicted at Spital Lodge when Charles was informed of his impending repatriation; the result being that Eleanor insisted on accompanying her husband to war-torn France. Where was the General now? Was he too, marching towards Moscow? Henri and John Bower were completely unaware of the mayhem taking place in Russia at this time, or that in the coming night General Joseph Exelman, who had escaped from Chesterfield seventeen months before, would be mounted on horseback all night, and with his men was surrounded by avenging Cossacks to the south of Moscow. Snow had already fallen days before and Napoleon's entire invading force was now made up of cold and hungry men, their horses dying from the frost and starvation.

Never did so many tears flow as they did over the following three days in the little house in Glumangate. Little Joseph found it hard to understand why his Mama and Papa were constantly wrapped in each other's arms, and although he loved to sit on Papa's knee he wondered why tears flowed down his father's face. 'Do soldiers cry, Papa?' he asked in his childlike way as he touched the tears with his small finger. Henri couldn't speak and just looked at Ruth for help.

'Only good ones like Papa, dear,' Ruth soothed the child and tried to conceal her own distress which would only have made things worse, 'only good ones!'

At the tender age of two, curly-haired Marie played quietly, occasionally staring with a bemused look at her parents from her position on the floor. The extra affection bestowed upon her by Henri was merely an added bonus in a long day of play.

So came the hour of departure, and with winter approaching Henri bade a sad and tearful farewell to Ruth and the children before travelling south towards the English Channel and thus to France, a country which had become almost foreign to him. He was no longer the half-demented, shabbily dressed victim of the deprivations experienced in San Domingo, who had arrived in Chesterfield on that cold December afternoon eight years before. He now held his head high again, his determination and sole aim being to simply survive until he could return to the arms of his family, and then provide for their welfare.

The journey towards his homeland was, for Henri, almost a blur, being one that stirred vastly differing emotions; from the deepest gloom at leaving his family behind, to the anticipation and curiosity over passing towns and countryside. He knew within himself that it wasn't wrong but quite natural for a man to look outwards, that was the spirit of mankind. Sadly his own horizons had been restricted for so long that he felt guilty at enjoying the experience. If only he had been allowed to venture freely beyond Chesterfield, to Sheffield or Derby, even London, then perhaps he would have felt more fulfilled and less claustrophobic.

This opening up of his mind to a degree excluded Ruth causing him some disquiet, making him feel almost disloyal. Before his capture, each new campaign in which he'd participated had stretched him mentally and physically; now he could not suppress his anticipation for the new challenge ahead. Henri fought the inner conflict between growing exhilaration and the sadness that he might never see Ruth and his children again. He was becoming a soldier once more, and a soldier should sally forth, complete the task in hand and, if his luck held out, return then to his home base. Perhaps such complications had held him back from marriage in the past but he would now have to adjust to a new way of thinking.

Finally reaching Portsmouth on the south coast, Henri reported to the Transport Depot as instructed. There, several days later, he was joined by other prisoners who were to be similarly exchanged by the Board. They were escorted under guard to board the vessel which was to take them to France. Their jubilation at being repatriated was almost infectious, but this had not yet reached the state of letting patriotism seem anti-English. Some, like Henri, had more reason than others to appreciate the hospitality and comfort that had been offered by their English hosts and were therefore more subdued.

Henri watched from the deck as eventually the shores of England gradually receded. For October the sun, although considerably weaker, still shimmered on the swelling waves, and it was a cool but pleasant day. He filled his lungs with the fresh sea air whilst his eyes moistened with regret.

Whilst Henri travelled homewards, Napoleon's 'Grande Armée' was stalemated in and around Moscow. When, five weeks previously, they had entered the Capital it seemed to be deserted, but the following morning, all around them houses and palaces alike began to burst into flame as the Russians burnt their own property and stores in order to prevent the French from getting their hands on them. This act did not prevent looting on a grand scale, but riches cannot replace food of which there was little. Napoleon soon realised that as the harsh, freezing winter progressed his men could starve to death, and so began the evacuation and retreat from Moscow on October 19th, 1812. With almost a hundred thousand men, all ill-equipped for winter, and with few supplies other than weaponry and munitions, they started the long and fearful retreat towards Russia's western border.

At least Henri was spared the deprivations and hardships suffered by these troops as they re-crossed the ravaged land, already laid bare by the original march to Moscow weeks earlier. Decomposing bodies still lay where they had been slain, now frozen stiff, and the first really heavy snows of winter fell three weeks into the march. Many men were in tatters, their boots worn through and some had no choice but to rob the corpses of anything that might prolong their own lives.

Due to the fact that everything seemed to have happened so quickly, Henri was unprepared for his return to the Loire Valley. Since his father's death there were few left now who remembered him, or who were overly concerned about his homecoming. Where in Saumur was he to go? At the Dépôt the Army Board had yet to re-assess his capabilities and were allowing him a period of rest and recuperation after his eight years in captivity. There had been interest shown in his mastery of the English language, although when he mentioned having a wife and family in England, he'd been told quite unceremoniously that according to French Law the marriage was not recognised and he should now find himself a good French woman. Henri ignored this remark, believing it best to hold his own council for a while at least. He did, of course wonder what circumstances had prompted his exchange after this length of time? Had General Exelman initiated the process after fleeing to France? The General had been friendly enough, although his opinion on marriages between officers and the enemy had not been favourable. Henri had no reason to suspect the fleeing Exelman to be behind anything but he couldn't help but wonder.

He finally arrived in Saumur after several days of arduous travel and having brought little clothing and only a few necessary items with him, Henri found himself in similar circumstances as on first reaching Chesterfield.

Installing himself temporarily in an inexpensive Inn he determined to settle his father's affairs first, if this had not already been done, then endeavour to locate any of his personal belongings that might still exist somewhere. There was no point in going to his parents' old home, for strangers would already be living there. He had an old uncle who lived several miles down river whom he'd not seen for years, and presuming that he was still alive, he decided that the meeting could wait a little longer. First he intended to visit his old mentor, the Abbé Rousseau.

As a result of oversleeping the following morning due to the exhaustion of travelling and his emotional strain, Henri decided to postpone business and stroll along familiar paths first.

The town had hardly changed in his absence, the Chateau de Saumur still dominated the river from its lofty heights, and unless the turrets had been moved he realised his drawing for Ruth was dreadfully inaccurate. He also made a mental note to count the arches on the bridge when he reached the Loire, and hoped one day to be able to correct the painting he'd done for her.

Within the town the mediaeval half timber-framed houses still lined the streets, which, in spite of the bright stonework at the base of each building were as dirty with human rubbish as ever. Most insanitary! Henri shrugged his shoulders, well aware that his countrymen had little regard for cleanliness. One thing in particular which had impressed Henri forcibly on his way back from San Domingo had been the contrasting state of English vessels to that of the French. The constant scrubbing of decks and the fumigations, although pungent and not particularly pleasant, did at least safeguard the welfare of the men as far as possible. Not that the streets of Chesterfield were a great deal cleaner than those in Saumur, but the frequent downpouring of rain there did much to swill the rubbish from the streets into the river Hipper below. He had taken pains to ensure Joseph never touched its waters as it was polluted by effluent from many sources, just as he himself certainly avoided some of the lower parts of town where open cess-pits were in evidence.

The Inn where he was residing was good enough for somewhere to sleep but he had no desire to dine there, instead he chose an eating house once noted for being the best in town.

When satisfied, his appetite appeased with a plate of freshly caught Loire salmon, vegetables and wine, Henri decided to walk down to the river. How he would have loved to have had young Joseph by his side to show him all the things he'd found exciting there as a boy. At that moment England was a very long way away! Taking the three miniatures from his pocket he held the one of Joseph towards the river. 'One day, my boy, I'll show you my river,' he said to himself.

Next morning Henri was woken early by the calling of a nearby cockerel. Thus disturbed he found it impossible to sleep again, and without Ruth by his side there was nothing to remain in bed for. He rose, remembering the day the caged linnet died causing Joseph to weep uncontrollably, until he had been forced to pacify him by going to 'Little Boney's' shop in the Market Square, and there buy a mechanical imported French bird with real feathers on. Twice afterwards Henri had been woken up early by its chirping and whistling when Joseph, always full of boyish mischief set it going.

Leaving the Inn, Henri made his way to the church of Notre Dame de Nantilly hoping to find his mentor the Abbé Rousseau still in residence there.

'Yes, Abbé Rousseau is still alive and well,' he was told on reaching the gate to the enclave. 'I'll see if he is free. Your name please?' The younger man bore no resemblance to anyone Henri had known there in the past.

'Please tell him Henri Pichon awaits his pleasure,' he said, happy and relieved that his old Priest was still in Saumur. Ten minutes passed before he finally heard footsteps on the stone-flagged passage leading from the main building.

The Abbé's face was wreathed in smiles as he came nearer. 'What a surprise,' he cried, overjoyed, his voice trembling. 'My son, you have returned to us at last!'

Henri's happiness at seeing his old employer and mentor from the past knew no bounds. He did, however, realise that the Abbé was no longer young, in fact he was becoming quite frail. 'Father,' Henri cried, embracing the man and kissing him. 'Yes, I am returned from England.' He released him and took a long look at the Abbé's face. He saw that time had increased the wrinkles on his aging brown skin and the eyes though alight with pleasure, had a tired look.

'Do I look so much older?' the Abbé asked with a wry smile as if reading Henri's thoughts. 'You called me father whereas it used to be brother.' This was no reprimand, mere a kindly acceptance that so much time had passed by. 'You were always a stubborn one.'

'I meant no harm,' Henri felt quite emotional as he reassuringly embraced the old man again. After a moment he released the Abbé who knew that Henri was deeply moved.

'You have been through much trouble, I think. Come inside and take a glass of wine with me,' the Abbé offered, 'I will be happy to hear of your travels.' He led Henri to a small plain room containing only a heavy wooden table, several chairs and a crucifix on one of the walls. 'Now tell me,' he asked, as he poured the wine, which had been placed on the table at his request when informed of Henri's arrival. 'How many years have you been away, ten at least?'

'Yes, ten, Father—may I call you that? It gives me great comfort to do so.' Henri took the goblet and sipped the sparkling white Saumur wine. 'That's wonderful, this is one of the things of Saumur that I missed most.'

The kindly old Abbé nodded. 'It would please me greatly for you to call me Father now!'

Henri continued. 'When I left the town last I was sent to San Domingo. Father, the atrocities and inhumanities there, on both sides I must add, distressed me greatly. I began to see that the black man had many reasons to hate the French, and of course treachery begets even more treachery. I was injured during a skirmish and hospitalised but then I caught yellow fever.' The Abbé listened intently. 'Because of the fever I could not return home with my regiment and ended up in a Fort which was without supplies. We were surrounded by infuriated natives intent on taking revenge on us, and were about to be annihilated by them when we were rescued by the English Navy. I was taken first to Jamaica then shipped to England. Once there I was confined in a terrible prison ship and would have died there if I had not accepted parole. Was that cowardly of me to do that, Father?'

The Abbé thought for a moment. 'What would have been the point of dying, my son? Providing you live a life worthy of being saved, that is the most important thing; that we become examples for good.'

'Thank you, Father. I have often tried to copy your example, but it isn't always easy, especially in the Army.'

'Would you have been happier in the Church, do you think? Though with conscription you had little choice.'

Henri shook his head and smiled. 'No, that never actually crossed my mind.'

'I never thought it had,' the Abbé smiled back. 'So, you were able to live as a free man in England?'

'It was frustrating to be constrained, and yet safe whilst France is so constantly at war.'

'It would seem that France will always be so, Henri! And what for? I think the reason has long since been lost. But tell me, I heard that you had found a wife, an English wife?'

Pleased to be able to express his feelings, Henri reached into his pocket, 'Yes, and I have two children.' He withdrew the three small ovals and placed them before his friend. 'I have done my best, a better artist would have made finer images of them but at least I will not forget their faces so easily with these.'

Taking the miniatures which Henri had so painstakingly created, the Abbé remarked, 'I never knew you could paint? They look good to me.'

'They don't do justice to their liveliness I'm afraid, but at least I am lucky to have such pictures when few men have been able to buy likenesses of their loved ones. My wife's name is Ruth.'

'Ruth was the loyal one in the Bible, of course!'

'Yes, and Ruth is a very loyal woman. We were married in a Protestant Church but of course here in France we would not in Law be married. We would have to marry again.'

'My son, if you married with the blessing of God then to me it would only be a legal necessity in France. In God's eyes you are married.'

'Thank you,' Henri said, and his face broke into a relieved smile. Finishing the remainder of the wine in his glass, he commented 'Ah! Such good wine, how I missed it.' A puzzled look then crossed his face. 'But Father, how did you know that I had married?'

'You seem to forget that your father and I were childhood friends. That is why, when the opportunity arose, I was able to find work for you here. We did not meet often, your father and I, our faiths being different, though I had hoped one day to make you one of us—but no matter, it wasn't to be!'

'I must have been very naïve, or too preoccupied,' Henri laughed.

'I prefer to think innocent. When you wrote from San Domingo your father asked me to read your letters; few that there were I might add,' this was not said unkindly. 'But this was not a chore.'

'Because he couldn't read or write I saw little point in writing too often, I believed he might have had to pay someone to read them to him, and it was difficult to put my feelings into words; especially so when all my letters had to be read by someone else. All my letters from England had to be scrutinised by the Agents before posting and it kills the spirit.' Henri paused, 'Did you write back for him on the odd occasions when he replied—was it you?'

The old Abbé nodded. 'You never needed to know. He was a proud man.'

'Then I owe you for your time, but for your kindness I cannot repay you, only thank you!'

'There is no need, your father made small donations when he could. You have no need to worry.' As from the past, Henri recognised the signs when the Abbé was determined to have the last word. 'Now, about this family of yours, what is to happen to them?'

'They are comfortable and safer in England than they would be here. Because I am unsure of what the Army wants of me now, as I have a bad chest when the weather is cold and damp, a consequence of the fever, things are uncertain. I haven't decided whether to bring my wife here after the war is over or go back there to stay. It is thanks to you that I eventually started to teach French in an English school. I owe so much to you!'

'My son, an Abbé should not have pride, pride is a sin, but I am proud of you. All those times I struggled to teach you when I thought you weren't listening, and quite often I was right! Nevertheless it has paid off.' The pair laughed, the Abbé's eyes twinkling merrily.

'But my mother, my father, where are they buried? Who saw to their affairs?'

'I did!'

Henri was startled. 'You?'

'It was no hardship. They are interred in the Protestant Cemetery as your father wanted. The cost was met by selling what furniture they had, their few personal possessions are here in a box. If you had never returned I would have raised money with them and sent it to England to your wife. I'm afraid your civilian clothes I gave to the poor.'

'It is a small enough payment to make for what you have done, Father!' Henri was humbled to think of the Abbé's kindness in his absence.

'You were in no position to do it. However, if you can return tomorrow I will have the box ready for you to collect.' The sound of a bell rang out. 'It is time for vespers, I must go. God Bless you my Son.'

Henri embraced the Abbé, 'You have given me encouragement for the future, Father!' he said, then kissed his mentor and left.

The visit had given Henri a boost to his spirits, just as speaking with his old tutor always had. Of course, as a boy, Henri found the Abbé's constant aim to educate and his lecturing irritated him, he would have preferred to daydream, but now he appreciated the benefits he had received. He was also intrigued as to what few possessions were in the box awaiting his collection. As he was free of the burden of taking care of his father's affairs, there remained little more to do before he could return to Paris to see what the future held for him. Evening was approaching and he returned to the Inn to read and while away the rest of the day.

The following morning, taking the Montée Du Petit Genève which ran alongside the Protestant cemetery, Henri was well aware that his task of finding his parent's grave would be difficult after all these years, as he couldn't know if there had been a headstone made for them. He entered the cemetery and eventually located the badly neglected family plot he'd been shown as a boy. He was quite moved to find both his mother's and father's names inscribed there very simply on his grandmother's headstone, no doubt done at the instigation of Abbé Rousseau.

Henri stayed for a while, savouring his memories and paying homage before proceeding to collect his box, the contents of which were still a mystery. These proved to be of little monetary value, not that Henri had expected any surprises, he just couldn't remember what might have been selected for him from the family home after ten years absence. Mostly they were mementoes which the Abbé considered worth keeping in the hopes of Henri surviving imprisonment.

There was his father's pipe, well chewed and discoloured and a treasured working knife, simple things, not much to show for a life-time's work. There were two sets of decorative buttons, which his mother had re-used several times, and the silk ribbons with which she trimmed her clothing on special occasions. These all lay on top of Henri's books, pens and papers with a few bits and pieces which might be of use. Henri packed everything back in the box which he then left for safe keeping by Abbé Rousseau, requesting that it should be sent to John Bower for Ruth, if anything happened to him, otherwise he would collect them when the war was over.

The more he explored his beloved Saumur the more he began to accept his lack of connection now for the place as, except for the old Abbé, he had no one here to whom he was close, no home, and no occupation other than his military service. The Army had been his life. There was no longer anything to offer his wife and family here in Saumur. Thus Henri decided that once his business was completed he would return to the Holding Dépôt in Paris, and be prepared to accept whatever orders awaited him there. He did not relish the prospect!

One final task remained before he moved on and that was to visit Hortense, and this was a totally different matter. Would she actually expect him to contact her? Did she even know of his return? He was ashamed of himself for not having written to her to say that she shouldn't wait for him, but she couldn't have read his letter even if he had done. What if she had waited, only then to be told he had married in England? It was a dilemma of his own making and only he could solve it. Having passed the message via his father telling her to forget him had simply not been good enough. Now, whatever the consequences, pleasant or otherwise, chivalry demanded that he at least made some effort to make amends.

Walking along the Quai Mayaud by the Loire the next day, Henri was exhilarated to be able to travel without the earlier restricting limits of his parole. Even so, ten miles suddenly felt like twenty to him in spite of pacing himself. At least his footsteps followed the river where there was much going on; from the trains of chalands, the flat-bottom barges each with its single square sail, battling the currents as they forced their way upstream; to the galiote with its fish-holding tanks which belonged to the fishermen. All manner of goods were being plied from town to town on this watery roadway as Henri proceeded towards the small village of Turquant where Hortense and her family lived. His fascination for these various activities on the Loire masked his weariness as he neared his destination and, considering it a necessity to boost his flagging energy, Henri fortified himself with some wine before approaching the house he sought.

As was customary in the region the door of the house stood ajar, and he recognised Hortense's mother as she sat on the wide doorstep, making the most of the fine weather before the cold winds ushered winter in. Only having met the woman half a dozen times previously,

Henri wondered if she would in turn recognise him now, after so long.

He need not have worried for rumour had already reached Turquant from the gossips of Saumur, that he had been seen in the town. Several passers-by had acknowledged Henri during the five days since his arrival, one or two had even passed the time of day. One man had talked at length, asking how he fared and what he was doing back in Saumur, when it was believed he was a prisoner in English hands? It was therefore inevitable that news had spread even this far out of town.

'Bonjour,' he said raising his hat and bowing slightly. 'I hope you are well?' The woman made to rise but Henri could see she was having some difficulty. 'Please, don't bother getting up, Madame. May I sit beside you?'

Shuffling along to make more room, the old woman indicated her acceptance. 'I heard you were back,' she said, 'so the English didn't want you any more?' She clucked like a hen, eyeing him sharply. 'You've got a few grey hairs now!'

Henri had never liked Hortense's mother's open way with words, it was as if she spoke first and thought afterwards. 'Is Hortense living hereabouts?' he asked, ignoring the remark.

'No business of yours, is it?'

'I came to explain the futility of her waiting for me when I was a prisoner in England. I had no intention of hurting her, but I couldn't write to her to explain that. I thought I might not survive the war. I wanted her to find happiness while she was young enough to enjoy life.'

'Very noble of you, but she got the message, second-hand of course.'

'But Hortense couldn't read or write, so how was I to tell her?' He was a little annoyed at her tone and began to wonder if he would have been better off staying away. 'I've come as soon as I could to see her, to apologise and to explain.'

'Funny prison, where you can marry and have children,' the old woman retorted sarcastically.

It occurred to Henri that she was probably incapable of understanding much beyond the village and Saumur, and decided not to pursue the subject but to find and talk to Hortense directly, and then return to his lodgings. 'It is to Hortense to whom I owe the apology. Where is she?'

'In Saumur, where else? There's no room here,' she waved a hand back towards the house. 'She's a married woman now with two children, and her husband's somewhere at the Russian front. You leave her alone, she's happy enough!'

'Madame,' Henri replied sternly, 'I will not go to find her. Just tell her I called and why. I shall be moving on within a day or two.' He got to his feet, 'I wish you all good fortune.' He replaced his hat and walked away after having the satisfaction of seeing the surprise and discomfort on her face over his chastening remarks. Ignoring her flustered protestations he continued on his way seeing little or no point in trying to excuse himself further. Had she become his mother-in-law he felt sure all would not have been well!

The result of such a long journey and his arduous exercise brought Henri to the conclusion that he was far from fit, but apart from the altercation with Hortense's mother he had enjoyed the day. Now, having partaken of a reasonable meal he retired to his room to contemplate his next move.

The longer he stayed in Saumur the more money he would spend, money that was precious to both himself and Ruth. The best solution was to return to the Dépôt where he would at least have his accommodation and rations provided free of charge, but before leaving he intended to pay one last visit to the Abbé who had been unavailable when Henri called to see his box. This time it was to check that his mentor was willing to keep it until the end of the war and, if necessary, to ensure that someone would carry out his request if anything happened to the Abbé himself.

The Abbé joined Henri in the grounds between the church and the high wall which separated it from the street outside. 'You look more contented,' the Abbé remarked as the pair sat on a bench near the wall, 'and I understand you've seen the box with your belongings. I hope I chose wisely, but I didn't know what was more important amongst what was left.'

'I think you chose remarkably well, Father. I can't even remember what was in the house after so long a time, and without your help I would have nothing left of the past, so I am in your debt, again.' Henri paused and looked around. The leaves on the trees were beginning to fall, thus heralding the approach of winter and frosty nights. 'I am going back to Paris tomorrow to the Holding Dépôt there, where I won't keep spending money which I cannot really afford. Will it be in order for me to leave the box here until after the war?'

'I have already put it back in storage along with instructions for its eventual disposal. If God is willing I shall be happy to hand it to you when the time comes; if not, all is prepared.'

'Father, your attention to my affairs has been a source of comfort, and I am very grateful. The names on the gravestone in the cemetery I presume was also your doing? I must pay you what it cost.'

The Abbé shook his head. 'No, my son, all the money from your father's goods and chattels covered that too. If you feel you must, then a small contribution to the Church would be more than welcome.'

Henri felt in his pocket, knowing that his already diminishing funds were becoming an embarrassment. The Abbé realised that after years of struggling to make ends meet as a prisoner, Henri could not have much money, especially with a family to keep, and added, 'Just slip a Louis or two in the collection box as you go, it will be sufficient.' He hoped this suggestion would help Henri to keep his self-respect.

At last the Abbé could be spared no longer from his duties and the two men prepared to part company. 'May God bless you and keep you safe, my son,' he said, giving Henri a blessing, 'and all the sons of France!' He bent and added softly to Henri, 'And England's. We're all God's children.'

For the last time Henri embraced his friend. 'If all men were like you, Father, there would be no fighting,' he said, his voice full of admiration. 'God be with you also. Good-bye.'

'Not Au revoirs?' the Abbé asked with a woeful smile. The remark had not been made through any intuition but Henri wondered why he had bid a final farewell to his mentor and hoped it was not a sign of foreboding.

When Henri left Saumur he did so wondering if he would ever return, and as the coach took the road North he sat back, enjoying the pleasant and familiar sights, only to realise that he had forgotten to count the number of arches of the Pont Cassart!

The journey back to Paris lasted three days and when Henri arrived there news was coming through that Napoleon had evacuated Moscow in order to avoid the approaching bitter winter.

When he reached the Dépôt, Henri soon found himself ordered to take a physical training course at the French College. Here he had great difficulty knuckling down to the fierce discipline and it wasn't long before it became obvious that the damage caused by his bout of yellow fever rendered him incapable of front line fighting ever again. Accordingly he was informed that an assessment would be made as to where his military experiences could be best used. These together with his mastery of the English language meant he was in a unique position, under certain circumstances, to be of service even now.

He was eager to explore Paris having been there only twice before whilst in transit with his regiment, times when there had been no opportunity to see the well-known sights about which he had heard so much. This situation he determined to rectify before being sent to some far-flung part of the world.

He found Sundays in the Capital were occupied in a variety of ways depending on each individual's choice. The religious went to church, the lonely became lonelier, and the happy and frivolous went to the parks. For Henri, alone once more, he thought a stroll in the park amongst families and young people might brighten his day. Without Ruth he had no desire to go to church, and so considered that a walk along the banks of the Seine first would give him greater solace. The two magnificent new bridges of Austerlitz and Jena had been completed across the river, and were suitable reminders of earlier French victories.

Henri was well wrapped-up against the cool breeze and he half expected the popular Tivoli Gardens to be empty now that summer was long past, so he was surprised to see so many there. It was hardly a peaceful haven within the walls of Paris as people of all social classes were mixed together for relaxation in their simple everyday clothes. There was delightful lively music playing and couples dancing; the only uniforms in evidence belonging to the patrolling soldiers. He stood and watched several performances by both excellent and poor jongleurs and comedians, mindful all the time of the difference between being alone and being able to share what he saw with Ruth and the children.

In spite of the happiness around him the gardens were still a lonely place for Henri so he rejected the idea of returning there later that evening to watch the firework display. For him to do so and stand beneath the light of a thousand lamps to watch the gaiety and listen to the music would be too much, and would evoke longings which he was striving to suppress.

It was actually hard to believe that there was a war going on and, in spite of the cooler weather, families still congregated on the grass and seats to eat what food they had brought. Children scampered into the woodland areas reminding him again of Joseph and Marie.

He must have looked a sad and lonely figure leaning on a railing admiring these activities because he was suddenly joined by two women who sidled up, one on either side of him. Aware of what they might be up to, he was mindful to be careful. Simultaneously both women began to edge closer and he turned to the tallest on his left, who flirted outrageously with him supposing him to be out for pleasure. Still very aware that there were two of them perhaps intent on robbing him, he turned quickly and placed his back against the railing. Neither woman could be considered anything other than coarse and of low class so naturally Henri wanted nothing to do with them. Had he been years younger he might have returned their flighty banter with a few quips before going on his way. Now though he was in no mood to be so accosted, but, because there were two of them it was difficult to disengage himself without causing a scene.

'I have no money, girls,' he stated bluntly with an air of authority, 'nor time for fun! I have been ordered to watch out for thieves and wanton women!' He must have suitably impressed them for they quickly withdrew and hurried off into the crowds. Henri smiled inwardly, prided himself on his quick thinking and left the park to explore further, an occupation which was giving him great pleasure after years of restriction.

He walked seemingly for hours then came upon the bronze column in the Place Vendôme which had been cast from 1,200 melted cannon captured from France's enemies. How many of these, he wondered, might have been made in Chesterfield and were now displayed before him here in Paris? It was such a small world.

On another day when the wind blew cold and biting over Paris, making it difficult for him to breathe easily without coughing, he visited the Louvre where he realised his own attempts at painting left a lot to be desired. He wasn't aware that some of the finest paintings in Europe that hung there had been brought from places the French had conquered and plundered.

Whilst Henri was exploring Paris, Napoleon's demoralised and depleted army, dressed in ragged summer-weight uniforms and wearing worn-out shoes and boots, plodded homewards.

News had reached Napoleon that a conspiracy had been uncovered in Paris to stage a Republican coup d'état and thereby overthrow him and his regime. As a result, he left his troops and returned post-haste to the Capital leaving behind in his wake a wretched trail of thousands of men struggling through freezing snow and blizzards, all the while being harassed by marauding peasants intent on revenge. These starving battalions in Russia foraged to find food for themselves and were ambushed constantly by Cossacks.

In Paris, meanwhile, Henri saw the approach of Christmas with a feeling of gloom. His cough was once again made worse by the winds which laid him low, and in his letters to Ruth he allowed this distress to show. When, eventually, these were read by her, Christmas had passed, the continental weather was at its harshest and she was powerless to help him. All she could do was worry and in the circumstances chose not to burden him further with the news that she was almost four months pregnant with their third child.

The news from Russia steadily worsened. The retreating army had already lost 5,000 horses which had perished and now lay beside the icy roads amongst the unburied bodies of men killed weeks earlier on the march to Moscow. It was also becoming increasingly obvious that the Emperor needed all the men he could muster if his regime was to survive, and if France was not to be occupied by the previously capitulating nations who were now turning against him. Might Napoleon become so desperate that he would call even the sick to arms? This was Henri's greatest fear.

If 1812 was a disastrous year for Napoleon and a heartbreaking one for Henri and Ruth, one good thing did emerge that would benefit mankind and could prevent future armies from starving. In London a businessman named Bryan Donkin established Britain's first canned food factory in Bermondsey, producing tin-coated iron cans that would preserve the life of food for long periods. He would later establish a large factory in Chesterfield.

Chapter 13   1813
A Changing World

*B*y 1813 the French Army that Henri had re-joined after his return from England was a very different one to that with which he had originally seen action in Egypt and San Domingo, the quality and capability of the soldiers was now showing a marked change. With war on so many fronts Napoleon's front-line elite, comprising seasoned professionals, had been decimated and these losses were now being replaced by hurriedly trained inexperienced conscripts. Those war-weary and disheartened soldiers who had survived the long and cruel retreat from Moscow were all mentally and physically exhausted. Europe had at last seen that Napoleon could be brought to his knees and if, and this was the crux of it, all countries affected by France's actions bonded together and remained firm in their resolve he could be curtailed, even destroyed. But Henri knew Napoleon would fight to the death using men from as many of his allies as were still with him, and these would be his gun-fodder.

In Chesterfield John Bower was Mayor again for the seventh and last time, and was a widower with three daughters on his hands who were intent on courting. He was no longer as robust as he had been during his previous terms in office, and still deeply missed his wife Isabella. He'd begun to think of his daughters as permanent residents in Spital Lodge, especially as within a year all would be over the age of thirty. Suddenly, with their mother's death, each one seemed intent on moving on, and suitors were beginning to call regularly at the house.

Poor Ruth increased in size as each month passed and she was grateful and overjoyed to receive Henri's letters and any monies he sent, as the latter saved her delving into the nest-egg which they had set aside for their future. This contact, tenuous though it was, also gave her assurance that he loved her! Henri was extremely cautious over what he wrote in case his loyalty to France should be thought in doubt, but he reminded her constantly of his intentions to return as soon as he could.

Ruth habitually read the *Mercury* and any other reports on the progress of the war, and was heartened to read of Britain's growing confidence as Wellington successfully continued in his actions to drive the French from the Spanish Peninsula.

Early in the month of June, Henri received a letter which amazed and immensely pleased him, for he was now the father of another daughter, conceived in the passionate but tearful days before he left Chesterfield. He understood why Ruth had not told him of her condition for fear of worrying him, but he was naturally concerned as to her health and her needs in coping with three children. That he fretted about this was obvious in the tender letter he penned immediately and sent by return. He also wrote out a copy of the letter which he posted several days later in case the first went astray. He now knew more emphatically than ever that he had to survive the war, he had to return, for how else would he see Henrietta, his new daughter?

By the end of the year, the war-torn countries that Napoleon had left behind him were starting to join together in anti-French alliances to drive him back and contain him in his own land. In fact, France was now in danger of being over-run and occupied by those joint forces. If Henri was dismayed that his beloved country was in danger, he was also heartened by the fact that the end of the war was probably approaching.

At home Ruth's optimism grew whenever she read of one of Napoleon's defeats and of the increasing talk about those nations ravaged by him, who were now considering banding together. There were other times, however, when she worried for Henri's safety, especially when she read that Napoleon was conscripting thousands of sixteen-year-old boys and retired veterans to increase the strength of his badly depleted army. Would he go as far as to use sick or weakened men? Was Henri at risk? Had Henri in fact told her everything, restricted as he was, or was he, as she had done to him, shielding her from the awful possibilities? He'd been gone over a year now, a year in which she'd carried their third child concealing her fears and discomforts from him, but how she longed for his presence at her side, to have him comfortingly and protectingly put his arms around her. Often in her lowest days she cried with fear that something untoward would happen to him and that she would never see him again.

Chapter 14 1814
A Time for Optimism

In the new year of 1814, over 100,000 Frenchmen, many of them being the sixteen-year-old conscripts, faced 350,000 allied troops on the Eastern Front as Napoleon widened his action once more. Brilliant though his campaign was, it was also a hopeless one against such large opposition, especially as Wellington in the south was already advancing on French soil. But Napoleon, becoming complacent and even foolhardy, had left the city of Paris badly exposed, and the invasion of France had begun.

As early as February 21st, Ruth read in a newspaper the exciting news that Napoleon had died and that the allies were in Paris! She was however frightened for Henri's safety, never knowing if the delay in hearing from him was due to problems with the mail or if he was ill.

Unfortunately Napoleon was very much alive, with the allies still fighting him, and it wasn't until March 31st that the French Capital fell into the hands of Russian and Prussian troops.

When this took place there were cries of 'Quel bien spectacle' at the sight of contingents of cavalrymen with their magnificent horses and the parade of awesome guns, as the allies entered Paris. The war-weary inhabitants gave a joyful welcome and applauded as the horses drank eagerly from the city's fountains. Amongst all this jubilation, Henri excitedly began to make plans. When things quietened down, he would resign from the army and make his way to England. In the meantime, prisoners would be returning and be in need of rehabilitation, food and clothing, so his job was not yet finished. That night he wrote to Ruth:

Paris 31st March, 1814

Mon petit Anges,

Have you heard the news! At last the war is over!

Now at last I can allow myself the luxury of believing that I will soon be able to return to my home and family. I can hardly keep my pen on the paper for thinking of that time to come. Today all of Paris is rejoicing that peace is here, there is much wild dancing after 22 years of war. Who cares now if we lost, all ordinary people wanted was peace.

How are you and my beloved angels, how I long to see you all. I write in stops and starts, so excited am I at the thought, I am having trouble thinking straight. I squeeze my own hand—it is true? I look out of the window and see the April sunshine and want to dance in the streets too, but I have no one to dance with.

I go too fast! I have not asked how you are? I do not know when you will get this letter as everything will be delayed and confused. I intend to find the best way to get this to England as fast as is possible. Sadly, I may have to stay here a while longer to help sort things out before I can resign from the army, but I will come as soon as I am able. I will write again in a few days when I know how things are going here. Now I can write unguardedly without my falling under suspicion.

I am overjoyed that I can finally see a way of getting to England, if only on leave for a short time. Everything is in the air. What can I say? I am too full at this unexpected news. Are you excited too? A longer letter will follow, in the meantime you must know that my thoughts are always with you. I live and work simply to this end. To think that my children will not know me brings tears to my eyes, there is so much time to make up for. Oh, I do become too excited and fearful that this happiness will not last!

I write no more because my heart overflows with love. Yes, I am well and Spring brings me further respite. I will sleep tonight better than I have since I left you. Embrace and kiss my angels for me.

Henri

The news that the war had ended reached London three days later but did not appear in the *Derby Mercury* until April 7th, by which time everyone knew that the country was at peace again.

The war was over! Chesterfield was buzzing with jubilation, even the prisoners rejoiced, not at France's capitulation but that as a consequence they should soon be returning home. But home to what?

Eager hands on all sides seized each newly-printed newspaper when it arrived, whilst those who couldn't read waited impatiently for someone to pass on any news of the developments in Europe. Would peace hold this time, and what of Napoleon?

In the small red-brick terraced house in Glumangate, Ruth laughed and cried simultaneously. She took Joseph and Marie's small hands in hers and did a little jig round the room. 'Papa will be returning,' she laughed almost hysterically as the children joined her in wild innocent happiness.

'When will he come?' Joseph asked. He was five years old now, with all the inquisitiveness of a small boy. 'Will he mend the bird for me?' he asked with implicit faith which touched Ruth and she laughed, a laugh which almost turned to a sob, resulting from the deep emotional relief the news had brought.

'If it can be mended,' she said gently, 'it may not be possible, the spring might be broken.'

'Papa is a soldier, he will do it!' Joseph insisted, leaving Ruth speechless at Joseph's faith in Henri. But when, and how? A shiver ran through her. Once before the war had ended but all her joy had been destroyed when the news eventually came through that William was dead. She dropped down listlessly on a chair, her face suddenly streaming with tears. She wiped them away quickly lest the children saw them. Please, not again, she prayed silently to herself. Please, not again!

Henri's letter did not arrive for three weeks, during which time Ruth waited, beside herself with worry. All around things were happening, rumour and her hundred tongues spread dubious information everywhere about everything, and no-one knew what to believe.

When at last Henri's all-important letter reached Ruth it was by the hand of John Bower, who made a point of delivering it immediately instead of waiting for Ruth to call at his office in daily expectation. John knocked on her door and waited, he was certainly not expecting the reaction he got, for as Ruth opened it and saw him standing there, she fainted.

When she came round she found herself surrounded by two fretting children and a flustered old man. 'Is it Henri?' she cried in anguish.

'Just a letter from him,' John Bower explained, completely bewildered by what had taken place. Ruth struggled to get up and John placed a steadying hand under her elbow to help. 'I thought I would bring it for you rather than wait until you called.'

'Oh, how foolish of me, for a moment I thought you had brought bad news,' she cried apologetically, 'I do appreciate your bringing it to me.'

'Would you like me to make you a cup of tea?' he offered, 'or would you rather be left alone to read Henri's letter?'

'I think I shall feel better prepared to read it if I had a cup of tea first, thank you!' She felt quite strained after weeks of uncertainty, and held the letter unopened on her lap. The colour, which had drained from her face, had almost fully returned when she took the tea from John and drank. 'Please do have one yourself,' she offered.

'I'll not stay if you don't mind. You look a better now, so I'll let you get on with your reading. I hope it's really good news.'

'I'm so grateful—do forgive my stupidity, but I thought fate had taken a hand once again.'

John Bower was now aware of the shock Ruth must have felt. 'Fortunately it does not seem to have done so. Well, I'll let myself out now and you must try not to fret so much!' Smiling at her he replaced his hat and left Ruth prising open the seal Henri had affixed to his letter.

Back in Paris Henri's near fluency with the English language was an advantage but he was also careful in letting it be known that he had the ability to use it.

Walking one day along the banks of the Seine dressed in civilian clothing, he heard a voice, an English voice, and decided to linger, fascinated by the man's accent for it reminded him of Ruth. He slackened his pace and fell in behind two men, one English, one Prussian, who were both conversing in English. They were obviously discussing some incident which had taken place earlier in the day.

'It seemed a little harsh to me,' the Englishman was saying, 'the war is over and I believe we must treat them with respect or it will all begin again.'

The Prussian quickly replied, a little heatedly, 'You English know nothing of the sufferings war brings, as we do! Your country was not over-run by French armies as ours has been, or you would feel the same. The French behaved cruelly in Prussia, destroying our homes, violating our wives, mothers and sisters, and murdering them when they'd satisfied themselves. They taught us lessons which we have come to France to put into practice!'

'I can understand your bitterness. Yes, England is fortunate in being an island, and I hope our soldiers had better self-control. However, we also have ruthless blackguards in our midst; I cannot say our hands are lily-white.'

The Prussian however, had not finished. 'There are thousands of allied soldiers in Paris, it wouldn't take long to stir them into action if the French don't keep their word.'

Henri, having heard the heated exchange and well aware of the atrocities meted out on all sides, let the men go forward without interruption. Had the conversation been light-hearted he might have introduced himself and exchanged pleasantries, including asking the Englishman about his origins. The war, however, was too fresh in everyone's mind and Henri considered it better not to become embroiled in the conversation.

The result of this encounter served to re-enforce something he'd begun to accept; he could not guarantee the safety of Ruth and the children here in Paris! It was also too early in the aftermath of war to contemplate moving back to Saumur where he would need to find employment. Thousands of men no longer needed by the army would also find it difficult to obtain work. His knowledge of English would not be of use in the majority of situations, thus he had a dilemma on his hands and until it was resolved Ruth and the children were safer where they were. He did not want to alarm Ruth and this meant that it would take some time for him to formulate in his mind just what he should put in his next letter home.

Several days after receiving Henri's letter Ruth received two more from Paris, the first being the copy of the earlier one which he had taken the precaution to write, the second written days later:

Paris April 11th, 1814

Mon petit Anges,

So much has happened here in Paris. I hope you are in receipt of my earlier letters written amidst all the excitement of the war's end. Always I am thinking that at last we will be together again, my thoughts are constantly with you. Somewhere I think any letters from you must be lost as I have not received one for two months now. I think that it will get better for writing soon.

Are you and the children well? Now the summer is coming they will be able to go walks with you. Oh, how I wish I could be there, for I would be allowed to explore the places which everyone said are so beautiful beyond the hills which I could see only in the distance.

But I must tell you of the happenings here. Napoleon has abdicated, as you will know from the newspapers, but I was there to see that happen! After all the anguish he has caused on France's behalf, the people of Paris are themselves now relieved to get rid of him. However, I am not so sure about the feelings in the countryside, there is a different attitude I think. Napoleon has gone to Fontainebleau until they decide finally what to do with him, and Louis XVIII is to return from England.

I do not think it wise for you to come here yet, for your own safety, for some months. There are too many foreign soldiers, thousands of them in Paris who, given chance might seek revenge. I would rather have you safe in England than by my side in danger. Please be patient, we have waited so long and have been lucky. Patience is a horrible word because it stops us doing what we desire to do. Please trust me. Embrace and kiss the children for me. I would that I could hold you in my arms again soon,

Henri

As the deposed Emperor Napoleon, once commander of a mighty fighting machine, said an emotional farewell to his elite guards at Fontainebleau Palace, he kissed their Standard then left, in order to board *HMS Inconstant* bound for the small island of Elba in the Mediterranean Sea. With only 86 miles of barren land to rule over, his restless spirit would be near impossible to suppress. What could he do with the rest of his life?

On May 2nd, Louis XVIII arrived at the Tuileries from Hartwell in England where he had been living in exile. The House of Bourbon had returned and the white banner bearing the ancient arms of France flew once more; whilst on the other hand the cavalry veterans considered that Napoleon was not so much in exile as 'away on leave'. There was too much still unsettled in France for Henri to do anything but bide his time and be patient too.

What Henri did not tell Ruth, however, was that according to the Treaty of Paris, which Napoleon signed, the strength of the French Army was to be drastically reduced in size. Consequently many officers would have to be taken off the active list and retired on half-pay, particularly those who were sick or wounded, and Henri held his breath knowing that the sword of Damocles hung precariously over his own head. Fortunately he had been selected to work in the Holding Dépôt's offices to help oversee and administer these reductions, payments and repatriations of prisoners, so that for a while he was safe in his lowly position, but for how long was unpredictable.

On the day the King returned to Paris, Henri, though not a Royalist, considered the future stability of his beloved France would be more secure in Louis' hands than it had been in Napoleon's. He too placed a white feather in his hat and joined the excited crowds that lined the capital's boulevards.

Returning home after the grand firework display celebrating the King's return and emotionally drained by the sheer enormity of the day's events, Henri decided to tell Ruth what had happened:

Paris May 2nd, 1814

Mon petit Anges,

Are you receiving my letters? Time is going very slowly and much needs sorting out. Are the little ones well and happy? I think of them and you always, you are always in my heart and I write in the hope that you do get all my letters. The coming of Spring finds my health improving and I am not bored, there is too much to do and many problems to solve—not mine but those for France.

The Bourbons are back! King Louis XVIII arrived from England and I went to watch with the crowds when he arrived. How I wish you were here to see the spectacle. The day dawned unclouded and delightful. Everywhere in Paris garlands of white lilies hung from window to window, tapestries fluttered from other windows above the gathering crowds who awaited the King's arrival. There were white cockades in everyone's hats, and cannons fired whilst bells rang out. Who could complain at noise when it proclaimed joy and excitement. Joseph would have seen something to remember for his whole life. The King's carriage and his entourage crossed the river so that he could enter the splendid cathedral of Notre Dame which stands on an island in the middle of the Seine. I waited for a long time for him to re-appear and followed the crowd to the Pont Neuf, where a woman descended from the sky in a balloon, releasing several white pigeons of peace to the sound of cannons. I pretended that you were all by my side as I followed the King to the Palace where eventually he appeared at the window, while musicians of the Conservatoire played beneath him on the ground below.

I have tried to paint a picture in your head so that we can share the exhibition because I fear it might be some time before I can see you. At least I am being paid, so many are not! Be patient, my love, I am eventually coming.

There is poverty here and the returning prisoners will not find it easy to survive. The Government will have to reduce the size of the army now there is peace and so far I am lucky to have been given employment.

Thankfully I have now received several of your letters, they are always precious to me. How glad I am that I painted your images, I keep them next to my heart but I am one short, for I have nothing of Henrietta, no picture or memory, this saddens me very much. I like it when you tell me about her.

I am pleased that John Bower is still receiving the Bank Drafts for you, or I work for nothing. Here is a little drawing I made of the woman and the balloon, for the children. My heart cries out in anguish sometimes at the distance between us, but I too must be patient.

Embrace the children and kiss them for me. For you, my love, I will always be, yours,

Henri.

Inspired by Henri's cheerful communication, and knowing that he was now receiving her letters, Ruth hastened to reply.

5, Glumangate,
Chesterfield.
May 18th, 1814

My dear, dear Husband,

I now have three letters! All received since peace was declared in March and how deeply thankful I am to hear that you are safe and well, and have at last got my letters. The newspapers here are full of rumours that take weeks sometimes to be proved right or wrong.

I love you to tell me what you are doing so that I can understand how you live. Thank you always for your letters, even though they make me cry. Also for the money which must be a great sacrifice to send, I will not waste it dear.

213

The prisoners are excited at the thought of going home, and appear more friendly now that we are no longer their enemies. Do you remember Monsieur Fleche who played the violin so well and Monsieur Labrosse and his horn? They were mentioned in the papers because, along with other 'French Gentlemen, lately prisoners of Chesterfield', they gave a concert in Sheffield which was well attended. This was despite an unseasonal fall of snow for May and then incessant rain. It sounded like a delightful and appreciated performance of good will. I did feel so proud to read of this, having known for so long that Frenchmen can be honourable and kind. This I learned from you, my husband.

The children miss you, but not as much as I do—they cannot possibly, can they? When you said you had no image of Henrietta I'm afraid I was very wasteful and paid to have a small picture of her painted for you. Am I forgiven? I don't think I will send it until you tell me it is secure for me to do so. Please tell me when!

The weather is improving and this puts a spring in my step. We often go walks now, past all the places we went to, and I stand there thinking that you are with me. You are not forgotten and I long to have you hold me in your arms.

I cannot write for too long without tears flowing, neither can I say what is really in my heart. Henrietta can walk at last, it is sad you cannot see her.

When the last Frenchman leaves town I will feel a deep loss because I pretend when I see them that you are still here. I will not then be able to hear your language spoken again. I'm afraid Joseph has wound the bird up too many times until the spring has broken. He awaits your return to mend it—do you think you could buy another before you leave Paris? Now that there is more light in the evenings I am able to take in more sewing, so we are managing in spite of the increasing cost of everything.

I am trying to be patient, yet I suppose I must try harder. I always hope that each letter will be the last and that we can be together again instead.

I think of you every night. The children kiss this letter here, as I do!

Good night my dear husband,

Your Ruth.

Paris was now a city of duels. A city of promenading, swaggering members of the Royal Household; and a city with poorly-clad, impoverished officers living and sleeping up to five in a garret, such were the miseries of half-pay. Some were no better off than the prisoners had been on parole in England. Henri's early return had given him an advantage in that he was already in a position to be useful to the authorities. Having been a prisoner of war himself, he knew what the men had been through and knew how difficult rehabilitation would be for many in the present political climate.

Towards the end of May the prisoners on parole were beginning to leave Chesterfield after their long sojourn on English soil. Most were desperate to return home, although many were a little afraid of the future after living with little to occupy their minds or hands for so long. Some saw no reason to return at all, whilst those who had married in England had the painful job of taking their wives and children away from loving parents and grandparents, who would probably never see them again.

All the French prisoners of war still held in Britain had received a letter from the commissioners who had arrived from France to regulate their return, to the effect that King Louis XVIII had applied to the Prince Regent for their release, and as fast as conveyances could be made available they would all be sent home. By this time about 3,000 men who had been confined in prisons and 86 officers from the parole system had already departed for their homeland. Unfortunately those that had died would remain on English soil as would 1,700 who had perished in the prison at Norman Cross.

The citizens of Chesterfield had long since accepted the presence of the prisoners, and many landladies missed not just the income from their lodgers but their company too. For years, many corresponded with their departed guests, but there were children in other towns who sadly never saw their fathers again, and wives who had been abandoned to their fate. Those men who did stay usually worked hard and raised respectable families in the towns of their parole. For women like Ruth, it was a matter of waiting until it was safe for them to travel to France or for their husbands to come back to them. This latter case was unfortunately a rare occurrence.

Just as France needed to reduce her military might after the war in order to reduce costs, so did England. Men returned to their home towns and villages and attempted to re-establish their lives and find employment. The financial impact was particularly bad in places like Chesterfield which had lost the small but useful income from the prisoners, and the falling demand for war materials hit industries badly.

There was an influx of unemployed ex-soldiers, some of whom were sick and wounded but all seeking help in their predicament. Ruth was extremely fortunate in having a home that was rent free, plus a small but important income from Henri and savings which the pair had prudently put to one side for emergencies. These, together with the income from Ruth's sewing, meant that she was more able than many to cope. She also realised that she could not ask Henri to resign from the army to come home to her, only to face unemployment. He was right, they would have to be patient. She knew from friends that some people in the town considered her to be yet another English wife abandoned by her French husband, but she held her head high and let it be known that she trusted Henri who wrote regularly to her.

As the year of 1814 progressed, extra or increased taxes were placed on such necessary commodities as soap, candles, paper, sugar and bread; wages were low and the Poor Relief Fund was stretched to the limit. Small farms began to go bankrupt and there was a genuine fear in Government circles that there could be a revolution in England, as there had been in France, because of the spreading poverty affecting all classes.

Ruth made a point of reading newspapers in the town's Reading Room, and often items other than those regarding the continuing economic gloom caught her eye. In August the British, still at war with America, burned down the White House in Washington DC, then on Christmas Eve Britain and America made peace.

Henri was now becoming optimistic in his thoughts and he began to plan for their future together. At last he felt that Ruth and the children would be safe in Paris where he was still in the pay of the army, so decided that as soon as Spring arrived he would fetch them. The house in Chesterfield could be rented out and the money sent to Paris to augment their income. Finally able to see an end to their plight, Henri endured the winter in a mood of quiet optimism.

With such expectations in view, Ruth tolerated the ice and snow of her winter also with a brighter outlook, and she worked with greater will.

Chapter 15   1815
Napoleon's Hundred Days

In Paris Henri struggled against the freezing cold, praying all the time that his weakness during the winter conditions would not cause him to be discharged before he was ready. All was set, their hopes raised high, and excitement mounted.

When the March winds roared in like a lion from Siberia, Henri was preparing to ask for a discharge from the army while his medical condition was still evident. He hoped to be back in England with his family by mid-April. However, the most devastating news was suddenly announced—Napoleon had escaped from his island prison of Elba, and had landed in the South of France. Henri was staggered by the effect the news had on many of the men and already new allegiances were taking place in their minds, albeit undeclared officially. Some Generals were vacillating over decisions as to where to place their loyalties, others were simply determined to rebuild France under the Bourbons, come what may.

However, as Napoleon marched inexorably northwards through France, gathering support all the way, Henri saw his dreams being slowly eroded. Not all Generals and their regiments were willing to break their oaths to the King and the Alliance, whilst others began openly to declare as being for Napoleon. Such was the quickening progress of Napoleon as he headed towards Paris that the mood was summed up in a clever musical composition satirically pointing to his progress the nearer he got.

The words being:

The MONSTER has broken out of the den;
The BRIGAND has landed at Cannes;
The GENERAL has reached Lyon;
NAPOLEON passed the night at Orleans;
The EMPEROR is expected hourly at the Tuilerie;
HIS IMPERIAL MAJESTY will address his
loyal subjects tomorrow.

Such was the mood of the people of France.

As a result, a few hours before midnight on March 18th, 1815, several carriages of the King's entourage rattled through the gates near the École Militaire and along deserted streets out of the city. In this fashion the king left Paris—in complete contrast to the adulation given at his earlier return twelve months previously.

This sudden reversal of fortune left Henri distraught! It was too late to return to England now without deserting and becoming disgraced. France was in turmoil once more. Napoleon's best Generals and Senior Officers who had been prisoners throughout Europe had returned and were still smarting from the fact that the House of Bourbon had been re-established in their absence. Many were quite willing to take up Napoleon's cause again and awaited his re-establishment with enthusiasm. Other Generals found their attempts to protest were untenable, even unwise, and so finally gave in. Henri was devastated!

Convinced that there would be further trouble and possibly an embargo on correspondence to England, Henri wrote one last letter to Ruth while he had the opportunity, reassuring her that he would return as soon as he was able.

Paris, 17th March, 1815

Dearest beloved wife,

(on reading this Ruth sensed a change in Henri especially as the intensity of his words increased).

I write in haste with the news that Napoleon has escaped and is making his way towards Paris. It may not be possible for me to contact you for a while, mail from the South of France was prohibited in order that Napoleon could gather men together and proceed unheralded to the capital. Even if I could afford to hire a coach in order to flee, there are none as they have all been requisitioned by the wealthy in their attempts to leave Paris with their riches before Napoleon arrives. I must post this today! In future I may not be able to write openly in a letter either.

No matter what happens, if I am spared the upheaval that there is all around me, my thoughts and heart will always be with you and the children. Let us hope that Napoleon's return will not result in another war that could go on for years.

I am sad always to be so full of gloom, but the rumours and opinions of my comrades are mixed and vastly divided. Who can tell how things will work out? Already touts have stocks of Tricolore emblems which they are selling secretly to people who, out of fear, are carrying both the white feather and the Tricolore, knowing that one or the other could be demanded at any time to prove their loyalty.

For so long now I have been awaiting the Spring so that I could return to you all, and now this has happened! Paris will not be a safe place for you and I cannot leave yet, I must support my country. There is so much unemployment and poverty here amongst the trappings of pomp. I am fortunate to have a job, but this brings responsibilities also. Must I go on without good news for you? Please, say a prayer for me, and for France.

*Nothing I can put on paper will ever tell you of my
true feelings for you all. I am lost without you, but I must
get this letter away whilst I am able to do so.*

*Soon beloved, I will return. Take care of our angels
until that time.*

*I am a very despondent yet devoted husband and
father.*

*Au revoir, I kiss my letter four times here xxxx, for
you all,*

Henri

Within twenty-four hours of Henri posting this letter to Ruth, the
King had fled to Belgium and Napoleon was installed in the Palace
at the Tuileries. The white feathers and banners had been replaced
with the Tricolore and those with divided loyalties soon realised
which side was the safest to support.

Henri had little time for boredom or frustration as the Emperor
was wasting no time in raising a fresh army of 100,000 men. Many
veterans were only too happy to leave ill-paid drudgery or reject their
soul-destroying idleness and march again in the shadow of
Napoleon's ambitions of glory. Such an army required clothing,
feeding and munitions. Clothing factories were soon turning out
uniforms at the rate of 1,200 per day, all of which provided work for
the unemployed poor, but the raw materials were in short supply and
largely unpaid for.

Long before Ruth received Henri's hastily written letter, the
news from France had filtered through and had been received with
foreboding. No-one believed that Napoleon was intent on peace and
it wasn't long before English soldiers found themselves en-route to
the continent again in readiness for what might come about. Many
were being transported by barges along canals from Ostende to
Bruges and then on to Ghent, before marching towards Brussels
from where Napoleon wanted to eject King Louis and Wellington's
Forces, and so regain control of the Low Countries.

Thus Henri, once a proud and dignified member of Napoleon's vast
fighting machine, was confined to the clerical work required in
supplying and overseeing part of the enormous baggage trains now
needed. Important though the task was and although his desire for

battle had long since burned itself out, he would rather have been mounted as before on some sturdy horse, with his head held high, but he hated no-one sufficiently to agree with Napoleon's desire for glory in some foreign territory.

In the Rue Saint-Dominique where Henri worked at the offices of the Minister of War, Marshall Davout, Henri witnessed with concern the constant bickering and rows between Napoleon and Davout; observed too the violent outbursts from the Emperor whom he considered was now not quite the man he'd been in his earlier campaigns. Neither was Napoleon having everything his own way, for the poorer people in the countryside were sullen and angry at his foisting another war on them, indeed they were having to be press-ganged into service. Whether sufficiently prepared or not, Napoleon was ready to force France into a war the nation didn't want.

Time was short and money extremely tight but the Emperor was adamant in his determination to turn Paris into a fortress, and then march into Belgium in order to get rid of the Bourbon King who was still a threat. Since the allies were not at war with France they were forbidden to patrol across the French frontiers, thus enabling Napoleon to marshal large numbers of his men without arousing the suspicions of his enemies. To Henri, however, it seemed that his Emperor was being driven by an inexplicable mania to control and conquer just as before, and there were many who doubted his ability to achieve either of these ambitions. Henri could clearly see inefficiency and incompetence in the administration brought about by the haste with which things were being done, but he daren't voice his thoughts for fear of censure. He dare not even write to Ruth lest he be thought suspect, and this both annoyed and distressed him, as he was still loyal to France.

As the Spring progressed so Henri's health improved, making it difficult for him to ignore the Emperor's call to arms. He was neither sufficiently fit nor experienced now to join the many veterans making up the fighting Brigades of the Chasseurs, so it was ironic that he suddenly found himself once more astride a horse. The War Minister had simply detailed him to accompany and supervise, along with other junior officers, the movement of the vast quantity of materials and food needed by the army heading towards Waterloo.

Almost ten years had passed since Henri had last ridden a horse and his body took some adjusting to the vigorous movement of the powerful animal. Not that he objected to riding alongside the supply and baggage train, it was certainly an easier method of checking things and urging on the slow, cumbersome wagons than it would have been on foot. Having spent his military life at the receiving end of supply trains Henri knew just how important these were to hungry, exhausted men, and this thought alone drove him on.

Slowly as he became more accustomed to his mount and the aches and numbness from riding began to ease, a re-awakening of the once familiar thrill of controlling a horse returned and he even felt fitter. The task of urging along such a large contingent of wagons, however, was not an easy one and time was of the essence if they were to reach the cavalry and troops up ahead each night.

Sadly the weather began to change for the worse, bringing heavy downpours of rain resulting in the wagons and horses floundering as the churned roads turned slowly to mud. Then, as night wore on, intermittent flashes of lightning and peals of thunder unnerved the horses drawing the wagons, whilst the driving rain reduced visibility slowing them down even more. This disastrous situation soon began to lower morale as men became drenched to the skin and covered in mud, yet the supplies had to get through. There was only one consolation, the enemy troops would also be at the mercy of the same weather conditions, and all lacked shelter and were unable to sleep on the soggy ground.

Arising from his sheltered bed at the farmhouse of Le Caillou on the morning of June 18th, 1815, Napoleon became both exasperated by unfavourable comments of France's chances of success made by his Generals, (including those of his brother Jérôme), and over-confident in his own strategic plan. After his defeat at Quatre-Bras followed by a victory at Lygny against Blücher's Prussian forces only days before, Napoleon now awaited the moment for the battle at Waterloo to commence. Mistakes and human error of judgement were soon to follow and not just by Napoleon. The lower fields, dividing Napoleon's troops from those of Wellington, had been saturated overnight. Thinking to delay the battle for several hours and thus allow the ground to dry sufficiently to prevent his heavy cannon and horses becoming bogged down, he thereby gave the Prussians precious time for their advance towards Waterloo to join Wellington.

When Henri finally found time to rest early that same morning he was soaked and exhausted. He could have done no more than he had in the nightmare conditions, in that he was content, but now he was shivering and felt quite unwell. As the day progressed he became feverish and bouts of coughing left him racked with pain.

At eleven o'clock the Battle of Waterloo began and Henri was growing weaker, yet in spite of this he worked with a will whilst cursing his own inadequacies. In the end his strength left him, he fell to the ground helpless, unable to rise and was soon oblivious to the chaos around him.

The engagements of battle raged bloodily on for nine hours until Napoleon quit the field and was chased back to Paris. The next morning found 40,000 men dead and dying after a battle that finally brought peace to Europe.

To Henri, lying with other sick and injured on one of the wagons, it mattered not. He had lost interest in his surroundings and realised that in all probability he would never reach Paris alive, nor see England again. He took what comfort he could from the fact that at least, for Ruth and the children, peace would become a reality at last.

Chapter 15   1815
Chesterfield— Mid July

The day was hot and by rights Ruth ought to have taken the children out into the fresh air for a walk. Instead the young ones squabbled and fretted crabbily between themselves in the heat. Ruth's eyes held a far-away look and she sat listlessly as if nothing was important anymore, only the welfare of the children keeping her despair at bay. There had been no more letters from Henri since the hasty one sent three months earlier in April. She felt deep down that there would be no more, and having read all the newspaper reports of the carnage at Waterloo, she knew he had to be dead. No, she would not be bitter, Henri would not have wanted that. She looked fondly at the children, his 'angels'.

'Come,' she heard herself saying, 'let's go for a walk.'

All the foundations she and Henri had created together seemed to be crumbling and although at least there was peace, with Napoleon banished for good to the far away island of St Helena, her life had to be rebuilt yet again. Her good friend and solicitor John Bower was dying, and news had reached Chesterfield that Charles D'Henin had a leg struck off by a cannonball at Waterloo. Poor Eleanor—but at least Charles still lived. She looked again at her children, hoping and praying that their future world would be different, a peaceful one.

Ruth forced herself out of the chair as someone knocked at the front door, perhaps another customer needed some sewing done because they couldn't afford new clothing. She opened the door lethargically, expecting and not ungrateful for more work, and vaguely saw a grey-haired man eyeing her rather strangely.

'What is it?' she asked, being distracted by Henrietta pulling at her skirt trying to see who was there.

'Madame, don't you know me?' the man asked good-humouredly.

'Oh, God!' Ruth cried, and looked closer. Of course, it was Henri!

She blinked in amazed disbelief and then stared, slowly realising that it was indeed him. Ruth simply stood there, her face drained of all colour, and Henri thought she might faint.

'Can I come in?' he asked quietly, initially bemused at this reception, then realising that the letter he'd sent immediately after his recovery must have been lost in transit; its arrival would have saved her so much distress as he'd intended it to warn her in advance of his home-coming. Gently easing Ruth to one side he entered the room and closed the door quickly, so as to prevent any passer-by seeing the tears flowing freely down her cheeks.

'It's Papa!' Joseph yelled in delight, as he ran in to see what the noise and delay was about and immediately recognised his father.

'I think you had better tell Mama who it is!' his father joked, and he took Ruth tenderly in his arms, hiding her face from the children. After so long apart he too found himself brought emotionally to tears as he held his wife protectively in his arms once more.

Henri then felt tiny hands clawing at his breeches and looked down, his eyes meeting a pair of blue ones exactly like Ruth's.

'Henrietta?', he whispered, knowing she was too young to answer. Gently releasing Ruth he reached out and lifted the child into his arms. As he had not yet received the miniature which Ruth had commissioned, this first contact with his second daughter was a strange and delightful one.

Holding Henrietta close he looked round and saw a shy Marie viewing him with suspicion and realised he was a stranger to her too. Henri knelt in order to encourage her forward, all the while observing Joseph waiting expectantly to be drawn into the group.

'My you have grown!' Henri said smiling with pride at the sturdy figure of his son.

'Papa, are you going away again?' Joseph asked in alarm. 'Because you are crying as well!'

'No, son,' Henri gasped, his voice choked with emotion, and stretching out a hand towards Joseph drew him closer. 'Never again!'

*The monument to the 1,770
French Prisoners of War who died
at Norman Cross Prison
between 1797 and 1814.*

INTERESTING FACTS

French Prisoner Numbers
The total number of French prisoners of war in England between 1803 and 1814 was approximately 122,440 of which 10,341 are believed to have died, and 17,607 were exchanged or sent home sick. Some of the men married and stayed in this country and the rest were repatriated at the end of hostilities.

Parole Towns
There was a total of 49 in all. 25 in England, 10 in Wales and 14 in Scotland.

Chesterfield
According to records available 420 prisoners came to Chesterfield under the Parole System, of which 65 attempted to escape, 6 died and 66 were exchanged and sent back to France. Many others were transferred to different towns for various reasons or sent to the prison at Norman Cross in which the conditions were appalling. It is almost impossible to ascertain how many were in Chesterfield at any one time after the first few months. Eleven prisoners married and one Chesterfield woman was known to have married a French prisoner elsewhere.
In Chesterfield Museum there are several beautifully crafted boxes made by the prisoners.

Norman Cross Prison, Nr Peterborough
Between 1797 and 1814, 1,770 French prisoners died there.
All that remains is a tall memorial to these men.

French or other ships (prizes) captured by the British Navy between May 16th and December 31st 1803
102 vessels were captured or destroyed, two of which were the *Franchise* and the *Duquesne*.

Franchise was captured off Brest returning from San Domingo with General Boyer on board on the 28th May 1803.

Duquesne was captured off San Domingo by *HMS Vanguard* on 24th July 1803. She was a 74-gun French 'Ship of the line' and became *HMS Duquesne*. At the time of her capture, on board was General D'Henin, his staff and others, also the ship's Commodore Pierre Querangal, all of whom came to Chesterfield. The *Duquesne* subsequently ran aground off Jamaica and was refloated and returned to England to be broken up.

HMS Vanguard

This 74-gun Ship of the Line was launched in 1787. She became Nelson's Flagship until 1799 when he transferred his flag to *HMS Foudroyant*. *Vanguard* eventually sailed to the West Indies under Captain James Walker. In 1808 she became Admiral Thomas Bertie's Flagship. In 1812 *Vanguard* was turned into a prison ship (Hulk) at Plymouth and then a powder hulk before being broken up in 1821.

Some important prisoners sent to Chesterfield

General Boyer was born 1771 in Paris and had a distinguished career. He was captured on May 28th, 1803 whilst returning to France from San Domingo, he was the first parole prisoner to arrive in Chesterfield from Castleton where he had been for a few days in transit. He was a troublesome prisoner and was constantly transferred from one parole town to another.

General Joseph Exelman was exchanged and warmly received by Napoleon on his return to France where he was given back his command. After Napoleon's escape from Elba, General Exelman re-joined his Emperor and fought at Waterloo. When the Bourbons came to the throne he was tried for his earlier defection and was sentenced to 20 years imprisonment, but this was subsequently reduced.

Brigadier General François Charles Joseph D'Henin. Little is known of his earlier personal history. He was exchanged and returned to duty in France, he also fought at Waterloo.

In Herne's *History of Napoleon*, D'Henin was accused of favouring the British at Waterloo, and was reported to Napoleon by a Dragoon that he had 'harangued his men to go over to the enemy', this occurred just before D'Henin had his leg torn off by a cannonball. (It is quite possible that he was neither traitor nor Anglophile, but like many other officers there, saw the futility of Napoleon's search for glory, and was shocked by the hopelessness and waste this ambition brought about).

Haiti
When the insurgent leader General Dessalines threw the French General Rochambeau and his soldiers off San Domingo he immediately issued a preliminary Proclamation of Independence and restored the original name of Haiti. In October 1804 Dessalines had himself declared Emperor, and in early 1805 the whites in Haiti were massacred on his orders.

John Bower
Died October 30th, 1815 having served seven terms of office as Town Mayor of Chesterfield.

Additional sources of information
Chesterfield collection of documents concerning the French Prisoners of War in the Local Studies Library, including the General Entry Book of French POWs.

Local and National Newspaper archives.

Port Royal Naval Base, Jamaica, letters and reports, National Archives, Kew.

Captains' and Masters' ships' logs—National Archives, Kew.

Recommended reading
Prisoners of War in Britain 1756-1815. Francis Abel. Oxford University Press 1914.
The Black Jacobins. C.L.R James. Allison & Busby, London. ISBN 085031 336 8.

In the churchyard of the Parish Church of St Mary and All Saints there is evidence of the prisoners stay in Chesterfield. Here stands a gravestone to the memory of one Francois Raingeard who died March 10th, 1812 aged 30. It was this gravestone which inspired the research and writing of this book.

Photograph by Rob Bendall

Other books available from
Marjorie Dunn

CALL OF THE LAPWING

A family historian's trail of discovery.

Intrigued by the mysterious ten year gap in her Great, Great Aunt Lizzie's diaries, and the news that her ancestors farm is to be demolished, Mimi Holden leaves Chicago for Sheffield. There she uncovers what drove Lizzie from her comfortable Victorian home and eventually took her to China. What was the guilty secret that had the power to destroy so many lives?

This dramatic voyage into the past is set in the 19th and 20th centuries in Sheffield, Derbyshire and old China.

ISBN 978 1 874718 67 3

Call of the Lapwing
is a sequel to Abe's Legacy

Abe's Legacy

An unusual and intriguing tale set partly in old Sheffield but mainly in the beautiful valleys and moors around Bradfield in the mid 1800s.

The collapse of the Dale Dyke Dam, in 1864 on the outskirts of Sheffield, was one of the biggest disasters in Victorian England and the huge loss of life and property had an enormous impact on the area.

This is a sensitive and fascinating account of 'The Flood' and its effects, especially on the three main fictitious characters. Edward is a man driven by his desire to comply with the unreasonable demands of a will in order to obtain an inheritance. Hannah and her daughter, Lizzie, hope to escape the poverty of Sheffield's slums, whilst Lydia, an actress of little talent, is prepared to play the most important role of her life to find security.

Once again Marjorie Dunn weaves a human tapestry in which adventure, romance and local history combine to keep the reader's interest right to the end.

ISBN 978 1 874718 42 0